W9-CJJ-315

MBA

F BAT
Battershill, Andrew, 1988-
Marry, bang, kill

JUL ▪ ▪ 2018

BANG
KILL

ANDREW

BATTERSHILL

GOOSE LANE

3 3281 01982 827 3

Copyright © 2018 by Andrew Battershill.

All rights reserved. No part of this work may be reproduced or used in any form or by any means, electronic or mechanical, including photocopying, recording, or any retrieval system, without the prior written permission of the publisher or a licence from the Canadian Copyright Licensing Agency (Access Copyright). To contact Access Copyright, visit www.accesscopyright.ca or call 1-800-893-5777.

Edited by Bethany Gibson.
Cover and page design by Julie Scriver.
HVD Rowdy font (title) and Nail Scratch font (author) by Eduardo Recife,
a.k.a. Misprinted Type.
Printed in Canada.
10 9 8 7 6 5 4 3 2 1

Library and Archives Canada Cataloguing in Publication

Battershill, Andrew, 1988-, author
Marry, bang, kill / Andrew Battershill.

Issued in print and electronic formats.
ISBN 978-1-77310-002-9 (softcover).--ISBN 978-1-77310-003-6 (EPUB).--
ISBN 978-1-77310-004-3 (KINDLE)

I. Title.

PS8603.A876M37 2018   C813'.6   C2017-906121-6
                   C2017-906122-4

We acknowledge the generous support of the Government of Canada,
the Canada Council for the Arts, and the Government of New Brunswick.

Goose Lane Editions
500 Beaverbrook Court, Suite 330
Fredericton, New Brunswick
CANADA E3B 5X4
www.gooselane.com

1 Victoria, British Columbia

Tommy Marlo was about this smart: if on a random Saturday night at the sketchiest nightclub in Montreal a stranger offered him drugs, Tommy would quickly size the stranger up to figure out whether the stranger was trying to roofie him. If he thought the guy was trying to drug and roll him in the alley out back later, he would fake-swallow and pocket the pills then surprise and roll the guy in the alley before the guy could roll him. This way, nobody else at the club would get roofied, and Tommy would have some loose cash for himself.

Tommy was also exactly this smart: he'd forget the pills in his pocket for about three weeks, pop one, say, while he was getting drunk at a bowling alley then have an incredibly weird night that he was lucky to escape without kidney damage.

So as he watched the teenage girl pack her MacBook Pro into her very large, very possibly real Gucci purse from across the street, he did a number of things that were halfway stupid and the rest of the way clever.

Having lost the holster, Tommy had to situate the hunting knife in his pocket so that he'd be able to pull it without cutting himself or accidentally slicing through the entire pocket of his sweatpants again. He scanned the street behind him and began moving towards the coffee shop at the perfect pace to intercept her at the perfect spot as she exited: far enough from the door of the coffee shop that she'd be hidden by the hedge of the patio, and far enough from the bus stop that nobody would recognize what was happening.

He also removed his glasses, an action for which smart and stupid were irrelevant judgments, since it was a thing he had to do. For Tommy, it was only possible to rob someone when they appeared to him a blurry, Caucasian shape rather than a living, 3-D teenage girl whose life was just as unique and special-feeling to her as his was to him.

His bad eyes were a big reason Tommy had gotten into mugging, as opposed to any other kind of theft, since it was the kind that didn't necessarily involve night vision. The kind where somebody with experience will tell you your first time: just close your eyes and do it. For Tommy, that was perfect, since he could stare people in the eye like a wild dog, and just be seeing what most people see when they relax their whole eyeballs.

Tommy wasn't sure what the exact definition of legally blind was, but he felt confident it would be insensitive to call himself that. He'd had too many prescriptions to keep track of, and none had fixed his vision all the way. Most helped most of the way, got him seeing straight with his glasses on or his contacts in, getting by, driving a car. But he never got the perfect pair—his vision always stayed that little bit askew, tilting off into swirls and vagueness. So he was not, probably, legally blind. Just very, very shitty at seeing things within twenty feet.

He'd prepared for the girl to be a bit of a tough nut, thirteen years old, bright blond hair and dark black eyebrows, leaving her crumbs on the table, shoving her way out the door and scowling into the welcoming brightness of the late afternoon. Already looking mean enough to teach middle school, let alone be in it. He reached her in perfect stride, at the perfect spot, and slid an arm over her shoulders, subtly twisting his body around to block her (and the fact that he was covering her mouth) from the street. She immediately bit his hand, and Tommy sucked in breath quickly, removing the knife from his pocket and directing her eyes towards it with his own.

"Okay, Bitch Face, give up the bag. Give it up. Give it up. I will stab you if you scream."

He retracted the hand and wiped it on his shirt, only succeeding in spreading her thick spit further across his hand.

The girl didn't look even a little scared, just grudging. She probably reacted the same way to movie theatre ads about turning off her cellphone. Her demeanour bluntly depressed Tommy. If he couldn't even put a scare into a thirteen-year-old girl, it really was time to get out of the game. She sullenly dropped the bag to the ground, and Tommy scooped it up with one hand, replacing the knife in his pocket with the other.

"It's not even my computer. You smell like onions."

What a little shit, Tommy thought, everyone smells like onions—calling people out on it was breaking the agreement we all make with each other each day. He turned to go.

"And I know I have a bitch face. People don't need to keep telling me."

This stopped Tommy, and he turned back to her. "How many people have called you a bitch face? I was just doing a thing here."

There are two personality traits required to stay in action as a street mugger for as long as Tommy had. The first is the one most people would think of: being careless or vicious or callous enough to threaten people with a knife and rob them. The second is just as important but more counterintuitive: being nice and easygoing enough to make and keep friends who are willing to help sell what one steals, and not dime one out if they get pinched.

These two traits exist on a spectrum, and Tommy was about as far as one could functionally be to the likeable side. He would have absolutely no problem fencing this computer and having a pleasant, personally meaningful afternoon with Bill, his computer guy. He would also, it was starting to seem, have trouble leaving Bitch Face without feeling bad about himself.

She toed the ground and tossed a heavy, limp chunk of hair over her shoulder. "But it was the first thing you thought of, right? Like, randomly, it popped in your head. Everyone calls me a bitch face. Or says I have one."

Tommy was spending much too long in the open here, but something about Bitch Face's prematurely jaded manner tugged at him. He scanned the street, and finding it empty, he looked her in the face, a vague chinook of paternal warmth wafting weakly through him. "You're young. Just...uh...it's also a posture thing. Like, hold your shoulders differently, maybe."

Bitch Face narrowed her eyes at him. "Fuck you, you greasy retard. Do you know who my dad is?"

Tommy turned his back on her and started hustling to his car. He felt stupid for hanging around too long and for not trusting his instincts about how good at hurting people's feelings Bitch Face would be.

"You're in big fucking trouble. You don't even know you're in big fucking trouble."

Tommy set off at a run, wanting to turn the corner, start his car, and get out of there. At that pace, the canopy of the trees melted into a mass of vague illuminated green. A blurry leaf-sky.

Bitch Face's voice, steady as a countertop behind him. A calm, penetrating shout. "They'll kill your whole family and throw them in a ditch in Delta. Watch the news." Tommy heard her through the breath in his ears, just as he hit the corner and turned it, the beige blobby blur of his car floating into view: "My dad will cut your feet off and throw them in the ocean. Don't you read Twitter?"

And Tommy Marlo was also this smart: he knew when a threat was specific enough to be terrifying.

Quadra Island, British Columbia

"Nobody cares. Trust me, I know you asked, you did ask, but I know better. I know in my soul that nobody cares. It isn't possible."

Grace nodded along. "Mousey, you're probably right about that."

Alan Mouse was balancing an empty highball glass on top of his head. He casually and carefully tipped his head over, reached out with one hand, and caught the glass. Mousey spoke with a vague but somehow harsh Middle American accent: a sort of slurred, directionless twang. If you found his corpse headless, but still with the jean cut-offs and white T-shirt on, you'd guess he was twenty-three years old; if you found the head, you'd say fifty. "Thank you."

Grace was in her early sixties, with tightly curly hair that stood in a short, straight column, black with a long streak of white through it. She always wore one of three loose, floral tunics. She weighed over two hundred pounds and had the most beautiful singing voice Mousey had heard in real life, concerts included. She drummed her fingers across the table in that smooth way people who have played thousands of hours of piano do, then she lifted all of her fingers to wag one in Mousey's face. "But that doesn't answer my question.

Hey, you're going to tell me something I don't really care about, right? Fine. I'll hear a thing I don't care about from you. That's fine with me, and it sure never stopped you before. That's for damn sure."

Someone who has earned a sad, small fortune as a corrupt cop and mid-level functionary in a poisonous and entrenched system of structural racism will tend not to want a whole lot of attention drawn to it, especially not when they're trying to maintain a somewhat new black friend. So Mousey was avoiding Grace's question about what his job had been. Also, he was avoiding the question because he had, over the years, evolved into that specific kind of friendly asshole.

"The past's the past. Here's a thing I've decided about society: I'm committing to thinking about the twelve or however many corporate oligarchs—who already own the world and control all the information and money on the planet—as everyone's dads. Like dads are when you're eight. They might be mean dads or nice dads, but it don't really matter either way, because you're eight, and they're grown-ass men. They're wearing polo shirts tucked into their shorts and compression socks because their legs are balding, but they don't give two shits tied together. They're driving."

"What about the moms?"

"To me, the corporate oligarchs are dads. Moms *take* you to the place you're going, y'know? It's a more inclusive vibe. The dads *drive* you. We're being driven, not taken. Society, I mean."

Grace had already signalled the bartender to settle the bill. It was her turn to pick it up. Their arrangement was this: they'd hang out at the Heriot Bay Inn drinking and talking, and when they were done, whether that was at the end of the night or the middle of the afternoon, he would help her with the stairs and walk her to her car. Once there, she would offer to drive him home, and Mousey would dither a bit before accepting. It was the sort of arrangement that people make who live on a huge, sparsely populated chunk of rainforest in the sea.

The Heriot Bay Inn was a bar inside the oldest hotel — and building — on Quadra Island. Various discarded pieces of boating equipment and an old British Columbia flag hung from the rafters. The shelves studding the walls were filled with trophies, more boat paraphernalia, and a coat of arms with a pig touching hands with an armoured knight and the phrase *in vino veritas* written below; across from the pig hung two replica fishes wearing tutus. There was a stage at the end of the bar, where local and travelling bands played and where the prizes for Rock and Roll Bingo Night were displayed. On the wall behind Grace was a framed, blown-up photograph of a man playing the piano, a young boy singing from a book of music, and a young girl playing the violin in that very building about a century prior. On the wall behind Mousey was another photograph, this one a smiling man in overalls who'd probably been dead since the 1930s, driving a train full of logs across tracks made mostly of other logs.

Mousey took a last hit of ice cubes and thunked the glass back down, letting his head hang. The tug of it felt nice on his neck. His breath came out ice-cube cold as he talked. "So now I'm just relaxing. The dad says he's driving us to the pool. I'm going with it. I'm getting in that minivan, I'm sitting low in the back seat, staring out the window, hoping to see a deer or a car accident or a pretty girl. Running it over in my head, y'know? What swimming's going to be like."

Grace sleepily considered her change on the bar-top before shrugging and turning back to Mousey. "You realize that driving-to-the-pool business started with me asking about your occupation, right? Like, a simple question. A census question. That's what I asked you. Someday your sweet flat little ass is going to tell me what you did to get here. That *house*."

"Is it really that flat?" Mousey craned to look over his shoulder and down his backside. The movement sent his bar stool off balance and clattering to the floor. He got one foot half under himself as Grace caught him firmly under the armpit. Mousey stood straight and bowed his head slightly at first, deepening the bow gradually as he bent over to pick up the stool. Grace smacked his rear so hard that he tipped forward and nudged the bar with his head. Behind them, a leathery kayak guide whooped encouragingly.

"Shit, son, you can't even sit on that thing. It's like a sheet of parchment. Swedish folks would wrap up a chunk of fish with that ass."

Mousey stood up smiling and rubbing the beginnings of a bump on his forehead. "I didn't even realize that one could sit on an ass. Did not know that until I was a good, say, twenty-four years old. I was watching an episode of *Roseanne*, and all of sudden I was like: 'Holy cow, you can sit on an ass, like it's a cushion.' Wild stuff. Really sit on it, y'know?"

Grace glanced behind herself now, with considerably more control than Mousey had. "Umm. Yeah, motherfucker, I'm familiar with the concept. Let's go. I'll drive you home."

"You'll drive nothing."

Grace reached over and slapped him across the belly. "Shhhhh. We both know I will. What did you do for a living? C'mon."

"You've never told me what you did. Why I gotta answer?"

"Who cares? I want *you* to tell *me.*"

Mousey moved his arms professorially, in an expansive and entirely pointless motion, bringing them to rest back in front of him. "I am not a man to live in the fleeting radiance of a time that is passed. Tonight I told you something relevant, something of the moment. A taste of me as me now. Under the glow of this night's moon."

Grace turned around and grabbed him by the elbow, gesturing gently at the door. "For somebody who hates people so much, you sure do like to talk."

"Don't be stupid." Mousey tilted his empty glass to check for more ice, then placed it back down noisily, spinning on his heel towards the door. "Talking doesn't have shit to do with other people."

Mousey looked back across the room as they left. He saw a woman reaching across a table, twisting one of someone else's dreadlocks, a long, fluorescent fishing lure dangling just above their table. He saw a skiff of napkin shreddings caught by a breath.

3 Victoria, British Columbia

Tommy realized relatively early in his career that mugging people on the street was a dying trade and that it was because of the internet. All he'd had to do was buy one basketball on Amazon to know people were going to be carrying less and less cash. And because he was exactly this smart, and no smarter, his solution hadn't been to find another trade but rather to start mugging people *for* their computers.

It had initially been a pretty successful strategy. He'd hit on the idea in Montreal, when he'd been hanging around selling coke to Concordia students. These kids all went to coffee shops, and they all brought their computers. They'd walk out of the cafés and the libraries with their attention occupied, laptops bulging teasingly against the sides of their bags. None of these kids had ever had a knife put to them.

The computer itself was an incredibly high-profit mugging, right off the bat, and after Tommy made friends with a few hackers, he was also able to get a solid cut of the cyber-theft: bank account access, credit cards, social insurance numbers. It was all there: passwords saved right on the browsers and all.

Cities got hot pretty fast for Tommy this way. Focusing on college towns, he'd hit a few coffee shops and a library or two over about six months, and then he'd skip to the next place. From Montreal he'd headed to Halifax, and from there he'd worked his way west, leapfrogging fences and connections from one place to the next. He was back in Victoria now, where he'd grown up, and was dismayed to have run out of west (not to mention money).

In his salad days of mugging people for their computers, Tommy had actually made a pretty legitimate income, but times had changed; now it was maybe a one-in-six shot to have saved passwords and no kill-switch or tracking apps on the laptops. For a while there, Tommy had been doing four thousand a month; now he wasn't even making enough to pay his expenses from city to city, reliant on small loans, big favours, and medium goodwill.

As was his standard practice, Tommy waited barely long enough to vacate the scene of the crime and get readjusted to having his glasses on to call the man who actually knew how to do anything with the computer Tommy'd just stolen.

"Hey, Bill, how're you doing?"

"I'm good, you?"

"I'm thinking sushi."

"Yeah, Japanese grocery store?"

"I'm going to call in to a restaurant. I'm feeling fresh." There was a brief, buzzing pause through the cheap plastic burner pressed clammily to Tommy's ear. He performed an extremely risky pass on the right of an old man in an old car. "I mean that I'm feeling freshness as, like, what I want in my sushi. I don't feel fresh in my own body, or whatever."

"No, I got that. I have cash, I'm paying for this."

"Nope."

"Tommy, seriously, you shouldn't be paying a commission of a restaurant meal every time you bring me business."

"It's valuable for me to show you that I appreciate our relationship. You're a skilled person and you do things I can't. I'm glad we work together, and I really mean that, and I probably don't say it enough."

"You actually say stuff like that a lot, dude. Thanks, though. Are you okay? You sound weird."

Tommy had been mugging people for a living since he'd left Victoria as a teen, and the only thing about the town that had changed was that the traffic had gotten worse. It wasn't surprising that he sounded weird. "Yeah, I'm sorry, man. I'm just...emotional, I guess. I feel emotional. But I guess anytime you feel something, you're emotional. Either way, don't ever try to pay for your soosh."

Tommy hung up the phone to prevent further arguing. Then immediately re-dialled to get Bill's order.

Tommy walked into the familiar dankness of Bill's computer dungeon/reasonably priced condo, shaking his head. He could smell the vaporizer bag already.

Tommy saw the television and Bill's expectant face. Tommy held a single finger out in front of him, wanting to get his question out before they settled in. "First, I have something I wanted to run by you, just to see if I'm... Okay, here's the deal, this is a thought I had when I was super-baked, but I want to bring it into the light of day. So, like, sober, I want to run this by you."

Bill spread his hands to welcome Tommy's idea into the room.

"Okay, so I was lying in bed, insomniacking a bit. And then I thought, like, if you take it all the way out of context, isn't sleeping really crazy? If you don't totally switch off your whole, uh, consciousness and all for a third of the day, you go insane and die."

Bill was already nodding along. "Right, and you need to do it all in a row. That's what's really weird. You'll still go crazy and die if you just sleep one hour at a time eight times a day."

"*Yes.* Totally on that page, man. And that whole time you're asleep you have to dream or it doesn't count. Because of REMs, or whatever. You don't just need to shut off or you go crazy and die, you need to shut off *and* all the shit in your brain needs to fire off randomly and make you see and act out crazy imaginary scenarios in your mind. To live, that needs to happen every night. That's a biological necessary thing everyone has to do."

"That's weird as fuck to think about, dude. Legit."

"Oh, awesome. I'm glad that held up to sobriety." Tommy placed the computer and the sushi gently on the coffee table then dropped down beside Bill on the couch, which was so punched out and sloppy that sitting on it you were almost at ground level. He took the bulging vape bag from Bill and inhaled happily.

"I'm sorry to bust your bubble, man, but I was already pretty baked when you got here."

The vapour hit Tommy's throat simultaneously with Bill's revelation hitting his consciousness, and both revolted as Tommy lurched forward into wracking, laughing cough. He weakly lifted his arm to pass the bag back. Bill grabbed it and rubbed Tommy's back with his other hand.

Eventually, Tommy regained his air. "Jesus, you are a piece of human garbage."

Bill laughed. "I do think that thought is legit, though, Tommy. It was just a little buzz I had on, I can still balance on the plane of the notional, brah."

"I'm sure, I'm sure." Tommy settled quietly into the depths of the couch, then pushed himself back up and started untying the knotted plastic bag around the sushi. "Oh, I was driving, so we didn't have a chance to debrief on this at the time, but you ordered a scallop roll. That's *gangster*."

Bill blew a smooth, thin line of vapour a discreet distance away from Tommy. "Is it?"

"See, man, see. That's how it is, when you're in it, when you're that scallop-ordering baller, you don't even see it. A scallop roll. The *gall*."

Bill grinned, passed the bag back, and carefully wiped some imaginary dirt off his real shoulder. The two men giggled for a while, then watched two episodes of *Paddington Bear* as they ate.

As Bill was pillaging everything he could off the laptop, Tommy was trying to play a video game where you start as a tiny ball that rolls and picks up dirt and turf, kind of like a snowball. You, the ball, grow and start gathering small trees and benches, and on and on until you have consumed entire people, then buildings, then cities, then continents, and then you end up in space rolling through light years gathering stars and moons and planets, and eventually galaxies. Then the game ends, and you get a score. Or at least that was what happened if Bill stoned or Tommy totally focused played it. As it was, Tommy was having trouble growing his ball. He kept taking runs at fences or businessmen and bouncing off, shedding whatever meagre lawn he'd picked up.

"Uh, Tommy…"

Tommy took a hard roll at a park bench and rebounded, dissipating back into his original form. He put the controller down and turned to look at Bill, who was staring deeply at the laptop. "Yeah, what's up?"

"Who did you steal this computer from?"

"Some chick outside the Hillside coffee place. You know, the one with those dope blueberry scones?"

Bill dug into his beard with both hands and stood, pulling the hands through in a way that Tommy couldn't imagine being comfortable.

"Did she give you the impression that she maybe was in, y'know, the most terrifying criminal motorcycle club in the history of the universe?"

"No, she was..." Tommy closed his eyes and failed to imagine dying because right in the moment, when you know it might really happen very soon, that's kind of an impossible thing to do. "She mentioned her dad."

Bill sat back down and angled the computer towards Tommy. "Look here, you remember that armoured car heist, all on the news, last week?"

"I don't have a TV."

"Well, an armoured car heist happened, they took, like, a hundred G's. Guard got fucked up, in a coma. It was bad, and it's here. The money's being stashed in a hidey-hole behind this address until it gets picked up tomorrow. That's...Holy fuck."

"How do you know that's the—"

"Because this computer is owned by a man who stopped learning after DOS, dude. Everything is on the desktop. His My Documents is empty, nothing is in code, and it's all very scary."

"I put a knife to his teen daughter. I called her a bitch face. Well, by accident...No, that—that was on purpose. It was all on purpose, if we're being real."

"This is literally the first file I opened, Tommy. And it's a thing people get killed over. Do you see that background image? That is straight black with white text that says: 'Don't let your tongue get your teeth knocked out.'"

"Yeah, I see that. This is not good. This is bad."

"I'm not going to open this jpeg, but just looking at the thumbnail I can tell it's a bloody crowbar. A picture of a bloody crowbar. A really very bloody crowbar."

Tommy got up to pace, but that only lasted a couple seconds. He dropped to his haunches and stayed there, looking straight at the stained carpet past his knees.

"Is that a severed foot?"

Tommy popped up and swiped the laptop off the table. He carried it precariously to the kitchen and began wiping it down with a loose, stained piece of paper towel. Bill followed a few seconds later.

"What are you doing? What's our plan?"

Tommy spun and grabbed Bill around his chest for a hug; he buried his head in the crook of the larger man's chest and closed his eyes for a second. "Okay. Fuck. I'm sorry, this is bad, and I wasn't here. Okay? Wipe all that shit, whatever you got off this laptop onto whatever computer of yours, and put that fucking computer in an oven. This is my problem."

"What are you going to do?"

Tommy had been scared for his life three times before this, but those had all been occasional. A quick flash, and then over. Once, a woman he'd been mugging had pulled a can of mace from a holster and he'd thought it was a gun. Once, he'd been jumped and shit-kicked leaving a nightclub in Kingston. Once, driving back from a hiking trip in the Okanagan, the van he'd been riding in had lost its brakes on the highway, and his quietest, most competent friend, a leather artist named Nic Gething, had almost magically glided the van up a hill and eventually stopped them. All of those times, Tommy had been frightened. He had felt it deeply in his chest, but the moments had gotten behind him before he'd known it, as if he'd blinked or looked the wrong way and missed them. The fear now was different. It was big and external and it didn't feel like it would be gone anytime soon. But he was somehow calm, able to think.

"Fuck it. I've split from plenty of towns. My mom's on Quadra Island, that's…remote, I guess. Hang there a couple days, y'know, say I'm sorry about the jumping bail that time and…just, also, sorry for my whole life, I guess. Then grab a boat. Get up to the Yukon or some shit, figure it out. Fucking just punch the clock. I'm fine. This'll be fine."

Bill bit his lip really hard. "Do you have the money to…"

"My problem, my problem. I'll… I'll take this computer, and I'll work something out. All right? Last time you'll hear of it. That's it."

They stood in the kitchen, breathing quickly, for several seconds.

"Are you sure about this?"

"It's done, I already went to Quadra, saw my mum, and I'm in the Yukon, man. Fuckin' staring at a rainbow. It's midnight, sun's up, all that. Having a party. I'm good. I'm already good. I'm over it, I'm fine."

Bill didn't say anything or move his head at all. He just stood there and looked a little like he might cry, but it's possible that Tommy was only thinking that because of how close to crying Tommy was.

Tommy didn't know exactly how making a life-changing decision felt. Like everyone else, Tommy had made such decisions every second he'd been awake as an adult. Like everyone else, Tommy's life was nothing more than a ceaseless, arbitrary stream of mortal micro-choices. Regardless, Tommy would afterwards remember ripping off the club not as a choice at all but rather as a series of stunning realizations, a short, slick conveyor belt of epiphany.

The first realization was that Bitch Face had not been exaggerating. In fact, she'd undersold the threat. Her father was the road captain of the local club chapter. His name was Jason Darillo, and he was not just a high-ranking member of the club but also a very, very crazy and gleefully violent one (that thumbnail was, indeed, a picture of a severed foot).

The second realization, almost simultaneous with the first, was that if he did not leave town immediately, he would not only be killed but—as Bitch Face had warned—his feet would be cut off and thrown in the ocean.

The third realization was that he did not even have the money to pay for the gas to get himself out of danger.

The fourth was that the money from the armoured car robbery was being held temporarily at a club-owned gas station in Esquimalt, not more than a ten-minute drive from Tommy's apartment.

The certainty he felt that it would take the club between thirteen and forty-eight hours to find and kill him overwhelmed Tommy's already pretty limited instincts to be careful and forward-thinking about the dangerous things he did. So instead of packing and preparing to go from robbing the money stash to Quadra Island—where he could appreciate nature and think about his life a little and, after things cooled down, hop on a boat and maybe get one of those fishing or oil jobs in Alaska where they give you money just to go there — Tommy left all his valuables at his apartment as he headed to the gas station, taking with him only his knife, a scrawled note to remind him of the stash's exact location, and his glasses.

Since his second week in Victoria, Tommy had been using a car belonging to the senile old woman down the street. After noticing that the Corolla never left its spot during the day, he had waited for a whole afternoon outside the house before finally seeing, frightening, reasoning with, and bribing the owner's baggy-eyed, slump-shouldered home care worker. For the $120 he'd had left in his wallet, Tommy had purchased himself unlimited, unsupervised use of a car with clean plates. It had been, easily, his biggest accomplishment since arriving in town.

Even as he coaxed the desperately underpowered seventeen-year-old car out of the senile woman's super-steep driveway, and even later, as he approached the gas station, Tommy did not feel very different than he had earlier in the day. The buzz of adrenaline made his legs and hands feel tingly and distant from his head, but his legs and hands often felt that way, like when he'd had a bit to drink or smoke, which, come to think of it, he had.

Tommy pulled into a parking spot at the gas station but left the car running. For the first time since he'd decided to steal the stashed money he felt like he needed a minute to think. He looked at the knife on the seat next to him. He was literally bringing a knife to a gun fight. Or — Tommy managed to hope solemnly — he was bringing a knife to no fight, which was almost as stupid.

The minute of thought Tommy took for himself was, in real time, more like three. Just enough time to catch a second look from the bored hangarounds assigned to guard the money.

The two men were smoking cigarettes outside the gas station, gossiping and making plans for after they were relieved, leaning against the gas station's freezer, chain-drinking the 5-Hour Energies that taste like grape cough syrup.

Tommy reversed his car out of the spot and towards the storm drain behind the gas station. This way he wouldn't have to back out of the tight space.

Seeing the weird, shitty car swing backwards across the length of the store and parking lot, the hangarounds followed it, each subtly drawing a large, not particularly functional handgun.

Tommy pulled his vehicle around more quickly than was cautious and narrowly missed a truck pulling up to the diesel pump, then he lurched the car backwards in three awkward bursts. He jumped out of the car, circled around it, dropped to a knee, and threw aside the grate covering the storm drain. Just as he reached the large canvas sacks full of money hiding under the lip of the drain, the sprinting hangarounds turned the corner, and in their excitement, both fired their booming hand-cannons without their feet under them. The shots missed Tommy (and all other solid objects) by a good margin.

The gunfire startled Tommy, and he hugged the money bags to his chest and froze, still on his knee. One of the hangarounds' guns jammed, and not knowing how to fix it, he just pulled the trigger while the gun made a series of loud metallic clicking sounds. The other loosed three shots in Tommy's general direction, hitting the side of the store twice and sending shards of grey brick dust into the glowing early-evening orange of the sky.

Tommy finally reacted, diving for his car, misjudging the distance, and smashing his face (and glasses) against the passenger door. The sounds of the world at large had boiled down to nothing but a long, sustained wail, the sights a blur of colours, the smells smoke, and the tastes only the metallic hints of his own blood. He wrestled the door open, tossed the bags in blind, and dove across the seats. The windshield exploded and glass spread enthusiastically across his back. Tommy reached down and pressed the gas pedal with his hand as the hangaround with the jammed gun reached the front of the car. The Corolla lurched forward, and the hangaround spun out of the way, instinctively reaching a hand out and smacking the hood of the car angrily as he fell. Tommy kept one hand on the gas and awkwardly swung the other arm back towards the steering wheel, hitting it with his elbow and succeeding only in making the car wobble slightly and resume its beeline path over the lip of the curb and then across the small patch of grass, the sidewalk, four lanes of light traffic, and one other sidewalk before slamming into the soft grass of a gentle roadside hill.

The collision threw Tommy forward, raking his ribs across the handle of the transmission. Now facing the back of the car, Tommy grabbed the seat and pulled himself up, kicking the still-open passenger door further open against its hinges, causing it to rebound shut. He twisted back and opened the driver's side, crawling halfway out, then kicking himself the rest of the way free, ending up face down in the grass.

Getting up, Tommy saw the guy he'd hit with his car lying still on the ground, and Tommy, an intuitively guilty person, knew right then that the smack of the hand on the car had been the sound of that hangaround getting hit by his car and dying. He knew it for certain.

The second hangaround headed straight towards Tommy at a full sprint, immediately tripping forcefully on the curb, sprawling out face first and sending his gun skittering across the ground.

Tommy grabbed the cash and made it around a long, countryish block with mostly grass and empty lots on it that he remembered clearly but could not see. He came to the next street corner, and in the swirling blur of car colours he waved his free arm as calmly as he could at the yellow blurs. A cab stopped, and then a skinny Indian man, too busy speaking loudly on a Bluetooth to notice or care about his passenger's bloody face, drove Tommy home.

Clutching the bags to his chest, Tommy closed his eyes, sunk into the back seat of the cab, and imagined the rhythm of the man's shouted Punjabi as long, violently twirled ribbons of silk, tracing arcs over his head.

Quadra Island, British Columbia

Glass Jar Jeffries was not a person who usually had much to say about the quality of a drawing, but he felt sure the one he'd had done on him was a genuine piece of art. The tattoo took up the entire surface area of his back. On his left shoulder was a roughly sketched person, an oddly visceral, slightly-too-thick-in-some-places figure representing St. Patrick. Away from the saint, snakes slithered in all directions, spreading down the length of Glass Jar's back, gathering towards the base of his spine, where one of them looked to be cresting the gentle, dimpled hill of his gluteus towards his asshole. The tattoo commemorated Glass Jar's distant, but deeply held, Irish heritage.

As usual, Glass Jar struggled to hoist the bag of shellfish over the lip of his truck. There were three seafood farms on the mostly uninhabited northern half of Quadra Island, and it was from selling old-fashioned kitchen-sink meth to the night workers at these plants that Glass Jar made his living. Rather than paying him in cash, the workers paid Glass Jar in shellfish. It was a humiliating but not necessarily financially disadvantageous deal for Glass Jar. It meant that he had to go to the trouble of selling the stuff under the table to a fish-and-chips shop in Campbell River, but also that he was able to get just slightly above street value for his meth.

After finally getting the shrimp into his truck, Glass Jar pressed his thumbs into two of the fleeing snakes and pushed hard against the bony, protuberant surface of his lower back, moaning with a deeply uneven mix of pain and relief as he reflected once more on how much he hated *Breaking Bad*. He had only watched a few random episodes of the show, but the notion of "high-quality" meth it had planted in the minds of consumers was putting old-school cooks like Glass Jar straight out of business. College kids were dropping out of chemistry degrees and cooking up huge batches that were "potent" and "clean" and "pure" and whateverthefuck. Glass Jar knew one way to cook, and it was dirty, low yield, and cheap, like meth was supposed to be. Like it was before everyone stopped living and started watching and gossiping about long-ass TV shows that you can't even follow unless you watch every minute of every episode. In the mind and world of Glass Jar Jeffries, meth was the thing you cooked in a sink in a shed, and television was *Jeopardy!*, daytime judge shows, and the local news. The way things had been in 1998, and always should be.

Releasing his back, Glass Jar stared down the long, black path of the logging road as dust from the gravel floated loosely around in the air, illuminated by his high beams, and soundtracked by the thick, chunking stutter of his truck's idling engine. He rubbed the top of his truck and brought his hand back dirty then wiped it on his jeans. Had he known the first thing about classical music, Glass Jar might have looked into the blackness of the unfinished road and thought about how fugue-like his life had become.

The same bags of subsistence fish, the same backache as he lifted them, the same drive home, and the same sad, sleepy shove of the fish into his freezer. Six days of drinking, smoking, driving around, hauling the same shit over to Campbell River, and selling it. The only variation on the theme recently had been that he'd started stealing scallops from the We Wai Kai Nation's farm, which was an extremely high-risk, extremely low-reward thing to do just for variety's sake.

Glass Jar caught sight of some movement in a bush. He fished his flashlight out of the shallow puddle of used bottles, wrappers, and cigarette butts on the floor of his truck. Even though it was summer, after the sun went down there was a vague, wet hint of cold in the air, and a ripple of shiver passed through the frayed nerves of Glass Jar's loose, sticky limbs. He plucked aimlessly at his bare shoulder and pressed on towards the bush. The beam of his flashlight wobbled onto a dog, lying on its side against a tree stump.

"If I'm not straight fuckin' a duck in the face. How are you, pooch?" Glass Jar dropped to his haunches. "You want some water? Hayzoo Chreesto, you're a drooler. A foamer, almost. Shit. You want a napkin? Hey, boy? You want some water?" He reached forward to pet the sickly fur, plastered flat against the dog's skull. "You got a big head. Big brain in there I'll just bet—"

In an unforeseeable burst of strength, the dog snapped up and bit Glass Jar halfway up his forearm. Glass Jar shook his arm out with a spasm, hurling the mutt to the packed dirt with a dull thud. The dog emitted an even duller half bark. Without cursing, crying out, or even checking his own wound, Glass Jar took one step back, found his balance, and punted the dog's skull. The beam of his flashlight was swinging around and illuminating random, glowing patches of the forest's green as Glass Jar continued to stomp and kick the dog's corpse. He expended so much physical effort that, without realizing how exhausted he was, Glass Jar fell backwards, sprawled out sideways, and vomited the perfectly clear contents of his stomach across the rainforest floor.

In spite of the hard years he'd put on himself and the fact that he was a six-foot-tall man who weighed 128 pounds, Glass Jar was still pretty resilient, and he recovered from the attack quickly. He pulled himself up slowly and in sections, like a set of soaked, knotted sheets being hauled out of a washing machine. He staggered towards the truck, poured himself into the seat, and examined his wounds for the first time. There were four small punctures, oozing thick, dark blood. He let the arm air itself out a minute as he struggled with the cap of his Oxies, then popped two, crushed one up on the dash using his flashlight, and huffed about half of it dry, letting the rest of it blow around the cabin with his jagged, jumpy breath. Composing himself, Glass Jar took a rag from the glove compartment (he usually used it to wipe his palm-grease off the steering wheel) and cinched it tight on his arm.

He admired his handiwork out of the corner of his eye as he drove home, barely even feeling the bites now. He spoke to the blazing circles of his high beams and into the deep, sequestered darkness behind them.

"Fuckin' dog. Bites like a bitch."

Glass Jar did not notice his own wordplay.

Grace had dropped Mousey at the side of the road, then been convinced to come in for more drinks, then floored her car down his driveway, leaving Mousey to walk the final stretch. This was the precise kind of asshole move Mousey enjoyed, even and especially when it was pulled on him. Following her, he ran the short distance in the drunken, downhill way that gets one feeling like one is a bird with very small wings, trying to glide. Now they were in the house, Grace another drink past her reasonable driving limit.

She picked up her empty glass and then put it back down. She stood and looked out the window. "Jesus. This *house.*"

Mousey's house was a small split-level built into the rock with pillars. The walls were windows so big and clean that from some angles they were difficult to distinguish from air. They overlooked three tiny wooded islands and an opening into the whole Pacific Ocean. The house was surrounded by evergreen trees, save the driveway and a small gravel clearing, where Mousey parked his car and chopped wood for exercise. Inside, the light fixtures were glowing white globes, all hung from the ceiling by imperceptibly thin cords. The kitchen had a stove that boiled water silently and flamelessly in two minutes flat, and Mousey's bathroom reminded those who saw it of what they imagined five-star Swedish hotels looked like: the bathtub facing a long, thin window overlooking the water, and the shower built into the centre of the room over bare wooden boards, no walls around it. A giant mirror with a square window cut out of the middle reflected the whole of the room back at itself, the walls squares of nearly opaque glass. His bedroom opened onto a triangular balcony, where he maintained a small herb garden. All the chairs and tables in the house were a small but sure amount too tall for comfort.

The house stood out, especially on Quadra Island, a tourist destination aimed at people already deeply enamoured with British Columbia. The island itself was about the physical size of Knoxville, with a year-round population of less than 2,500. Most of the people and activity were concentrated on the bottom third of the island, clustered around the prettier beaches and the two ferry docks. Mousey and Grace lived close to one another in a residential area for year-rounders, which started down by the dock and sprawled leisurely all the way up past the fish plants and the logging camp, the only businesses on the northern part of the island. The houses were generally wooden-framed, overlooking large gardens and woodsheds, most of them showing the awkwardness of design common to all structures hanging in that liminality between house and cabin.

Turning away from Grace, Mousey linked his hands in a Gable grip and awkwardly torqued his body to the side by pulling harder on the left than the right in a probably fruitless attempt to loosen what had become over the years a very shitty and rigid right shoulder. To avoid thinking about the foreverness of the shittiness of his shoulder, he started whistling.

Mousey loved to whistle. And since he'd retired, he'd taken to it even more. The problem was that he couldn't remember more than a verse of just about anything. So the tunes he whistled were almost always indecipherable, skipping back to the beginning of some half-remembered song that wasn't really a song. He piped out a good third of something that sounded way less than a third like "Shave and a Haircut."

Grace laughed, even louder than usual. The loosest window in the house vibrated softly. "You know you're tone deaf, right? You're the real deal, son. A lot of people claim it, if they don't want to sing the anthem. But you are the thing. You're as deaf to song as a sheep. As a whole herd of sheep."

"Nah, that's an urban legend. Tone deaf. Not a real thing."

"No, boy, no. Have you heard yourself on tape? You modulate a *lot*. People who hear pitch don't modulate that much. Even a lot of actual deaf people don't. You have a confidence you don't deserve, in the whistling department."

"Okay. So, you're a music teacher and I...I am a learner. You should teach me how to whistle."

"You want a whistling lesson?"

"I'll pay you good, promise."

Grace waved him off and looked out the window again. She turned back to him sharply as if he'd just dropped something heavy. "How'd you know I was a teacher? I said musician, is what I said."

"You have a Royal Conservatory sticker on your windshield."

Grace turned back to the window. The sky was dark at the top, sloping down into a soft, luminescent blue above the trees. They could both see many more stars than either of them was used to, and they could hear the tops of the trees swaying in their tall, second-growth thinness. She reached out and left one precise fingerprint on the glass. "I'm retired."

Mousey hopped to his feet and clapped twice. Grace sucked her teeth at him like he was somebody else's dog shitting on somebody else's rug.

"C'mon, Gracey. We're all retired here. Teeeach me."

"No."

"I want to whistle. Like a salesman from the fifties would whistle."

"No."

"It's a public service! I see other people when I whistle. I'm not deaf to sentiment."

"How did salesmen from the fifties whistle?"

"It was a different time. People could look across land-scapes—and this is a science fact—people could look across beautiful landscapes and not think about every animal and plant in the world dying."

"People could?"

"Fact."

Grace drummed a tight, perfect rhythm on her lips then leaned forward and put her hands on her knees. "I would be a hero to this community."

"I'll pay you so much money."

"You know about my disability cheques, I can't be work-ing for cash, so you supply the booze and shove your money up yourself somehow. And you tell me what exactly the fuck job you retired from so early to this goddamn house, and you have a deal."

"Deal."

"You did the financial crash, didn't you? You're one of those. You hedged a shit-ton of funds. Come on, you can tell me. I can take it."

Mousey raised a loose, shambling arm as if to swear on something, then he just let the arm fall. In spite of the reality of what he'd done, of all he'd done, he had not hedged a single fund. So at least there was a baseline. "You want to know? Huh? I'll tell you: I was a detective."

"Fuuuuuck you. No, you weren't."

"I guess I retired a lieutenant. I think of myself as a detective." Mousey was always of the mind that if you've got to do something, it's always best to lean into it. You're going to tell someone your sad story, you should tell all of it, and tell it sadly.

"In this house? You were a cop? No, sir."

"I can only tell you the truth."

Grace leaned back in her chair, crossed her arms. "Okay, so you were a cop, then tell me about it. Tell me about becoming a cop."

"Becoming police? That's pretty boring. Basically, I got super into working out this one summer. And my buddy at the gym was training up for the physical test, so I started doing all the stuff with him, and why not, right? I took all entrance tests, and I passed. Did really well, actually, and they wanted me. Not much else was happening, so I joined up. That's not the good story, though."

"And just what on God's green earth is?"

"The story of how I made the Special Investigations Unit, working bodies, task forces, political hit jobs, all that fun stuff. Sergeant Alan Mouse," he jabbed his chest forcefully with both thumbs, "this guy."

"And how'd you do that?"

Mousey could have kept his mouth shut. It was always an option. But he liked Grace, and at some point she'd have to know him. Besides, it was a phrase he liked and hadn't said in a long time: "I shot a pimp in the knee."

"You what?"

"You heard me fine."

"Why would you do that?"

"I was working Vice at the time and he — guy's name was Ripple Henry — he was a bit portly, y'know, why they called him that. So I failed to clear a room properly on a cathouse raid, and Henry got the best of me a little bit. He was choking me out, maybe strangling is the better, uh, y'know, word, but anyhow I shot...well, shooting implies a bit of distance. These terms, always hard. So let's just say he was strangling me, and I put my gun against his knee and fired it."

"And that got you promoted?"

"Yup."

Grace's eyes flicked briefly out the window behind his head, then back him. "You're lying."

"Nope. That's true. I acted with meritorious valour in the line of duty. Quote unquote."

"Then how'd you pay for the house?"

"I live on my pension, and I bought the house with a

bunch of payoff money I took. Also, I worked as an investigator for a law firm for a year. That was ritzy."

Grace sighed. "Payoffs? How much in payoffs, Mr. LA Confidential over here, how much?"

"Approximately $267,000, after the laundry. And I'm from Chicago, hah-ctually, not LA." Mousey had been staring at his hands as he talked; he couldn't believe how soft they still were. They were delicate, refined, the hands of a prince. He shoved one in front of Grace, who shoved it back. "Seriously, though, these things are great. Can you believe I grew them myself?"

"Yes, yes, yes. We've covered it. They're soft, all right? You have the hands of a child who hasn't worked a day. Congratulations."

"I know you meant that as a put-down, but thank you very much. I appreciate those words."

"What happened to the guy?"

Mousey was once more fully distracted by his own hands. You could barely see pores, the fingers all thin and straight, like they should be holding a cigarette in a really long holder. "What guy?"

"The guy you shot, the pimp."

"Oh, Ripple Henry? Yeah, he ended up getting killed in prison. Eighteen or so months later."

"Wait, he was murdered?"

"Yuh huh. A couple guys, they jumped him in the showers and shanked him in either kidney. Both? Do you say 'either' when you mean 'both,' y'know, for kidneys?" Mousey looked up from his hands and then back. He sensed Grace staring at him. "What? That kind of stuff happens in prisons fairly often. Probably something similar happened yesterday or today. If not, definitely tomorrow. Statistics are weird, hey?"

Grace bounced an open hand off the top of her hair. "I really have no idea with you, with that face. Be straight. Are you telling the truth? It's so fucked up if you are."

Mousey grinned. "No. Just kidding. I was a garage-door-opener salesman. I'm living off a modest garage-door-opener fortune."

"Whatever, man, whatever. You're right. I'm sorry I asked. Either way, you're retired now. Hell of a word. Tired again. We're a couple newly tired again people."

"You're not retired." He languidly fell into a straight posture on the couch opposite her. "Remember, Grace, you're giving me whistling lessons."

"I mean, you just told me what I wanted, so I'm good now. I don't feel like I have to do anything."

"I'll give you $15,000 cash."

"With your garage-door money? Fifteen thousand?"

"Do you remember how annoying it was to get all the way out of your car to pull open your garage? People *love* garage-door-openers."

Instead of rolling her eyes, Grace rolled her tongue around her mouth like it was an eye and her lips were lids. She pointed at him and moved as if to talk, then stopped. She left her hand dangling over the open space between the couches. Mousey wondered if her shoulder was getting tired, if it was burning. Past the hand he could see his own face in the glass.

Grace did two more full tongue orbits. "We've got a

lesson to get to. Start off, man, unpurse your lips. You don't get to whistle right off. Close those little lips, you have to hum before you can run."

The next hour and a half moved along slowly but with a distinct progression. The humming and learning-some-differences-between-some-notes portion of the lesson failed and was abandoned after just a few minutes. Grace, being an experienced and adaptable teacher, moved swiftly on to rote instruction. She taught him the exact physical way to manipulate his mouth and breath to whistle the theme of a Sergio Leone film, the name of which they had both forgotten.

The lesson finished before too much refining had been done and too much of the bourbon was gone, both because they were tired and because Mousey got distracted by how much of the Milky Way was visible from his living room. He sprawled across the floor and motioned for Grace to follow. She shook her head firmly.

"People with double knee replacements don't just lie down on the floor."

Mousey raised a flat hand above his head and then dropped it with a slap against his forehead. "I forgot! Sorry! Thanks for the lesson. Oooh, reminds me." He sprung up quickly and rushed towards the pantry, his socks slipping against the hardwood floor a couple times. Grace pulled the plastic-topped cork out of the whiskey bottle and threw it, hitting him square in the back of the neck. Mousey skidded to a stop. "That was nice. Good arm on ya."

Grace twirled a hand through the air, bowing without moving any other part of her body.

Mousey walked the last couple steps to the pantry and pushed open the fake wall panel. He twisted the dial to open his combination safe. Inside were three bundles of $5,000 in Canadian fifties, a .38 revolver, a quarter ounce of marijuana, an almost empty bottle of methadone, another of Dexedrine, and a half-full one of codeine cough syrup. He took the money out, stopping to look back at the mostly cleared-out safe. He looked at where the money had been, and he ran his finger over the cold surface. Then he closed the door without locking it.

When he'd been getting his money laundered, Mousey had asked the amazing Chinese accountant to give him the cash in fifties instead of hundreds because he liked the red bills, having grown bored of the homogeneity of American cash. He was into the Canadian fives, tens, twenties, and fifties; he thought the gold hundreds were a bit on the nose.

Even looking at the money, even looking right at it in his hand as he was about to give it to Grace, Mousey wouldn't have said out loud that he felt guilty. He would have said he was guilt-full. You don't give away stacks of cash because of how you feel. You give it away because of what you know you are.

Grace was in the middle of a very gentle sip straight from the bottle when he placed the bundles on her leg. She almost spit up when she saw them, and all three fell to the floor. The money sat there for a while, both of them looking at it, until Grace raised her eyes to Mousey's and he winked. She stood with considerable effort, took two steps back and another conservative sip from the bottle.

"Just what the fuck is that?"

Mousey picked up the bills and laid them out side by side on the cushion Grace had just moved from. "It's your money. For the lesson. I'm really confident about the song." He whistled several sounds that resembled, but were not in fact, music.

"I'm not taking that. I'm not taking anything, that's really …I don't like it, Mousey. I don't like this."

He stayed looking at the money. "I don't want it, I don't need it, and it's clean. You don't have to worry about it. I promise it's clean."

"That much cash money doesn't exist clean."

Mousey smiled again; it was less charming this time. "I have a pension. I don't need it, and I want to give it to you. You don't want it, give it to charity."

"You want rid of it, *you* give it to charity."

"Can't."

"Why not?"

"Don't believe in it."

"And your pension, that's a garage-door-opener pension, right?"

Mousey knew better than to talk or nod or move his head at all.

"Fuck you. I need the money, so no. I'm not taking nothing I need from you."

Mousey finally looked up from the money. He pointed at her. "What's your favourite dinosaur?"

Grace smiled. "Just when I'm ready to treat you like the asshole you is, you pull me back." She spread her arms opera-singer wide. "I'm a brontosaurus girl, from way back. I ride for the brontosaurus."

Mousey shook the money stack at her. "See, I already knew that, actually."

"For real? Damn, son. If I'm forgetting telling you my favourite dinosaur, I know we're having way too many of these dumbass conversations."

"Nah, it was early days, forgetting is fair. See, not to brag, but I have a pretty amazing memory. I agreed with you back then, and I agree with you now. I'm a brontosaurus boy. They're so big and so gentle."

Grace toasted him with the bottle and took another tiny sip. "When you're right, you're right. But you already knew that, because you've got your gold star for memorizing shit."

"See, after we agreed about the brontosauri, you went home and diddled around on the piano or whatever, and I researched the hell out of those dinos. And guess what?"

"I'm grown. I don't guess."

"They're not a real thing."

"My son was in elementary; I saw the homework, Brontosaurus is real, man."

"They're just little apatosaurs. And those fellas might even have had feathers."

Grace shrugged. "Names are whatever. They still roamed, eating grass and harming nobody, correct?"

"Correct."

"So I still love 'em. What's your point?"

He flipped the money packet onto the couch next to him. "It's a tough world out there for dinosaurs. And the gentle ones deserve more" — Mousey winced — "than the other ones."

Grace sat back down beside Mousey, putting him between her and the money. She grabbed his hand and held it. "Just promise me this is safe money. You can't tell me about jail murders and then make me go to jail. It's mean."

"I promise. For real. I promise. Plus, and don't take this the wrong way, I think you'd be a momma. Get a couple sweet young things in your stable; it's not a bad life. I know this gal, she's doing some time up in Logan now—"

Grace squeezed his hand to stop him. Then she laid her other hand flat. Mousey put the bills in it. "I'm too drunk to drive or hear the rest of you talking. You got a guest room in this greenhouse?"

"Bed's made and everything. Don't say I'm not thoughtful."

"I wouldn't say that about you, my friend. That's one of the ones I wouldn't say."

Grace flapped the cash at him, and Mousey recoiled theatrically, flipping himself all the way over the back of the couch and hitting his head on the floor. They both laughed.

"Think that'll hurt tomorrow?"

"I think everything will hurt tomorrow." He stood and his vision went black for a quick second from the head rush.

Grace hauled herself up and started towards the stairs. "When you're right, you're right."

His vision cleared and he wiped his dry face with his dry hand. "What about the rest of the time?"

Grace didn't turn around; all she did was snort, wave the last of his dirty money at him, and turn the corner.

5 Victoria, British Columbia

As the wails of the sirens slowly died down, and the shuffling and slams of people coming home from work dissipated into the occasional shuffles and slams of people coming home from the bar or the gym after work, Tommy Marlo stared with watery, unseeing eyes at his floor.

In his mental rerunning of the situation, Tommy had become fixated on the sound of the bump on his hood as he'd floored the car past the two club members at the gas station. He'd been face down across the seats with his eyes closed at that exact moment, and now he imagined the guy bouncing over the roof in the way people who have been killed by a stupid, reckless driver would bump over the roof of a car.

Having never killed anyone before, and being completely sure that the hand he hadn't even hurt with the hood of his car was an entire person he'd killed, Tommy felt a kind of bottomless guilt that he had never before imagined.

Asking Tommy what it felt like to be a murderer on the run from the most dangerous criminal motorcycle gang in history would have been like asking how it felt to be fifteen on his fifteenth birthday. You never have an answer to give, but you do feel differently. It's just too soon to explain how.

Being a murderer on the run from the most dangerous criminal motorcycle gang in history felt like arms and legs and breathing. It felt like nothing at all.

Although it seemed so long ago, Tommy could remember how he'd felt that morning. Tired, sad, worried, annoyed by little things, and, as was usual for him, a little bit hopeful. Now Tommy was sitting on his sagging pullout bed, feeling nothing, in the way that arms and legs and breathing are nothing. He looked up from his floor to the indistinct blur of his closed curtains. Finally, he stood and put in his contacts, then he flaked the long, dried patch of blood off his face with a fingernail.

Since coming to Victoria three months prior, Tommy had been on a haphazard self-improvement kick, which had mostly consisted of doing sit-ups and push-ups sporadically and buying a peel-off word-of-the-day calendar to improve his vocabulary. As his eyes reluctantly dragged themselves back into focus, he saw the calendar. It was over a month behind. Tommy slumped into his desk seat and without looking peeled three days off, letting them scatter themselves across the desk.

Winsome Gaping Nightwitch.

Tommy felt no need to read the rest of the card for the definition of *winsome*. His eyes and brain were tired, so he satisfied himself with a phonetic knowledge of the word. For the first time in a couple hours, he used his mouth to make a sound on purpose.

"Winsome Gaping Night Witch. Winsome. Gaping. Nightwitch. Night. Witch. Gaping. Gaping. Gaping."

Talking perked Tommy up a little and snapped him

partially out of his trance. He spun his chair around and rose gingerly, remembering his bruised ribs (or really his body at all) for the first time since he'd left the gas station. He reached into his pocket and, after almost bisecting his finger, lifted his hunting knife out. Tommy had no idea how the knife could have ended up there. He specifically remembered leaving it out on the passenger seat. Tommy shrugged off this miracle, now equally numb to the joys of the uncertain and unlikely. Using the knife, he cut the cord on the first bag of money, peeked in, and nodded glumly at more money than he'd ever seen in one place before. He didn't bother to count it, but he eyeballed it at about fifty grand. He let the floppy top of the bag drop back down and moved on to the second bag.

The second his hand entered the bag Tommy's entire sensory world once again exploded, this time into a suffocating world of scalding green dye. He whirled away, coughing and ineffectually grabbing at his eyes, which really just pushed more dye below his eyelids and knocked his glasses to the ground. He fell to the floor and used his hands to guide himself to the sink beside his bed (his bathroom was just a toilet and shower). He vomited green dye into the sink and splashed ineffectually at his eyes.

Using the wall and bathroom floor to guide him, he flopped over the edge of his bathtub and through the mildew-highlighted plastic shower curtain, pulling it down with him into the tub. He got the water running and let it soak across his head and face. The shower curtain was wrapped around him, gathering pockets of diluted green ink and water and spilling them as Tommy contorted and continued to mash at his eyes. Eventually, his eyes settled into a lighter, more passive burning, and he stopped thrashing, letting the water soak his shaved head, forming small streams down his face and into his shirt.

Tommy laughed, choked on some water, and finally pulled his head out from under the faucet. He propped himself up on one elbow, like a movie cowboy around a movie campfire, and looked down at the drain and the watery ink sliding past him and into it. He started singing, with perfect pitch and a confident, trained voice.

"Winsome gaping night witch / Winsome gaping night witch / I will find you / I will find you / I will find you / and then you'll know / and it'll go to show / a whole lot of nothing at alllllllll. Winsoooooommmmme gaping / I missed you before we met / and I'm getting awful wet / and I hope you miss you / too."

Tommy wept for a long time into the blanketing context of water.

Greta was picking up Sergei outside of the Spaghetti Factory he owned. He was a very short, very wide man with a very full beard. He always wore a suit with no tie and expensive runners that he hoped would pass, at first glance, for dress shoes. He'd had set Greta up with a short-notice find-and-kill gig, some idiot named Tommy Marlo who'd knocked off a stash of stolen money from the club, and she needed a face-to-face with Sergei to talk it out.

Sergei waved and hustled around the back of the car with an unlikely, compact agility before opening the door and coming to rest gently in the passenger seat.

"Hello, my dear!" He spoke with a pleasingly heavy accent. Greta reached over and shook his hand before shoulder-checking past him and pulling into the empty street. "So you wish to speak with your elder. It is business?"

"'Fraid so, sweet knees. This job is hot. I don't want it."

He rubbed his beard. "You feel you have a choice?"

"Serge, what's the point in having you…hang on." The car was coming up to a very stale yellow left-turn signal. Greta sped up and hit the turn wide, screeching across the intersection immediately after the light changed. Sergei gripped the armrest tightly, digging his nails into the leather.

"Jesus, woman!"

Greta evened out the car and gunned it towards the next light. She laughed and punched Sergei in the arm. "You're such an old ninny. I know the suggestion light was red, but that's in the past now. We only have so much time in this world, Serge. Don't spend it worrying about things you can't control, like dying in a car crash because of my reckless driving. I've crashed three cars and I died less than one times."

"And once more we see there are reasons you are employed as you are, and reasons why I am but a humble chain-restaurant owner. My heart is open to all things and thus is fragile. Drop me at this corner." Sergei didn't speak in buildings he owned, so the meetings were always in cars, or restaurants, or alleys. Greta liked that, never having been a huge Spaghetti Factory fan in the first place.

Greta pulled over and spun to look at him. "You think I'm going to do this hot mess of a gig?"

"Carton of loveliness, there are some things I think, and I do so tremblingly and with uncertainty, but there are also other things. Things I know. This is an other thing."

Greta nodded. "Why don't they put their guys on it? I'm expensive."

"As one does, they appreciate finesse. They have a man at his apartment for the rest of this day, in the unlikely event that he returns to it. You start tonight. You are to search the apartment in the hopes of finding what a policeman's mind would call evidence of his whereabouts, and what an artist's mind would dub 'the goods.'" It really was a very thick and beautiful Russian accent.

"No, I don't. We both know this Marlo kid rabbited

already. I don't start shit tonight, except maybe this needle-work project I've been thinking about…"

"Three times your usual money is not enough for you?"

"They're giving you that?"

"A portion from my own pocket, dearest." Greta cocked an eyebrow. Sergei looked to have changed species and swallowed a domestic bird whole. "There are favours I wish owed to me. Also, if I may be so bold as to inquire: needlepoint?"

"It's for an ironic gift."

"Ah. Of course."

Greta twisted her ring, a long oval plate with a Jan van Calcar woodcut on it. "Fuck. Fine. I'll take Marlo. From the pocket, hey? You really want this one, hey, Mr. Spaghetti?"

Sergei was already out of the door and putting on sunglasses. He paused a second then looked straight at the sun. "If I had been twenty years younger and we had both used the same alphabet from birth, our love would have burned hotter than this gorgeous star which sustains us, and lasted for twice as long."

Greta spent the afternoon cooking dinner and preparing reheatable meals for the week, then she exercised and did some myofascial-release stretching with a foam roller.

Late in the afternoon the hitman leaned out her window to take a picture of a garbage can lid that had somehow ended up in the branches of the tree across the street from her house. The photo did not capture the way the branch swayed and trembled in the wind, and it did not convey the thin, high-pitched trembling metal sound that Greta imagined as she looked at it, but it was a technically competent photograph. She had effectively framed the lid between the branches holding up the power line hanging above and in this way managed to suggest the fleeting, subdued awe that had hit her after she'd caught sight of the object out of the corner of her eye.

She pulled up to the apartment complex, catching the biker's eye on her first circle of the block and then sliding smoothly into his spot as he pulled out. The moron was still wearing a bandana. No leather jacket, just a jewellery-store-robbery hoodie that suggested, fully and precisely, the full patch cut he wasn't wearing. Subtle as a Baptist church service.

Although contract murder was her business, there were a number of aspects of this particular contract murder with which Greta was unfamiliar, and of which she was wary. The job was less simple, less "here's an address now go squelch a human soul" than she preferred. The involvement of a truly terrifying, surprisingly sloppy criminal motorcycle gang worried her from a logistical standpoint. Then, on top of all the complications, there was the potential of having to find, restrain, and maybe lightly torture Tommy Marlo.

Since her particular brand of malevolence was of a negative, as opposed to an actively sadistic, type, characterized more by the absence of standard human feelings for the people she hurt than a delight in their pain, the prospect of finding, restraining, and maybe lightly torturing Tommy

Marlo troubled Greta in a distantly revolting sort of way, the way the idea of cleaning up day-old vomit would trouble her.

The hitman chain-smoked organic cigarettes, read a somewhat spewily written small-press crime novel, and drank ginger root tea from a thermos as she staked out Tommy Marlo's apartment, waiting for the whole street to go to sleep.

Around four o'clock in the morning, Greta slipped out of the car, walking slowly in a loose, upright posture towards the apartment. She picked Tommy Marlo's lock in less than forty seconds.

Greta had killed twenty-one people, and when she was twelve years old her family had been driving home from camping, and she'd looked out the window at the exact perfect second to see a golden retriever disappear under the wheels of a pickup truck and spit back out headless with its neck now wider than its body. Tommy's apartment was still, by a good margin, the saddest thing she'd ever seen.

For starters it was an airless third-floor studio next to the garbage chute. Even a pretty good decorator would have had trouble, and Marlo obviously thought feng shui was a dish you ordered for takeout. The bathroom was so small they put the sink in the main room, almost hanging over a double mattress about as thick as a slice of cheese. Marlo'd triggered the ink packs and left the green slime all over the floor and sink, a thick trail leading into the shower, which was stained fluorescent. Looking at the spatter, she guessed he'd taken the ink pack straight to the face, gotten confused and remembered the shower late.

The closet was empty, so he'd obviously split. Dyed green like that, most of the cash he'd stolen was about as useful as an asshole to a jellyfish. Marlo had been around the block, he'd know better than to try to buy a plane ticket with cash the day after an armed robbery, so Greta figured he either had a hot car or was hitchhiking. Greta tossed the place for receipts or relevant documents and didn't find anything; Marlo wasn't a conscientious tax guy. All told, it took Greta an hour. She did a quick double-check, scanned for her own hairs, and left. She backed out the door, hoping to shut it as quietly as possible. Having pretty strong natural instincts, she sensed the landlord's presence without seeing or hearing him. She turned around smiling.

He was an older guy, late fifties, janitor-skinny, holding a bucket of water in one hand and a long, ratty-looking cleaning tool in the other. The old guy looked like he'd been scared for a second. His whole body relaxed when he saw Greta's breasts, or, more accurately, that she was a person with breasts. She made an embarrassed expression cross her face, then held a finger over her lips. The old man smiled and nodded at her a bit sympathetically, knowing Marlo. He looked at her as a man who'd seen thousands of mistakes from a distance and judged almost none of them.

Greta stayed in the doorway and made a show of searching through her fanny pack. The landlord kept coming, he got to the trash chute and put the bucket down, dipping the tool in, and then he reached up to open the chute. He leaned in, and before he had time to scrub one wall, Greta had already closed the distance and stabbed him twice in the lungs. The garbage chute banged closed, and she heard the wet sponge-on-a-stick bang down the sides towards the bottom. In one motion she'd covered his mouth and nose and started dragging him into Marlo's apartment, staring with a distant aesthetic admiration at the bright red trail he left across the filthy hallway floor. Dust bunnies oblivious, playing in a field of blood.

Having grown up in Victoria, Tommy knew exactly how necessary it was to bring a raincoat with him as he hitch-hiked up island. But—as was happening more and more, lately—the things he knew were smart to do had very little impact on the things he ended up doing.

As most people would expect, spending his early child-hood as half of one of the approximately 750-and-a-half black people in Victoria, British Columbia, had been alienating and confusing in a medium-mild sort of way for Tommy. Not the kind of thing you think about every day, but something that's always bubbling near the surface, turn-ing up in ambiguous interactions that stick in your mind for months on end. As fewer people might expect, spending his early teen years as half of one of the approximately 750-and-a-half black people in Victoria, British Columbia, had been, initially, awesome.

Because Tommy's mother coached the choir to Nationals every year, Tommy had started attending a private high school in grade nine on scholarship. And here, instead of being a normal kid who occasionally elicited a weird, quick-ly hushed reaction from people, he became a straight-up celebrity.

The clique of hottest girls in grades eleven and twelve loved rap and basketball and the far-off idea of black guys. So as his friends from middle school struggled through a first term of white-boy pimples and wet dreams, Tommy, in just a couple months, had been passed between three impossibly attractive young women in button-down shirts and kilts rolled up at the waist to show more of their thighs.

They were wild girls with a lot of money, and so Tommy had also started smoking weed with them, and then started doing coke with them, and then, because the girls would get nervous, started carrying their money and picking up the coke for them and making friends with the low-level dealers who would always want to talk to him and drive around with him and dap him up and sing along, every "nigga" included, to Three 6 Mafia songs.

But the thing about celebrities is that they're also commodities. Even as a fourteen-year-old, Tommy had had an inkling of just what he was to these girls, which was a gift. They loved him, but they loved him the way they loved the Mini Coopers their fathers had given them after they'd passed their road tests. And that love is small and sincere and present, until they crumple the fender.

They were older than Tommy, older and more confident and more soft and more lovely than anyone he'd known until then, but they were still very young. And they were brave, but brave in the way a buffalo is brave, because their whole lives are so strong and sturdy and slow their brains can't even process predators. So when Jasmine and Sam got caught pounding lines while they skipped chapel, and the locker search turned up two balls of coke and seven pills of ecstasy, they'd learned suddenly and in a panic that they had a lot, and that losing any of what they had would hurt way more than keeping it felt good. So they'd snitched on Tommy, and because they were the beautiful daughters of commodities traders and he was, still, half of one of the 750-and-a-half black people in Victoria, British Columbia, he'd been expelled and told by five consecutive fat men in short-sleeved dress shirts that he was lucky not to go to jail, and Jasmine and Sam had gone to rehab, and then Dartmouth.

The world these girls had showed him had stayed fun for a while, but it had not stayed awesome. Tommy had credibility with drug dealers, and he still had an appeal to all the girls who wanted their lives to feel like a music video for about the length of a music video, but those girls weren't rich girls anymore, and the drugs stayed the same price. And his mom was still there, hearing the smoky shred of his vocal chords, her patience draining and the space it left filling with rage. So he'd started scamming college kids who wanted to buy down on the corner of Douglas and Yates.

After he'd put together a little stake, he decided to go in on a half ounce of blow with his girlfriend. Heading back to her car after the pickup, he was stopped by two uniformed cops and asked why he was in a hurry and what was in his bag. And he said I'm not, and my gym stuff. And the older cop had smirked and said oh yeah you're going to the Y to shoot hoops? And Tommy had taken a little toot picking up the blow so he was riding an edge, feeling a little sharp and a little quick and a little bit sick of being half of one of the 750-and-a-half black people in Victoria, British Columbia, and he'd said no, fuckhead, I'm going to Pilates. And then there was the side of the building pressed on his face, and then there was air and free space and enough time to start to run, and then there was the sidewalk pressed on his face and about fifty thousand volts of Taser in every part of his body at once, and then there was another expulsion, a youth magistrate, another nineteen consecutive thick dudes in sweaty short-sleeved dress shirts telling him he was lucky not to go to juvie. And then there was his mom, not patient anymore, not mad anymore, just empty, just drained, saying do what you like, Tommy, it's on you, I'm done. Just done.

Tommy decided that if done was a thing he and his mother were letting each other be, then he was about done with about every part of being half of one of the 750 and a half black people in Victoria, British Columbia, and the only part of it he changed was the being in Victoria, British Columbia, part.

And now he was back, and the light drizzle had started, as it always will, at the exact point at which Tommy was too far from his home and too close to the bus stop to turn around. Even right then, Tommy felt what he knew was coming: a long, slow soak that just settled over you, and that you didn't understand the depth of until you caught yourself shivering. And even knowing what was coming, he stayed at the stop, waiting fifteen minutes for the bus that came every sixteen minutes.

He rode all the way to the end of the line, waiting through a driver change and a random stop where they kept the driver but changed the number on the front of the bus. He hoped for his hoodie to dry, which, being thickly knit hemp, it would in another nine to twelve hours.

The driver turned off the bus without saying anything and waited for Tommy to rouse himself and wrestle his huge, misshapen bag onto his shoulder (he wasn't a good packer). Tommy spoke for the first time in what felt like a long time and thanked the driver in a weak, phlegmy voice, and the driver grunted in response.

Tommy figured that the Greyhound bus, while comfortable and not illegal, was probably being watched and staked out by both the club and the cops, and that hitchhiking, while cold and dangerous and definitely illegal, was off the grid and impossible to watch from a parked cop car or blank-panel gang-murder van and was therefore the best of his bad options.

Tommy hadn't hitchhiked in a couple years, but it's not exactly a skill you lose, or really a skill at all. He waited patiently in the wide shoulder of the road he'd selected, just far enough away from the Langford Superstore to avoid the big crowds, but close enough to get a decent runoff of cars driven by lonely people.

He was there for just over an hour before two girls using a cardboard box as an umbrella walked up to the hitching spot. He smiled and waved at them, pointed at their box, and said: "Jealous." The girls laughed more than was reasonable, walked all the way up to him and nervously rushed through asking him if he'd been waiting long and what his name was and if he had any K or molly to sell. Both of them were wearing thick flannel work shirts unbuttoned and tied so that their pierced bellies showed. One of the piercings was a stylized spike with a purple plastic diamond as the cap. The other was in the shape of a very thin dolphin.

Kaylie and Rodha gave their ages as eighteen, which Tommy pegged as a couple years bloated. The girls were hitching up to a camp-out party in Duncan. Out of concern, Tommy asked them if they were meeting anyone up there, which set off an invitation to the party and some flirting from Kaylie that made him feel like he was watching an SPCA commercial. Tommy pretended that he might hit up the party then gave the girls some advice about buying safe party drugs that bored them and sent them both into their phones.

Tommy finally flagged down a nice car driven by a pretty middle-aged woman in a high school soccer sweater. He dropped his bag and rushed over.

"Are you with these girls?"

Tommy reached across the plane of her open window and gratefully touched her arm, which felt like a huge mistake even as it was happening. "No, no. It's good that you're thinking like that, about their safety, I mean. They need a ride, I do too, but I'm...separate. They're not with me. But, like, myself too, I've been out here..." He'd shot his arm back to his side a while ago, and now found himself with it suspended oddly, his elbow up by his head. This was not going well.

The woman looked at Tommy suspiciously, which, he reflected sadly, actually probably meant she was a kind and ethical person who worried more about teenage girls trying to hitch than the adult male dirtbags standing near them. "I only have room for two. One of my seatbelts is broken."

"Oh, that's fine. Five seatbelts, right? So four of us, one for each..." Tommy paused and had a little, defeated smile for himself. Maybe hitchhiking is a skill you can lose. "One for each of us."

"Um, no. I meant two are broken. That's what I meant. I only have room for three people total. So I'll take just you or I'll take the girls. I'm not taking you with the girls."

Tommy nodded and looked back at the girls, who were moving slowly towards the car, hugged together under the cardboard. "Uh, I get it. I get it. I'll, uh... I'll wait it out. Just, shit, they're better off riding with a woman than some random creepy-ass trucker, right?"

The driver smiled at him and raised her eyes in a way that made Tommy realize he'd been leaning over her car in a not strictly socially appropriate way. He took a couple drifting steps back. "That's what I think too. I hope you catch a lift."

"I will. Thanks for stopping." The girls arrived and Tommy opened the back door and held it for them with a jokey sweep of the arm. The girls piled in, laughing and not looking at him.

The car started pulling away and Tommy waved. Kaylie blew him a kiss, and flashed him one cup of a very normal blue bra, which was a thing he hadn't wanted her to do. He'd just wanted to let the girls know he didn't mind giving up the ride, and that he didn't mind as a real person, not just as somebody who hoped someday to put his dick in or around them. He'd wanted to tell them that even in the sketchiest scenes — like hitchhiking with a fugitive who would have mugged them if he hadn't had $55,000 in his backpack — girls like them could still find people who would cut them a break for honest reasons. He'd wanted to tell them that he hoped they'd only let people put their dicks in or around them when they (Kaylie and Rodha) thought it would be fun. He'd wanted to tell them they could think of favours and good breaks the way Tommy himself thought of them: as just a part of life, a small uneven counterpoint to all the bad randomness they were already used to, not as things they always had to earn or buy with one cup of a very normal blue bra.

But from the side of the road you can't always convey thoughts that long and that sadly won. You can just wave and accept whatever soundless thing the person does back, and hope you both understand each other better than you can show right then with just your arm and the look on your face and the way you hold your body upright against the slow drizzle of rain soaking you through with only persistence and the whole sky and time.

Marlo had not left a big paper trail, which was to say that there was literally nothing written down in his entire apartment. There also hadn't been any pens. But it had only taken Greta one short trawl of the Dark Web to find Marlo's guy in Victoria, a small-time fence and hacker, and a big-league prog-rock and television-file pirate, named Bill in real life and Jumanji87 on 4chan.

Or that was the way it seemed. Sitting in her car outside Bill's Fernwood condo building, Greta had to acknowledge that there was a very small chance that Bill wasn't the only person selling credit card information and old-ass stolen laptops in Victoria, British Columbia. But she had weighed even that almost infinitesimal possibility before she brought her paintbrushes and giant bottle of what looked exactly like, and could even actually be, human blood into this poor guy's cheap condo.

It wasn't so much that Greta was nervous but more that she was protective of her own image and pride. You bring a bottle of something that definitely could be blood into a guy's house, paint an original and not terrible picture on his wall, and it sends a very strong message, communicates your intent. You do the same to some torrenter who happens to have gotten his hand on some used computers, and then you just look like a ditz. A weird, psycho ditz, which is one kind of ditz that nobody likes.

Greta opened the sack and took a last look at the bottle of what could even actually be human blood, which was sweating in the heat. The hitman closed the bag and, as she often did, spoke to herself as if the other self was sitting on the hood of her car and could hear through glass. "Commit. The idea's the idea."

The actual home invasion couldn't have gone any better. Bill was out of the apartment, his hallway was empty, and his lock was easy. To top it all off, he was extremely well organized, all his stolen laptops arranged in a long, wheeled file folder. Marlo's laptop wasn't there, as she'd figured. Even he had to know what he had. There was also a ton of medical-grade marijuana lying around, and after considering deeply and finally dismissing the idea of stealing Bill's Volcano, Greta pocketed three individually packaged joints of Sativa before she settled into thinking about where to paint the blood portrait.

The best spot would probably have been the dingy, tight hallway between the front door and the two bedrooms in the back (it had a claustrophobic feel that she thought would really work to highlight the intensity of the colour palette), but she had to make sure he got all the way inside so she could contain him in the apartment. So she settled for the living room wall. The living room had good light, the wall primed with a pale single coat of beige paint. The room was a bit too spacious for her liking, but it did have a bank of computers and a bunch of fans buzzing and a huge, stained couch that was collapsing in on itself, all of which would, hopefully, help to give Bill the claustrophobic, night-terror feeling she was hoping for.

The living room would be a fine spot for the mural.

There is no way to be brought into the world of contract killing that is more or less usual than any other.

Four years prior, Greta had graduated with a master's degree in art history from a prestigious US university. And for the six years it had taken her to go through her university education, she was considered a successful young woman, having gotten her degrees from schools people had heard of. Then, all at once, she became just a young woman with $41,000 of student debt, no employable skills, and no desire to do a PhD.

For about a year she stayed in her parents' basement, working in a call centre and going to indie rock shows and doing a ton of MDMA. On a rainy fall night, smoking and trying to even out beside the doors of an Empathy Pig concert, Greta found her career. The stairwell outside of Grumpy's Tavern had flooded in the rain, so Greta was standing on a milk crate, poking the dwarf statuette above the door in the nose. A woman's voice emerged from the doorway, the existence of which Greta had forgotten as she looked into the cracked paint of the wooden dwarf's eyes.

"Excuse me, can I get the fuck out of this bar now?"

Greta suddenly remembered that the true purpose of

the milk crate was not to allow one a better vantage on Grumpy the Wooden Dwarf, but to let people move in and out of the bar's flooded stairwell. She felt a depth of contrition that was, perhaps, exaggerated and she reached out to touch the sound of the voice as she apologized.

"I am so sorry. You want to go outside into this beautiful rain that makes you remember childhood and I'm on this crate andandand oh man, have you talked to this dwarf? He has soulful eyes and a nose that could sink a battleship." Her hand was already unimaginably deep into the woman's hair, which was thick and wonderfully complicated. "You have fantastic hair, my hand is lost in it like in a forest, except my hand won't die of hypothermia and people do that when they get lost in the forest, even though being lost in a giant forest must be a sweet feeling until you start getting cold. All those trees and mosses and air."

The woman was laughing and gently pushing Greta's wrist out of her hair. "Greta?"

Greta wiggled her fingers around in front of her face for a moment before looking past them and realizing that the woman was actually Karen, whom she'd known in grad school. "Karen! You have a really strong grip."

Karen gently guided Greta to a dry spot that was all the way under the awning. "How are you doing?"

Greta allowed a happy shiver full sway over the length of her spine. "Super-good! I mean, shitty normally, but super-good right this second! How are you? Are you on vacation? Where did you find such a textured shirt?" Greta's hand, having stopped wiggling, had found its way into Karen's open coat and was now running up along both sides of Karen's red corset-style top.

Karen laughed and once more gently guided Greta's hands to a less personally invasive location. "I am super-good too, and I'm only in town on business for like a week. Do you want a smoke?"

Greta found herself severely lacking saliva, and was also trying not to grind her teeth, so she nodded instead of speaking and twisted her head around in a completely unsystematic attempt to find her drink. Karen reached over Greta's shoulder and handed her the glass, which was now mostly full of rainwater. Greta finished the drink in one swallow, and as she turned around, a lit cigarette was placed smoothly between her lips. The smoke tasted metallic and sharp, and Greta tried to focus on the blooming feeling in her chest. She looked down at Karen's rainboots, a small repeated black-and-white headshot of Elvis Presley covering them.

Greta exhaled straight up into the doorway. "What do you do for work? I call people on the phone and ask them if they've had cancer and things like cancer or if they're happy with the community college they went to. Those are different surveys, though."

The smoke from Greta's cigarette was floating back down in thick wisps, shrouding Karen's hair. Karen held her non-cigarette hand out into the rain, letting the water run down her arm. "I kill people for money." She slowly pulled her hand back in, reached through the smoke and poked Greta, wetly, on the tip of her nose.

Greta giggled and wiped her nose aggressively. "You would be perfect. Who would think the cute girl with a massive lady-boner for Hieronymus Bosch is there to kill you? You'd be like a wolf in a sheep's hairdo."

Karen grabbed a piece of her own bangs; she pulled it out slowly, watching the strands of her hair curl back towards her head one by one. "*The Seven Deadly Sins and the Four Last Things*, all day, errday. And you're absolutely right, they don't. They wouldn't expect you either."

Greta was a little busy exploring the ice cubes remaining in her glass, but she listened to Karen. Greta felt a strong desire to sound like a woman talking to another woman in a novel written by a woman using a man's name. "These days, my dear, nobody expects a thing of me."

The two women slouched closer together, threw aside their cigarettes, and held both of each other's hands. Karen said: "You shouldn't be by yourself playing with dwarves outside of bars."

"I came with my friend, but she's having a skinny-jean-covered penis folded into her in one of those booths now…"

"You shouldn't be working a shit job and feeling like a loser. Listen, I've got a job. And I can get you work, if you want really, really strange, fun, uber-fucked-up work."

Greta took a long, fluttery breath and relaxed her neck, leaning back into the wall and feeling all the bumps and drops of paint with the back of her head.

"So tell me about it."

ø

Greta had learned very early on that there's no point having a preconceived idea of what someone will look like when all you've done is stalk them on the internet and search their apartment and paint in what could easily be blood all over their living room. Nonetheless, as a small person who saw things through the eyes in her own small head, she was never fully prepared for people to wind up huge, especially not people who do jobs that tiny people can do just as well.

Bill was about six-foot-four, wearing thick glasses and a T-shirt that just as easily could have been any of the prog-rock album covers decorating the walls around him, tri-toned beard sprawling off his face like a suburb. He made it all the way into the living room before he saw the wall, and he saw Greta only in the panicked glance he shot around the apartment right after.

The hitman waved in a friendly way she actually felt. From looking at him and searching his apartment, this was a guy she could imagine making class-friends with in a second-year history course and genuinely liking until he invited her out for a coffee that was definitely actually a somewhat awkward date and then never seeing him again. "Hi. I'm a person with a name you will never learn. Your name is William Harbough and your mother lives at 2427 Foul Bay Road, basement suite. I broke into your apartment, there's a catch bolt on your door, so when you closed it behind you it locked, and now only I can open it." The guy was staring at the painting, shaking already. This was going to be an easy one. "I see you looking at this really quite bloody-looking mural that I painted on your wall. So,

first, some words on the piece: I'm calling this one *Gimme!*
That's the title, and yes, before you ask, the medium is very
human-blood-like substance on drywall. And yes, this is a
painting of a pipe." She turned back to admire her work,
then nodded back at Bill. "It is not the 'this is not a pipe'
Magritte pipe, or not-pipe. That's a fine painting. Does it
deserve to be the most famous of the famous? Probs not,
but that's a matter for scholars of that movement. This is
my own pipe, that I drew and thought of myself. It's an
original. Plus, Magritte was a pussy and did his with paint,
not with a mysterious human-blood-like substance that I'd
be curious as fuck about if I were you, Bill. You go by Bill,
right? But I won't tell you if it's blood, Bill. And if it were
blood I wouldn't tell where the blood is from, Bill, because
that's the last thing anyone cares about, where the blood
came from. I'm just going to tell you that I'm here about
Tommy Marlo and the last computer he stole. And I broke
in here, used that fancy equipment to lock you in, and then
I, painstakingly and with the love of a talent never quite
mastered, painted a passable picture on your wall to get
your attention about this very serious matter with Tommy
and the computer he jacked from a young girl. I'm not
going to be a hack and threaten you or anything, I'll let you
connect the dots—hey, paint your own picture—and think
about how seriously me and the people paying me many,
many dollars are taking this." She took a long pause that she
kept from being pregnant by half humming, half breathing
a bouncy tune she had come up with when waiting for a bus
some time ago. "So we'll go through all your computers in
there, then we're going to have a chat about Tommy."

Six huge, heaving breaths later, his glasses totally fogged over, Bill found his voice. "I don't have the computer."

"Why not? You're Tommy's fence, right?"

Eyes still locked on the pipe, "I'm his fence, but once we saw what was on the computer he didn't want me to ... He took it himself. In case he could ..."

"Use it as a chip to deal with the cops or the club." She clicked her tongue against her teeth. "We'll see how that works out for him. Where is he?"

Bill was feeling his oats now, his eyes flicking towards her behind the fogged glass, setting his weight in his legs almost as if he wanted, or had any idea how, to fight. "He's my friend. I ... I won't do that."

Greta smiled genuinely. "Okay, so here's the scene, my dude. You've got at least a buck forty-five on me, weight-wise. The tippy top of my steady head standing on my tippy-toes doesn't reach your collarbones. I've got nothing in my hands. And I'm standing three feet away from you in your living room telling you, right now, that you're going to give up your boy. I'm not telling you *to* give him up. I'm informing you that you will. See the difference?"

She took a step closer to him, placed her head gently into his chest and moved him surely back until he fell onto the couch. She leaned over and tapped his nose with her index finger.

"Smile button!" His upper lip trembled, but not because he was fighting a smile. "What I'm trying to say to you, Bill, is that you should look at this as a favour, right now. That's the way to see this thing. You live in the internet; you know the deal. This is a world of unceasing subjectivity. A world of opinions. But right now, right this very second, I'm giving you the gift of living in fact. There's no two ways to see the world right now. There's no choose-your-own-adventure end to this little scene we have here. There's one ending, and it's up to me, not you, how we get there. I'm letting you exist in the presence of hard truth, for just a little while. And I think you should appreciate that." Greta gracefully flung her leg above her shoulder and used the momentum to flip onto the couch, settling with her legs crossed on the armrest and across Bill's lap. The lower angle let her see the thick line of wetness creeping down his jeans. "Plus, you can probably get a lot out of this, jerking-off-wise, later. A really shameful, sharp, humiliating load. I hear those're all the rage these days. So take a deep breath and try to bank this whole scene. You're going to be okay."

It's true of cats and it's true of people: if you really want to train them, you can't just shout and hit them, and you can't just give them treats and hugs. They won't hear one note, no matter what that note is. Pet, pet, slap. Do that once, and they never, ever forget it. The hitman popped over onto her other hip, uncrossed her ankles, and slammed a short, sharp, barré kick into Bill's face, not breaking his nose, but bending it with a light cartilagey crunch at the end. His watering eyes stayed looking away from her as Greta swung around and sat upright.

"Man, you need a new couch. This shit is about to swallow me. Need some life in your cushions, dude. So I'm going to let you chill a minute, fire up that Volcano for us, and we can vape a nice leisurely bag together while you tell me where I'm going to find your friend."

ø

Sergei agreed to meet at Greta's favourite brunch restaurant, a loss-leader and passion project supported by the (mostly) BDSM sex store on the first floor. The owner, a friendly man sporting leather chaps and a handlebar moustache, brought her a full pot of coffee as she waited, and then he complimented her shoes. She saw Sergei take the stairs two at a time. He nimbly swung himself into the restaurant and settled down across from her with a flourish, like someone's father in a European film musical.

"Hello! You have worked quickly and beautifully and had a long and troublesome day and night, I trust."

"You trust right."

"Indeed, it is my greatest gift. You look perturbed."

"Well, it got a bit messy. I assume the cleanup crew comes out of my end."

Sergei tilted his head to one side, thinking, then he shook the head. He gathered his fingers with a loose twiddle. "Not this time. Your other work has been excellent. And that cost has been spared, following your little mishap with the janitor, as it affords us the opportunity to lay the blame on Mr. Thomas Marlo and further damage his credibility, should he be apprehended and attempt to barter with the police." He flicked the edge of the menu then twiddled his fingers. "The breakfast, they serve it all day, yes?"

"You really want something out of this one, hey? As long as you have the cash, I'm good."

"So you are confident of his destination, our idiot thief?"

"Yep. I'm heading to a northern Gulf Island. So's he."

"How pleasant."

Greta had not been to bed and was in a species of mood that had been hitting her more frequently lately. "Not for anyone I meet along the way." She looked back into her coffee, which was dark black with small currents swirling around in it, like oil in a barrel.

Sergei theatrically spread the menu out to its full size. "Now that the vulgarities of business are behind us, we must eat." He paused as he read the menu and then quickly closed it and looked deeply into Greta's eyes. "I will have the Big Bear Breakfast."

Greta laughed into her coffee. "Serge, do you understand what *bear* means in this context?"

"Of course. It is a large omnivore who lives in the woods."

The corners of her mouth pulled into a smile. She put her coffee cup down, rested her hand firmly against the hot metal pot, and closed her eyes. "I burn hotter than the sun, and I'll live twice as long."

Sergei clapped his hands together. "You speak nothing but the truth, dearest girl."

Greta relaxed into the scalding heat.

10 Quadra Island, British Columbia

By the time Mousey woke up, Grace and the last of his cash nest egg were gone, and he was ten minutes late to meet his drug dealer, who was already lurking at the top of his driveway.

Mousey had been (barely) allowed to punch his twenty-year ticket from the Chicago PD mostly because senior police officials and mid-level political hacks were terrified both of the things he knew and of the people he was willing to tell. Mousey had spent a year as a criminal defence investigator, burning whatever bridges he had left, and after the last exposé dropped in the *Tribune*, had left Chicago, retired at the age of forty-three, firmly blackballed from the only city and profession he'd ever known.

A tall contractor and a tiny old man with a giant backhoe had spent a year clearing his land on Quadra and building the house that his ex-girlfriend, who was now a professor of architecture in Muncie, Indiana, had designed for him. All told it had cost him about half the money he'd saved from work and bribery and stealing, and he'd moved in a year ago but had been on the island for just nine months of that time.

A lovely bike trip down the Amalfi Coast, a three-city wine tour with a group of his lawyer friends, and a solo train trip to Germany had taken up a couple months. He'd also flown down to Chicago to speak at a slumlord's parole hearing and turned that into an emotionally intense Vegas trip with a woman he'd met on the internet.

His retirement was, in its material niceness and its harsh, lonely barrenness, not one Mousey would ever have imagined for himself—waking up every day with that feeling of having gone to bed in a hotel in a different time zone and continent and culture than the one he'd woken up in, and sometimes hungover and already ten minutes late to meet his drug dealer.

Once, a very long time ago, Mousey had asked the Most Disgusting Man in Chicago how it was that he (the Most Disgusting Man in Chicago) had been able to get away with all the disgusting things he'd been doing for all the disgusting years he'd been doing them. Mousey had asked the question in a way that, looking back on himself now, he found charmingly genuine. He had asked because he really wanted to know—not because it would help him manipulate the suspect or gain information about potential accomplices; just out of simple curiosity. And the Most Disgusting Man in Chicago had seemed to like the question, the way one likes being asked questions one has imagined answering. The guy smiled, looked Mousey up and down, and told him.

The way to avoid being seen is to be something no one wants to look at. You can't try to be a thing nobody wants to look at, because you're a person, not a thing. You can't turn yourself into a thing on your own, from inside. Nobody has that power. You just have to be it, from the start.

Every time he bought drugs from Glass Jar Jeffries, Mousey thought about that conversation. He thought about people who were only things, and he thought about the way the Most Disgusting Man in Chicago had thrown the words out in his usual downcast way, as if trying to ping-pong them across the table. How certain he'd sounded. Then Mousey would think for an even quicker second about how odd it was that he could think about what the Most Disgusting Man in Chicago had said, think about the Most Disgusting Man in Chicago's posture and his odour and his tiny creepy hand movements, without thinking about all the terrible bodies and terrible weeping relatives the Most Disgusting Man in Chicago had made him see and touch with a latex glove on and smell and talk and listen to. The way everything could be separate and far away and still just as weird and specific as reality always is. Of how years that felt like decades and decades that felt like seconds could be managed and stored and swept away. And by the time Mousey was just starting to get a little sad, Glass Jar would usually have splayed his way across the gravel of Mousey's driveway to hand him the drugs and collect his money.

As straightforwardly as viscera escaping midsection, Glass Jar flopped his seeping arm out towards Mousey, offering the two bottles of pills in his hand.

Glass Jar had the leathery and unwanted look of some sort of fruit that people don't usually like to dehydrate. His skin was puckered with abuse and stained with an extremely deep tan. His hairline was the sort that never recedes, no matter how prudent a full-scale retreat might be. The hair itself was slick and thin and ropey, its colour made indeterminate by the grease. It dangled skimpily to just below his ears, the kind of hair that needn't be cut because the ends split at a faster rate than the hair grows, giving the impression of very long, very lazily assembled fuses, smouldering listlessly towards explosion.

Mousey had never much admired the professionalism of drug dealers, but now that he was paying for drugs instead of stealing them from evidence lockers, he began to find himself irked by its absence. He snatched the drugs from Glass Jar, and with the casual, practised style of a person who has handled large amounts of illicit cash, flipped his pre-counted roll of bills out towards Glass Jar.

Glass Jar allowed some words to fall over the tip of his lip, like a winded marathon runner spitting. "Thanks to you, boss man."

Mousey grunted and, with a slight tremor he was not deluded enough to ignore, popped open the bottles and counted the pills inside.

Glass Jar, to his credit, was actually about as smart as a six-year-old who can smell a parent's distress and start misbehaving. He reached across and tapped Mousey oddly on the shoulder with a closed fist.

"Don't stand and ceremony, big man. I won't be, whatzit, offended if you gotta pop one of those puppies now. Seems like a sweaty day for you. But that might be the pot calling the kettle metal. My pots are metal-coloured. Like metal if you don't touch it."

Mousey capped the second bottle, spun it into the air, and caught it. "You're a courteous guy, but I'm good, thanks."

Glass Jar tried to jam his tongue through his cheek then smiled. "If you say so. Hey, don't mind me asking, what TV you watch?"

"Sports. Baseball and basketball mostly. And just whatever, sitcoms, dramas. What everyone watches."

Glass Jar coughed and spat quizzically into the air. A thick globe of lung waste floated away from him in a comet-like parabola before splattering aggressively across the gravel.

Mousey tossed the bottle of Percocet from his right to his left hand. "Why?"

Glass Jar sucked his teeth and took a second, more reserved spit at his feet. "You watch that *Breaking Bad*, don't you? Watch that shit and feel hard, right? Like you know about fuckin'…the game, right?"

Mousey tried to keep his smile steady, not let it peak with too much amusement. Glass Jar was a marvel, thirty years a junkie and still couldn't spot a cop from a foot away. "I don't think I know anything. I just get blasted and watch TV. I'm retired, done with the hustling."

Glass Jar laughed, his ribs rippling like a shredded-up flag. "Where I come from, hustlin' means a different thing, boss man. Or maybe the same, I don't know your life."

Mousey spun the Dexies in the air and caught them. "I guess I better be careful." He winked at no one in particular. "You seem like you're from a tough place."

Glass Jar nodded absently, "counted" his money at a speed that Mousey wasn't fooled by for a second, and turned to leave.

Sometimes a thing happens that can defeat the imagination of even a person who has seen the Northern Lights and a family-annihilation murder-suicide scene and several orcas in the wild who seemed happy. And Mousey was seeing one of those things: Glass Jar's jeans had slumped down below his ass cheek while remaining on his body, somehow suspended by the bone-wide girth of his legs; meanwhile one leg of Glass Jar's boxers had ridden well above the waistline, held up by their own waistband, like a snake biting itself halfway down its body.

It raised so many questions in Mousey, and so little desire to answer them. A long time ago, he might have asked all those silly whys, but he'd had so many beautiful, hilarious, and brutal lessons pressed into him since then. How could he ever have wanted to know things like that? It would be like looking through the centre of the sun.

11

Constable Mike Richmond still had an hour of paperwork left to do and only half an hour until his scheduled patrol started. He let out a long, sad breath, looked to the thin, plywoody bathroom door, and returned to work.

Paperwork wasn't always a bad thing, and Mike, by nature, had the patience for it. It killed time and was often a sign of a good day spent. An incident or arrest report to be filled in, maybe a search warrant to apply for, the fleeting seconds of accomplishment made solid by their recording. But the loose, shambling pile of single-ply papers currently filling Mike's desk did nothing of the sort. They were his boss's union paperwork. They signified not good work done but work that could only be finished. They evoked no pride in Mike, only the inevitable aftertaste of hopelessness that so often taints the palate of the passive, ambitious optimist.

Mike's supervisor was Sergeant Arnold Reubens, who was as demanding and unsympathetic a boss as he was useless a worker. So Mike knew not only that he had to fill out the union paperwork for his boss in order to get his vacation days right but also that he wouldn't be thanked, and that, in fact, the work was sure to be attended with some sort of vague, unreasoned criticism.

A particularly horrifying aspect of working under Arnold Reubens's command was that the man shit more often, and for longer, than Mike had ever imagined a person could or would without having to see a doctor immediately. So Mike spent a good amount of his time trying desperately not to listen to painful, alternately loose, amorphic-sounding and long, spiky, rock-hard stools passing from his boss into the welcoming and resonant soundscape of their shared office toilet three to six times in a given day.

In an effort to ignore the familiar and polyrhythmic anti-music of his boss's desperate straining, Mike closed his eyes, spun his office chair in a slow, smooth circle, and imagined his future, his life as a high-ranking RCMP officer, and then maybe later a judge or an MLA.

Richmond was a huge, gentle man of certain but flexible professional ambition. He'd joined the RCMP early, seeing it as the most exciting and easiest way into either a civil-service or political career. He liked the variety of directions his life might take, but only if that variety came with the sureness and stability of a rigidly hierarchical command structure. But of all the arcs he'd imagined for his career, none had included a long detour driving a boat around looking for expired licence tags under the nagging and inattentive supervision of a man with the stupidity and gen-eralized malevolence of Sergeant Reubens. Mike had always known the two-to-four-year hardship posting was part of the deal when you joined up, and he wasn't opposed to it on principle. But in his imaginings, the hardship postings were more solitary, more rustic. Up in Nunavut, hunting food for the old people, jumping cars with frozen batteries, scaring away polar bears, and getting a head start on LSAT prep in the off-hours.

His current posting instead presented him with the twin curses of too much busy work and a complete lack of useful training or experience. And since Quadra Island was so temperate and scenic, it was a posting of four instead of two years.

At length Reubens emerged from the commode as Mike was conjuring a mental picture of his future wife reading a book on the couch. Mike looking up at her from his gardening as she held the book with one hand, the fingers of the other playing absently against the soft front of her foot, tucked back towards her. Mike had been about to imagine his future wife looking up, seeing him blurry in the distance as her eyes adjusted, and then smiling at him, at the long streak of workdirt across his cheekbone — when Reubens emitted a long, wet belch. The sergeant then slammed the window open and spit through it thickly.

With his head still halfway out the window, Reubens said. "You aren't done yet?"

The young cop didn't bother looking up. Because Mike had not made eye contact on his first day, Reubens had pegged him as untrustworthy, and there was no possible action Mike could take to change or even gently modify this first impression. Sergeant Reubens believed in trusting his instincts.

Reubens tucked his thumbs into his belt loops and surveyed his command. They worked one-on/one-off usually, with a twice-a-week overlap for collaborative projects, like road checks or calls to Cortes Island. Today was Mike's day with Reubens, and there hadn't even been a call to get him out of the office. Mike was sitting still and quiet, watching the stiff, familiar gears of his boss's mental engine grinding oillessly in their futile, screeching battle against inertia, when Mousey knocked on the front door so hard they both jumped.

Mousey slouched in and threw out his usual clipped, Midwestern slur. "Am I interrupting a punitive moment, Sergeant Reubens?" He raised the box of donuts he was holding and started to spin it on his finger, and then stopped the box from falling with his other hand.

Here it is, Mike thought, the tumbleweed rolling right across the long, sad, deserted street of Detective Heaven. The tumbleweed was in his mid- to late forties, soft in the middle, drawn in the neck and face, with weirdly toned legs wrapped in jean shorts he must have borrowed from his niece. According to Mike's extensive internet research, Mousey'd been a genuine Chicago Detective Bureau hotshot: old-school Vice Squad legend, homicide case man, DA bagman. An escape artist who walked out clean from three of the biggest shitstorms in the history of the hurricane alley of cop shitstorms with his twenty-year pension intact and a beautiful house in the Gulf Islands. Now the kind of burnout case your dead grandfather warns you about in the boozy nightmares you have after a wake or a high school reunion.

The tumbleweed blew across the room in his usual stoned, half-skipping manner, dipping low to offer the donuts to Mike, and then swinging with a certain junkie grace up to Reubens, who, having just rid his body of several ounces of congealed gluten, began filling it up again. Mousey pulled a weird half pivot and perched on the corner of Reubens's empty desk and crossed his legs in a long, showy motion. He winked a droopy eye at Mike, having obviously taken a stronger than usual combination of whatever pills he was popping these days.

Mousey fired off a few of his standard bits, a combination of whimsical, child-like nature insights and super-callous and disturbing Chicago law enforcement tales, and Reubens, as always, ate it up.

Sergeant Reubens, for all his years of service and tight-leash supervisor cop pronouncements, was not cagey enough to realize that Mousey was not some good-old-boy cop coming in to swap stories but rather a junkie who sometimes got loaded and popped off shots into the bushes around his house and knew he needed to be tight with the local PD. Mike, for all his inexperience and small-minded ambition, was.

Mike gently escorted the remainder of the donut into his mouth then reached his boot out to tap Mousey's crossed shin. "How's it going, Mousey? Like, today?"

Mousey turned slightly, eyeballed Mike for a second, and then looked back at his shoes and shrugged. "Ahhh, the usual, Constable — few strikes, few gutters. But it's all good at the bowling alley as long as you give those shoes back. Y'know what I'm saying? Sometimes you're the sock, sometimes you're the foot, and all anyone cares about is the shoe. Y'know what I mean, Mickey?"

It was the first time anyone had ever called him Mickey, and judging from the tumbleweed's eyes, Mike thought it would probably be the last. He returned to his paperwork, and the conversation between Mousey and Reubens gradually petered out. Mousey left the donuts behind, threw Richmond a crisp salute and shuffled out of the office.

"Get out on the road, Constable. If you're this slow, you're gonna have to come back and finish the paperwork. Don't cut corners."

Mike only needed his peripheral vision to see Reubens's beer belly stretched tightly against the buttons of his shirt in a way that always made Mike think about the last second when you're tearing a donut apart and it almost seems like the thing has seams. Mike had spent literally hours, maybe days, if you added it up, staring at that belly, thinking and dreaming.

If donuts had seams.

12 Victoria, British Columbia

Greta had many skills that were fairly unique, if not necessarily all that prized, in the world of contract murder, one of which was an honest, deep, and overdeveloped talent for self-analysis. She hardly looked like anyone's first choice, and had Karen and Sergei not trained and advocated for her, she would never have had any contracts, let alone a six-figure payday for a quick kidnap or kill job.

She was used most often in situations that required some combination of stealth, the element of surprise, and most importantly, research and computer skills. Greta's work, as quick and as good as it had been, had only established Marlo's planned destination, not his actual location. It was also impossible to know if he still had the computer with him, but on the off chance that he'd been either dumb enough to hold onto it for no reason or smart enough to hold onto it as a bargaining chip, Greta was the best choice for recovering the computer intact, and if at all possible, bringing Marlo in alive to be tortured/debriefed about what he'd seen and who he'd talked to about it, and doing all of that without drawing any (more) heat.

So Greta was taking the GHB with her, just in case she took Marlo alive and needed to sedate him, but she was also bringing her shotgun, just in case she didn't and had to blow huge holes in him and anyone who saw her do it. She'd been on some tricky jobs but never one this high profile. The hitman wasn't nervous, but she also wasn't as calm as she was used to being.

Relocating her tools from her storage locker to the trunk of the car, Greta was thinking over her options and, she would readily admit (to herself), worrying about the stakes of this gig and was paying a little less attention to her surroundings than she usually did, so she only saw the thick-bodied manshape behind her reflected in the rear window of her car as she unlocked the trunk and barely had time to drop the unloaded shotgun and grab a low single leg on the guy, sending his considerable bulk off its already tenuous balance, dropping her knee on his spine as he hit the ground. She pulled her ankle-piece and jammed it into the knob between his neck and brain stem and waited for him to settle, which he did after he stopped coughing.

It was only then that she saw the patch on the back of his leather cut and the RC stitched just above it. "Fuck."

Jason Darillo was the road captain of the Victoria chapter of the club, and now mostly helped manage and supply cocaine to the city's two strip clubs. He was also the whole reason she'd been hired, since even the club knew he was too crazy to unleash on his daughter's mugger. He croaked out a breathless "Cunt." She eased off him to let him sit up, kept the gun pointed at his head.

Darillo rolled to a seated position and coughed intentionally down between his legs. "You get it? Who I am? Drop that bitch-piece and let's talk."

"All you've shown me is a Halloween costume, sir. Slowly grab your wallet and throw it to me, and if you get frisky, I'll put two in your throat. My trunk's not full yet."

Darillo moaned and reached with exaggerated caution into the front pocket of his cut. He pulled out a slim wallet with a stylized AK-47 sewn onto it and tossed it over. Greta caught the wallet with her off-hand, her eyes staying locked on Darillo. She took two lateral steps and brought the wallet into her vision through the side-mirror of the car.

"See, see who I am, you stupid fuckin' twat?"

Greta winked and tossed his wallet back to him. "Okay, Jason — Captain Darillo? — let's meet halfway, I'll lower this gun but keep it in my hand, and you just at some point privately consider why you go right to harsh vaginal expletives to express your frustration." Greta cocked the gun up playfully then spun it once around and lowered the barrel to the ground, like a cowperson would.

Darillo stood and didn't wipe himself off or adjust his clothes, which had pulled to the side and bunched in a thick, awkward lump. "I'm your fuckin' boss, I'm paying you."

"Listen, it's your girl got mugged, right? Your daughter. So I'm giving you a break. But you are not my boss. You're not Sergei's boss either, and he's the guy you're paying. And you're not paying. Other people are paying me because they want you out of it, because, as evidenced by you sneaking up on someone you know to be a killer for hire, they think you're a little too emotionally invested in this situation."

Darillo finally straightened his shirt, jeans still weirdly low-slung and gaping to the side. "You're right, and you're wrong. I'm here to tell you that they trust you. And if you can do your cuteshit and get them the computer back, you'll get your money. But they're also letting me take my six oldest, ugliest friends to Campbell River to wait this out. And you're gonna keep me updated, upfuckingseconded, on your progress. And if you take too long, or make a fucking cunt-ass nuisance of yourself…"

"I'm as vulgar as the next person, but was that necessary?"

"They will call it in. And I will take the ferry over with my boys, and we will make it rain all over that island. And if you get wet, that's no one's fuckin' concern but yours and your priest's." Darillo paused for the medium-horrible second it took for Greta to know he wasn't bluffing. "Call whoever the fuck you think your boss is and check it out, little girl. Sergei was supposed to give you the news, but I'm a hands-on sort of a guy, and this fuckin' Marlo held a blade to my daughter's throat. So I thought I'd let you know." He took a step forward and Greta raised the gun evenly.

"Okay, scary man, that might all be true tomorrow, but how about you try to keep in mind that right this very moment you're talking to a person with the means to take whatever scraps of flesh you've got in that skull of yours out and spray them anywhere she chooses. And with that in your little mind, you turn on your cute boot-heel and ride that toy motorcycle on home."

Darillo nodded, smiled creepily, and finally straightened his pants as he walked away.

13 Quadra Island, British Columbia

Glass Jar left his meeting with Mousey in unusually high spirits. His bankroll as flush as it had been in weeks, nothing could spoil Glass Jar's mood, not even the obvious fact that he would have no further income until at least next month and had exhausted his supply of meth fixings.

He knew the Mousey's type, "functioning" junkies with slight hand tremors and a serious look down their noses at him, and knew from this last meeting that the guy would only be calling him more often and for more product from now on.

He decided to stay out, drive around, and look at the water for a while. Glass Jar's preferred point of view on the Pacific Ocean was from the familiar vantage of his truck, so he drove straight down an abandoned boat launch and parked. Glass Jar marvelled at the dark, sun-soaked richness of the ocean's blue through the thick, forgotten streaks of dirt and bug guts his never-before-cleaned-or-attended-to wipers had spread across the windshield.

Whether he knew it or not, Glass Jar was a person who, in spite of his almost limitless free time, was parched for quiet and reflective moments. And just as the clean, cold water of thought had started to wet his dry, frothing mental palate, the thick bile of a not-swallowed-soon-enough belchpuke choked him in the form of his ringing cellphone.

Glass Jar hated and cursed his phone, which was now just as it had come to him, but with a thick layer of congealed dirt spread over it. He had been a relatively early and extremely grudging cellphone owner, his trade necessitating it years ago, but he had never, in all the years he'd owned one, opened the settings menu. When a phone inevitably malfunctioned, or was not loud enough (the wax that had clogged Glass Jar's ears since late adolescence was by now visible to the naked eye of anyone who passed within a few feet and chanced to look directly at him), he became unreasonably filled with rage, and without thinking about it further or consulting anyone for help, he would buy a new one.

He'd never owned anything other than a Motorola flip phone, and had never adjusted the default ringer. Sometimes a brief spark of curiosity would throw itself vainly against the brick wall of his thoughts when he heard another person's ringtone. These tones were inevitably less offensive to him than his own, but the spark would flash only briefly before falling dead to the cold, dusty floor of reality. So it was not unusual for Glass Jar to curse loudly and smack the headrest next to him, as he did now, when his phone rang. It was also not particularly unusual for him to answer the phone abruptly and viciously, not having taken enough time to compose himself.

"What in fuck do you want?"

The man on the other end of the line used a satellite spinning through the infinity of space to transmit the coldness of his silence to Glass Jar for several long seconds. "I'm going to go ahead and assume you're still too stupid to have caller ID working on your phone. I'm going to do you that favour, Glass Jar."

Darillo had known Glass Jar in their younger days in Vancouver, and had not a soft spot but a remotely flexible spot for Glass Jar in his heart. It was Darillo who had, in exchange for a little taste of whatever Glass Jar earned for the rest of his life, allowed Glass Jar to operate on Quadra Island and hooked him up with the fish farmers.

"Oh shit, sorry, Jay, sorry I..."

"Shut the fuck up and don't say any more names, for the last fuckin' time in your life. Okay?"

"Yeah. Yeahshitsorry."

"Okay, fuckskull"—it had long been Darillo's assertion that to call Glass Jar fuckhead was to do him the overly generous compliment of assuming he had the component parts of a human head—"listen up and don't fuckin' talk. So there's some heavy shit going down here. There's a professional person with a temper coming to where you're at, you get me?"

"Yeah, I—"

"Did I say you could talk yet? Shut your cunt lips, fuckskull. Sew them fuckin' shut if you have to. This person with a temper, this professional person, they're coming to your spot, and they can't have any attention, anything going on, got it? That means stay in your house. That means, if you have to, holding your fuckin' breath until I tell you it's all right to sigh. You hear me?"

"Yeah, I—"

"If you say one more word, I swear to fuckin' Christ, Glass Jar, I will feed you your own hamstrings like they're fuckin' pork chops. Shut up. I'm telling you not to earn, not to use outside your house, not to fuckin' piss in the woods without permission. This is very serious. Do you understand?"

Glass Jar silently glowered at the tree-studded mountains in the distance. After a few seconds, Darillo's voice boomed back on the line.

"Holy shit, he proves he's as smart as a fuckin' British bulldog who managed not to roll over her puppies in the night. Good. Wait for me to call, all right. You can get back to whatever it is you do to earn the twenty-eight fuckin' cents you earn up on that fuckin' backwater."

Glass Jar kept the receiver of his phone, gummily, against his ear for several seconds, listening to the dial tone. As an avid evening news watcher and a slightly higher form of sentience than he was commonly believed to be, Glass Jar knew this was about the guy who'd ripped off the club's gas station in Victoria, some half-assed shootout behind it. The kid was coming to Quadra and they had a hitter en route. That kind of daytime robbery—Bonnie and Clyde shit—had never been Glass Jar's scene, not even when he'd been young and relatively functional, so he resigned himself to a trip to the grocery store for supplies and a super-marathon of booze or meth-fuelled cable television viewing. He took a look back at the ocean, sighed, and reversed his truck up the launch with unusual caution, then he drove the speed limit to the store.

Six boxes of Pizza Pops, a huge plastic tub of wasabi peas, three chicken pot pies, and two bottles of Russian

Prince Vodka cost more than Glass Jar had anticipated, and he had to dig back into his roll and count twice before he managed to hit the number.

There was a little girl wearing a green cape in the lineup behind him, and Glass Jar could feel her judgey look. She was no superhero, she wasn't even a person yet (not really), she had no right to look down on him. He felt angry and feverish and disoriented. As he struggled his bags into the crooks of his elbows, he turned and walked backwards a couple steps, baring the bareness of his gums at the little girl, who ducked defensively behind her mother's leg.

Glass Jar did not usually feel upset about his station in life, or resentful of the man who bullied him and took his money, until he had contact with the general public. But as soon as he'd been in a citizen's gaze for few seconds, the injustice of it, where he had ended up after all the work he'd done, would reach a critical mass in his chest.

Glass Jar put his bags in the back seat, slammed the door, and glowered at the empty nets and buckets in the bed of his truck. Without thinking about it too long, he opened the back door of his truck, and in full view of the largest parking lot on the island, took a huge belt off the Prince. He rolled the jutting bones of his spine pleasantly against the frame of the door, slumped into the driver's seat, and peeled out of the parking lot towards the scallop farm. He allowed the wind to slam the tiny back door of his truck closed for him.

11

Once he was out on the road doing it, Mike never minded the patrols. He was very easily made motion-sick as a passenger in the car, and especially on the boat, so driving himself was the only way to get through a patrol without feeling like he needed to lie down and just watch sports. The problem with doing the patrols solo was that Reubens was making him do it. Had his boss not made it so obvious that this was a punishment for being an insufficiently "straight shooter," Mike probably would have asked for it.

As he listened to a motivational book on tape about the equity potential and deep spiritual rewards inherent to a Zen Buddhist approach to stock trading, Mike coasted his truck up the swaying, unpaved road overlooking Rebecca Spit, glancing into driveways and wondering casually what exactly he was ever looking for.

As he slowed to check out the We Wai Kai scallop bed, Mike recognized Glass Jar's tattoo. The band's harvesting area was explicitly not any of Mike's business, but somebody had been stealing scallops from the farm, and the RCMP had been asked to keep an eye out. Now there was Glass Jar, hoisting a large net full of shells into the back of his truck; his shirt off, his pants hanging off him as if he was an ankle and they were a tube sock with a broken elastic. Mike pulled his truck off to the side of the road and got out, then he crept over and hid behind a tree.

Having stashed his rowboat on the beach and loaded a pearl net full of scallops into his truck, Glass Jar was just now rewarding his hard work with a sustained belt off a bottle of Russian Prince. Glass Jar finished the drink and chucked the plastic two-six into the bed of the truck, then he leaned deeply back towards the ocean, pressing the small of his back firmly in the other direction, his methy ribs looking ready to poke through skin.

Mike returned to his car and peeled quickly and quietly away. Glass Jar must be heading back to his place, since he couldn't take the five o'clock ferry, easily the most crowded of the day, with an open truck full of stolen scallops. As he drove, Mike pumped his fist twice, felt lame even though he was alone, and then contented himself with banging the steering wheel with an open palm. This was it. His. Reubens would be off shift, so he wouldn't come even if Mike did radio it in. He was alone.

His plan was to beat Glass Jar home, hide his car up the road, and take him as he unloaded the scallops. If he collared him getting out of the car, he could book him for the scallops and a DUI, and he'd get to search the car, where he was sure he'd find a felony drug charge. And it would all be his, no Reubens taking credit; it would be Mike's. At the very least they'd tie Glass Jar up for a year; there was no way he could make bail.

Mike spied Glass Jar's horrible little home, a one-room aluminum-sided hovel in the middle of an empty forest. He bumped his car further up the road, pulled it a short distance into the trees, and sat a minute to compose himself. He breathed deeply and unevenly, pulled his service weapon, checked and re-holstered it. Then he looked himself in the eyes in the mirror and set out towards the house.

The cop settled himself behind a thick arbutus tree and watched the road. Eventually, Glass Jar's truck turned the corner, its engine labouring as it sluggishly listed towards the shoulder. Glass Jar over-adjusted on his steering, and after almost dumping his car in the ditch on his right, narrowly grazed the lip of the ditch on the left before swinging the truck around in a long and surprisingly fluid arc into his driveway.

Mike took off running up the road, stretching his long, always almost cramping legs to their full stride. As is common to men of his size, once Mike had a full head of steam going it was easier to run through an object than around it, so as he reached the driveway Mike simply dipped his shoulder and plowed bluntly through Glass Jar's swaying reclaimed-wooden-plank address sign.

The two men caught sight of each other at roughly the same time, as Mike's vision cleared from the collision, and as Glass Jar's customarily dulled reaction time at length alerted him to the sounds of a 235-pound police officer barrelling through signage.

Glass Jar was mid-hoist on his third attempt to pull the scallops out of the bed of his truck. The first two had seen the net flirt with the lip of the truck bed before landing back in the bottom when he lost his grip on the wet ropes. By the time he saw Richmond, Glass Jar was just about ready to give up on his task anyway, so he dropped the net, raised his hands casually above his head, and drifted a few feet away from the car.

Richmond skidded to stop, spraying loose gravel and dust. A few of the pebbles shot towards Glass Jar's feet, and the junkie began a loose-limbed jig. Mike's summoned enough heaving breath to shout at Glass Jar.

"HANDS UP RIGHT NOW!"

Glass Jar straightened his elbows above his head but kept his feet bouncing in a stilted rhythm. "They don't go much upper than this, boss."

Mike took a breath through his nose. "Stop dancing."

Glass Jar stilled his feet, then he tried to rub a scab off his face with his shoulder as Mike caught more of his breath. "I'd turn myself around, boss, but then you might think I was doing the hor-key por-key." Glass Jar's entire rib cage rippled with mirth. Then he snorted deeply, considered spitting, swallowed, and looked back at Mike.

"Turn around, and drop to your knees." Mike was coming back to himself now, his right hand hovering over his holster, his left twisted out involuntarily towards Glass Jar in a Bela Lugosi vampiric-spell-casting sort of way.

Glass Jar's gums grinned, abscessedly, at the cop. "And that's what it's all about. Do do do doo do."

"On your stomach, and shut up about the hokey-pokey."

Glass Jar keeled straight over sideways, landing with a hollow thud in the grass and rolling onto his belly. "Make sure you cinch those cuffs up tight, boss. My weight's been losing itself."

By the time Mike was done searching the truck, Glass Jar had gotten upright and picked the small patch of his lawn behind his back bare. While Glass Jar had sobered sufficiently to begin worrying, Mike had relaxed. Since he enjoyed organizing things, Mike laid out the objects he'd found on the gravel in front of Glass Jar in an ascending order of the severity of charges they represented.

Mike dropped to a crouch. Feeling the tug in his knees, he stood back up. "Okay, Glass Jar, it's time do some counting. We have open liquor in a motor vehicle, plus a huge Dee Wee, plus theft, plus simple possession of stolen prescription narcotics, with the labels on, plus possession with intent on the bagged-up meth. How's your math? That equals a year and change for you, and a nice note in the service record for me, by my count."

Glass Jar bit his lip back into his mouth, folding it briefly into the pocket between his teeth and gums. "My math says you don't waste time on a show unless you want something from me. Your fuckin' problem is you don't even know what that is. Only I know. So book me or shut that face-hole, swole-chest motherfucker."

Mike looked all the way down at Glass Jar sitting at his feet, his cuffed hands canted against the dead grass, and a long-forgotten feeling surged through him.

That feeling was middle-school basketball.

By the age of twelve, Mike had already developed the height and musculature of a mediocre varsity athlete. Playing on eight-foot nets, and with prepubescent boys, Mike had been such a dominant hard-court force that the league had been forced to change its rules, banning dunking and restricting a player's minutes to less than half of the total game time.

Mike smiled and leaned heavily against the truck. "Swing away, Glass Jar. But you're the one that needs to give me some felony skinny, and I'm the one sitting on a clean shit-head arrest. You're a big shit-head fish in a tiny shit-head pond, bud. The community will love me. Hell, I might even get a free flax seed bread at the Saturday market for running you out of town. You're not popular."

There was a reason Glass Jar lived in a Quadra Island shack. A few years back, he'd been an Andegg Brothers hangaround in Vancouver. Not high level, but up there enough to know a lot of people. He did a few border runs, but mostly he cooked decent meth and helped run bets. Around the time that whole gang went down, Glass Jar got caught when his boat ran out of gas crossing the border with sixteen kilos of coke. He'd actually played it pretty smart, snitching half a dozen guys who were probably going down anyway, making it out alive and (rumour had it) with a shoebox full of cash, bets he'd been holding for one of the bookies he'd ratted. So Glass Jar was being given a pass; he'd waited out most of the gang purges that went down in the early teens, and kept to himself. The word on him now was that once in a while the club chapter from Vancouver

Island would throw him a bone in the form of some pot and pills to sell, or take meth off his hands when he got himself together enough to cook a decent batch.

The point, from Mike's career's perspective, was that Glass Jar knew how to do business and would have about six shank-free minutes in jail.

Glass Jar's face contorted, as if he was staring at an unexpected hydro bill. "All right, all right, all right. Few things I've heard. I'll give you two cookhouses, one in Campbell River, the other in Comox. They're small, but I know the people, and I can give you easy PC to search 'em. I can't testify, though. I can't do that again."

"That's a start. Keep it running."

Glass Jar looked up at Mike and rolled his eyes, yellowly, at the cop. "They don't tell me shit, man." Glass Jar tilted his head to the side in even-handed consideration. "Guess they're right not to, hey, boss?"

"Gimme some details on the cooks and I'll kick you on the driving and crank. I still have to run you in on the theft and the scripts, though."

"Come on, man. I . . . That's what I got."

"Then I guess you're going for the whole biscuit. I'm not kicking you outright for a couple of kitchen meth cooks." Mike raised his hand sympathetically, savouring the moment. "What can I do?"

For a long time after that the two men remained silent as Mike watched huge trees swaying slightly and firmly in the wind and Glass Jar aggressively scratched the top of his chest using his chin. After a few seconds, he straightened his neck and spoke to the side of his truck.

"You remember sugar. Like, as a kid, you remember sugar?"

"Sure, kids are nuts for sugar."

"*Right*, boss, *right*. Kids go mental for it. And nobody says it, but it's because they're getting fucked up. When you're a kid, you plan it, like getting fucked up, and then you get really high and you pass out. At least, I remember it like that. It's a shame you outgrow getting high on sugar. Because you don't have that thin kid-blood anymore."

"What?"

Glass Jar looked up at Richmond like he'd just expressed ignorance of the Holocaust. "Kids have thin blood. Then you get older and it gets thicker. Yeah . . . kids have thin blood, that's why they're not supposed to fuck or lift weights or nothing. Because of the thin blood. Aren't you a cop? Like, you should know that for first aid or whatever."

"Enough, Glass Jar. What do you have for me?"

"I have a rumour."

Mike glowed internally with pride as he turned his nose up and away from the news, like it was an unexpected smell. "Rumours. You're giving me rumours."

Glass Jar rotated his neck in a sickening fashion. "One rumour. It's a big-un, though. Maybe the biggest un you're ever gonna get. So stand me up, take these cuffs off, and let me keep my shit."

Mike yanked Glass Jar to his feet, wiped the vodka-permeated sweat off his hand, and undid the cuffs. He wagged his finger. "Keeping the stuff depends on what you tell me."

Glass Jar smiled, and instead of rubbing his wrists he

shook them loosely, as if messing around with two tambourines he didn't quite know how to play. "So I guess you mighta heard about the money-stash robbery. Down in Vicky-toria. Dumb fella did it got the whole outfit and law after him. You mighta heard?"

Glass Jar paused as he cautiously and systematically loaded his valuables back into his truck before remembering his initial intention to take them inside. He fished a cigarette out of a long-forgotten pack on the floor.

Mike took a long, stilted breath. This was, indeed, somehow a big one.

Glass Jar swung himself unevenly onto the corner of his truck bed and after six tries got his cigarette lit. Trying to look like a man with a lot to say, he took a long drag and flipped the end of the cigarette theatrically. No ash fell.

15 Victoria, British Columbia

Greta had, at various points in the last few years, been made aware of a number of common-sense crime maxims that she felt certain did not apply to her. Her thinking was that most of these rules were meant for criminals who looked like criminals, men with scars through their eyebrows and upper lips, giant elevated calluses on their lighter thumbs. Thick ethnic white guys with phlegm in their throats and jackets slightly too thin for the wind.

Speeding was a big one. As a general rule, when one has two unregistered handguns and a switchblade on one's person, not to mention a shotgun, some blow, and a jam jar full of GHB in the trunk, one is not supposed to blast down a crowded highway at an average speed of about 145 km/hour, weaving between trucks and trailers and small cars driven by old men whose necks are too stiff to let them shoulder-check. The speeding rule didn't apply to Greta, not only because she was totally confident that she could talk her way out of any ticket, but more importantly because she would never be pulled over.

People Greta's age were growing fond of complaining, after a couple drinks, that they'd been raised to think they were special and were now finding out that they weren't. It was a complaint with which Greta could no longer remotely empathize, because she didn't feel that she had been raised to believe anything in particular and, more importantly, because she *was* special. If she didn't want a ticket, she wouldn't get one. If she needed someone dead, she killed them. Ever since Karen had showed her the ropes and referred her to Sergei and she'd shot that defenceless teen who'd ratted to the cops, Greta had stopped knowing or caring about struggle. There was no struggle, just different stages of a plan, spiderwebs of coincidence branching off life's neat flow chart.

Greta wanted to buy herself a new work jacket before hitting the highway, so she did. She'd wanted to make the seven o'clock ferry onto Quadra, so she drove the Island Highway in two hours flat, and she did.

Although she'd never heard it as a set-down rule, Greta was pretty sure that if you ran it by them, most wise criminals would tell you not to shimmy out the sunroof of your car with two handguns on your person (plus a shotgun, some blow, and a jam jar full of GHB in the trunk), and roll sideways to the ground on a crowded ferry. But in recent years Greta had come to appreciate her physicality. She liked to flex her flexibility whenever she could, just to feel it, like when cats dig their claws hard into carpets and then just let go.

After dismounting from her car, Greta straightened her clothes, swept the hair out of her eyes, and leaned on the ferry's guardrail, feeling the cool summer breeze against her skin, and looking out as the mouth of the strait opened into a wider part of a much bigger strait.

Greta didn't believe in struggle, but she did believe in luck, so she'd have no trouble admitting she was lucky her reflexes didn't take over and that she didn't instinctively deliver a crushing knee to the head of the five-year-old child who brushed against her leg as she looked over the water. Instead she flinched, controlled herself, and said "Whoa, now."

The child's hair was the kind of blond that doesn't get past the first two weeks of puberty. He nodded up at her, and then looked straight down at his feet. Greta looked briefly around and saw the boy's father leaning against a nearby minivan. He smiled and nodded at Greta. Nobody ever thought she'd kill anybody, it never even crossed their mind. Greta spoke to the top of the child's head.

"Hello. How are you today?" The kid dug the ball of one foot into the top of the other. Then he lost his balance a little and went back to standing normally. "Are you on vacation?" His shoes were still more interesting to him, and now that Greta saw them, they did have a large anthropomorphized truck on them, so that seemed fair. She tried one more time. "Do you go to school on the island?"

The boy finally looked up, holding Greta's gaze. His eyes were the colour of the ocean in a painting that doesn't quite have the light right. He spoke, a halting, high-pitched voice. "No. I had a rash on my whole body."

Greta would have laughed if the boy didn't look so serious. "Oh."

"I had a rash on my whole body and I wasn't allowed to be around kids at school. I had a rash on my whole body."

The boy's father arrived and gathered the child around

his leg. He had long, thick, dark eyebrows that wrapped almost around to his temples, and he seemed kind enough to be embarrassed for everyone all the time. "I'm sorry if he bothered you."

"No, no. I don't talk to kids much, it's cool."

"Sure, sure, sorry." He guided the boy a pace in front of him, then turned around, his head cocked to one side. "And, uh, yeah. I...He never had a rash. I don't know why he said that."

Greta indulged her long-standing habit of leaving people hanging, socially. Eventually, the man turned around and got back in his car, carefully buckling his son in. Greta turned to look at the ocean again as it disappeared behind the stand of trees around the bay. She waited until the man behind her honked before she got in her car and drove off the boat.

15 Quadra Island, British Columbia

After leaving Glass Jar and anonymously returning the scallops, Mike returned to the office to find a note from Reubens sending him right back out the door on one more distasteful errand, disposing of a rabid dog that had been haunting the seafood plant and that some cranked-out night worker had kicked to death.

Mike pulled up, and the circle of identical men in identical coveralls identically unbuttoned and draping from the shoulder split to accommodate him. The dog was splayed across the ground, its neck twisted sideways, head caved three ways in on itself, a long, thick line of foamed-out saliva sitting oddly on the ground, like surface runoff. Mike took a knee beside the body, craning his head wearily to the side as he examined the head wounds.

The young cop looked up and saw a broad, grim-looking man who was not wearing coveralls but rather a short-sleeved button-down with a pocket protector. Mike stood and motioned to his truck and the supervisor followed. Once they were out of earshot the pocket protector reached to awkwardly shake Mike's hand and said three first names to introduce himself before beginning an apology. Richmond shook his head until the pocket protector stopped talking. He hadn't taken in any of the three first names.

"Okay. So, listen…sir. Listen, in normal circumstances, and I'm sure you know this, in normal circumstances we'd be shutting your plant down until public health came up here and checked all your guys for bite-marks and workman's comp came up here to check on the conditions and your hours and all that. Since we're a boat ride from the nearest health unit, and it's five p.m., you'd be down for four days minimum. We both know all that, right?"

Three First Names didn't nod; he took one step back and spoke. "And what do we need to do to make this not a regular situation?"

"Answer my questions and do what I ask, that's all."

"Okay."

"So this is the dog? Right? This is the one you've been calling about?"

"Never saw it myself, but that idiot who called it in, couple of the other guys have confirmed it, yeah."

"Nobody's ever seen two, right? Just the one dog, which is the dead dog over there."

"That's right. Yeah."

"Now, this is the key spot, and seriously, seriously, seriously, you've got to tell me if you know who did this. Somebody kicked that dog to death, which means somebody put their boot on a rabid dog's face. We'd need to check that guy."

"Listen, we ran it down before you got here. Everybody's saying no, and I believe them. I'll check the night shift for bite marks as soon as they come in. Everyone else is getting a physical, ASAP. I just need to have the plant open while I do it. I can't close. I need this place open, please."

"Hey, I understand. Sounds good. So here's what went down: I got out here and the dog's body wasn't around anymore. Wow, weird, right? Because somebody double-bagged the body and buried it at least a foot into the ground, right?"

"Sounds like what happened to me."

Mike let out a long breath. "If you see another one, tell them to just call it in, all right?"

"I'll tell them, yeah."

The guy didn't seem quite relieved enough. Mike took a hard look at him. "Anything else on this? Do you know who did it? They won't get in trouble, just have to check 'em."

Three First Names chewed his lip for a second and then shook his head. "It'd just be speculating anyway. I'll take care of it. This is handled."

Had it been the sort of thing that could benefit him personally, and had he not been otherwise occupied, Mike might have pushed a little harder, tried to get whatever the guy was holding back, but it was, after all, just a dead dog. So instead of pressing the manager or talking to any of the other workers, Richmond nodded, got back in his truck, without another look at the dog, or the men, or the long, lovely tunnel of forest leading straight to the sea.

As he drove back to the station, the young cop wasted a good amount of mental energy beating himself up for not just taking the easy win. Using the drug stuff Glass Jar had given him, taking the good note in his service jacket, and moving on. If he'd done that, he could have finished his stint on Quadra and left with a decent chance at a halfway decent posting. The way things were going in the RCMP these days, it wouldn't be enough to guarantee him anything; even with the busts, he'd likelier end up giving out speeding tickets in Moose Jaw than land on a task force.

But, Mike firmly reminded himself by pounding an imaginary table with his canned-ham fist, he hadn't taken the quick, easy flounder. He'd landed a big fish, and he hadn't really meant to, but once it's on the hook you have to pull it in. This was a career collar. If he could book Tommy Marlo, if Tommy Marlo even showed up on Quadra, he'd be fast-tracking it to inspector, and after that as high as he could go.

Nothing was for sure, though, and this uncertainty plagued both Mike and the wet and increasingly frayed collar of his shirt as he chewed it. Glass Jar didn't really know anything. He'd heard that the club had one hitman they wanted on it; everyone else was supposed to stay away from Marlo and off Quadra altogether. It was a sensitive situation, and they didn't want anyone going off half-cocked. They wanted the money and the computer found, and they wanted Tommy Marlo dead, and they wanted both done cleanly and quietly.

Hours into his research, his eyes bleary from the screen, and his focus ragged from the legalese and jargon and pointless known-associates reports, Mike finally did the math. Two plus two. Marlo's whole history started when he skipped bail in Montreal. To skip bail, he had to make bail.

To make bail, he had to have money, or, more likely, a blood relative with money. What Mike finally figured out was just whom Marlo was coming to see on Quadra. What he didn't know was how the club could have guessed. But they had, and their hitter was on the way.

As he drove home, and as he once again allowed the shirt-collar to drop out of his mouth and land stickily against his chest, Mike realized that he was in over his head, and he was alone. He couldn't ask Reubens, who'd just take it from him, run it up the chain. Plus, Mike would have to explain how he got the information, and he was nervous enough already about leaving Glass Jar loose. What he needed was off-the-books help from someone with big-case experience, and as he'd reconfirmed towards the bottom of a huge internet sinkhole, there was one person like that on the island.

Mousey's driveway was as long and scenic as the entrance to a national park, and Mike took the drive slowly, looking up at the treeline against the light blue glow of the early night sky. Mike stopped, turned off the truck and stared absently at the mossy bluff under Mousey's house. He relaxed, and in his floating, computer-screen-raw vision, imagined his future house, and future wife, but he imagined them as one of those houses you see on the back of a truck, speeding down the highway. He imagined looking at his wife again, her reading something, hands drumming against the edge of her lip, not thinking about him watching her, the side of the highway slipping past, framed in the window behind her. Mike imagined his hands empty, watching the thinness of her dress, and the easy, green-brown blur of ditches and fields and trees that she also wasn't thinking about.

When he heard the gunshots, Mike's first instinct was to duck, but the seatbelt arrested his movement and kept him propped up in his seat. Another two shots echoed around the trees surrounding the driveway. Mike mashed his hand against the seatbelt and finally unbuckled and dove out of the car. The young cop flattened himself against the truck and scanned the area around him as he reached for his gun and, attempting to un-holster, dropped it. Mike froze in his crouch for few seconds that felt like waiting for a few tectonic plates to move a few inches, then he reached down, picked up the weapon, and moved in as low and quick a crouch as he could manage towards the source of the sound. Mike reached the rippled metal siding of Mousey's house, braced himself, and spun around the corner.

Mousey was sitting in a lawn chair precariously wedged between two uneven rocks, a huge set of puffed-out 1990s ear protectors bulging out from the sides of his head, legs stretched all the way out, one hand holding a smouldering joint, the other sighting a small revolver at an empty whiskey bottle hanging off a tree branch. Mike cursed and dropped to his haunches as he tried to get his breathing back on track.

The old cop placed the joint in his mouth and held it there without dragging as he tried to steady his swaying aim with a two-handed grip, and squeezed off four shots that didn't even move the bottle, splintering the bullet-ridden trunk of the tree in a loose group. Mousey sighed earmuff-loud, re-engaged his safety, and replaced the gun in his Serpico-era ankle holster, hauled on the joint, and finally caught sight of Mike. Mousey did a pretty good job of bluffing off his surprise while finishing and then coughing out his hit. "From what I hear about small towns, it's best not to roll up on someone after dark."

Mike was breathing normally now, but his hands were tingling. He forced a smile across his face. "It isn't dark yet."

Mousey laughed, clearly home-for-the-night stoned. He hopped out of the chair, almost fell down the rocks, and righted himself, somehow keeping the joint wedged in the corner of his mouth. He pulled the joint out and wagged it at Mike. "You got me on the technicality, counsellor. You're the one wants to be a lawyer, right? Yeah, of course you are. You're not the fat one."

"Thanks. I appreciate that."

Still laughing, Mousey tucked the joint back between his lips and loosely pulled his wrists together, offering them to Mike. "You got me, officer. I surrender." Mousey reached up and grabbed a small portion of Mike's quivering, tense shoulder and shook it companionably. "Sorry, sir. I'll cool it on the gunplay for a few weeks."

Mike gave him a gentle push backwards, towards the house, and Mousey play-stumbled theatrically before performing a technically solid triple jump onto his elevated back deck. Mike shook his head. "Mousey, there's a range in Campbell River, it's not even far."

Mousey considered the joint in his hand, then he carefully pinched the ember off and put the roach in his pocket. "I mean, I'm going for a different sort of, uh, phenomenological experience with it here, but yeah, you're right. I appreciate your cutting me a break like that. It's a party-foul, I know. You want to come in?"

"Yeah, something I want to talk to you about."

Mousey waited for the young cop to climb the stairs. Mike watched impassively as Mousey moved first to put an arm around Mike's shoulders then reconsidered and slipped the arm around Mike's waist. The stoned middle-aged man took on a serious air. "Is it about girls?"

Mike turned down three drink offers as Mousey spent almost an hour studying the folder Mike had assembled at the office. He accepted the fourth offer and bolted his entire drink nervously before Mousey was finished with the file. Mousey looked different than Mike had seen him before, more serious, his eyes focused instead of doing that half-present junkie scanning. Mike was busy looking out the window through the bottom of his glass when Mousey finally slid the folder back across the table. It passed in front of Mike, off the table, and landed with a thick slap on the ground.

Mousey closed one eye and held up both hands in apology. "Sorry buddy, you've got me a little juiced up here."

Mike put the glass down and picked up the folder. "So what do you think?"

"About what?"

"The case."

Mousey shook his head and moved to stand. He paced in front of the reading nook. "There's no case. What you have there is a situation."

"About the situation, then."

"You don't want me in on this, buddy. I'm sorry, but you don't."

"What do you mean?"

"So this Marlo cat, he starts out his adult record with a strong-arm robbery in Montreal, and he has a juvie file from out here. Suspicion, suspicion all over, but nobody bothers to pick him up. He's a purse snatcher with a half-a-brain. He's a known associate in real guys' files. Dumb enough to get picked up, smart enough to skip his bond and stay skipped for a few years. Not a high achiever, but he's a survivor. Never thrives, because he's got the warrant and skips town pretty regularly. He's stealing computers, probably a decent gig a few years ago, but it's getting played out now. He moves west, hemorrhaging money. So he's in Victoria, he's broke, he steals a laptop. Looks for credit card numbers, or whatever, and somehow he stumbles onto a money stash. I'd guess he's not a hard junkie, but he's probably a lifelong substance abuser. If he was a citizen, he'd be barely holding down twenty hours a week at a grocery store, something like that. Whatever load he likes to get on, he gets that on and, without thinking about it too much, he knocks off the stash. He's smart enough not to take an accomplice, too stupid to think about what the money's actually for. Y'know, like maybe the club isn't just leaving a hundred grand lying around behind a gas station on a whim."

Mousey was on a roll, and Mike wanted in on it. "Stupid enough to mess with the club."

Mousey paused and tilted his head to either side, then kept pacing. "He's broke, probably pretty desperate, and I bet, because his half-a-brain's taken him this far, he's got a plan. Skipping town, skipping the whole country if he can figure out a way. He'll have a hundred-K head start and maybe he'll clean up his life and get work, or whatever it is he thinks. Kid like this, he's never gonna get another shot at that kind of money. Anyhow, his plan gets fucked up because half the money is covered in green paint. Now it's a fifty-K head start, and he's so hot it'll probably cost him half that just to get out of the province. Instead of leaving the country he changes his plan, and now he's coming to an island. So he's got someone on Quadra, girl he's fucking, guy he's fucking, or a family member he ain't fucking. And judging from the look on your huge, adorable punum, you know who that is, and nobody else does. That's your card here, right?"

Mike scratched his head. Mousey, all appearances aside, was no joke. "You got all that from the file? Fine, fine, but what do you make of him killing the super in his building?"

"How does that timeline feel to you?"

"Uh…"

"He didn't kill the super. If he was around in Victoria that long, he wouldn't be alive. And we know he's alive because the club would have run his body up a flagpole by now if they'd found him. Wasn't him killed the super, it was the hitters they sent after him. Which would be why he's 'missing' and not, y'know, a really gross corpse doubling as an object lesson about the consequences of fucking with criminal motorcycle clubs." Mousey sat back down, bent back his hand and cracked three knuckles, shook out the hand, and waved Mike off. "Continuing, you know who Marlo's heading for, and you got that li'l nugget a sketchy way. What? Worked a deal? I know you don't have informants, so you did something fucked up. You're keeping it from Reubens, and you have dreams of running Marlo in solo, taking the glory. As opposed to being a good civil servant and taking this up the pole and doing your best to get nobody killed. But it's your first time, you're driving home, and you feel this swell in your tummy like maybe you aren't ready for a thing like this, so you come to me. Am I right?"

"Ballpark."

"So you want my advice?"

"I'd appreciate it, yeah. Yeah, maybe an extra pair of hands would help too, if you wouldn't mind."

"I'm a generally stimulated man, Richmond. And I quit this shit for a reason. You get advice from me one time. And you're not going to like it."

"Let me be the judge of that. I'll give you the connection, right now."

The old cop dropped his hands to his sides, letting them hang like apples clinging to the end of a broken branch. "Do not tell me that, Mike. This is the whole point of what I'm saying to you here. Do not tell me who he's here for. I have no reason to know, and I don't give a shit." Mousey looked away. He let the pause float a long time. "Your instincts aren't bad. Cutting out Reubens, that's a good move. Sitting on your informant, also good. Getting your research in, okay. You did the right things to make a run at this. And you realized you're not ready. That's absolutely correct. You don't want this, Richmond."

"That's your advice?"

"It's the best you'll ever get. Drop this now. You are looking to put yourself between a cornered, desperate man and a large, ruthless criminal organization with its ass hanging all the way out. That's not a good spot to be in."

"You don't think I know that? I know it."

"You might know it, buddy. But you don't get it. You hear the words, and you say the right words back, but the gravity of this is not working on you. You are floating. On a thing like this, when you take it on yourself, what are you doing? The only advantage you have as a cop is resources. You have no resources on this. You have a full-time job. You can't follow anyone. You can't talk to anyone. You can only work this for like two hours a day. In case you forgot this part, Marlo, the button-men they send after him, and your snitch, could all, easily, be in a spot where they have to kill you if you do somehow get within sniffing distance of Marlo and the money. And if you want to keep your job and life, you might have to kill one or all of them and bury their bodies in the woods and never tell another person you did it."

"I don't think so. I think you're wrong about that."

"You don't *think* so. Based on what? This isn't about thinking. This is about being ready. You run Marlo in, he's dead in a day. You run whoever kills Marlo in, they're doing life. Your informant gets nervous and tells the wrong person he talked to you, he's killed and you're killed. None of that will be wrong. If you're putting someone in line to have their life wrecked or ended, they can do whatever they want to you, and the last thing it'll be is wrong. These are the stakes you're playing, and you're playing them alone. You come to me for help on this. Why? Are we friends, Mike? Am I your dad? No. I'm just some guy with big-case pedigree, and you flocked to me like you were a fly and I was some shit. And you wanted to bring me in. If I come in on a thing like this, big boy, I'm coming in hard. If you're not ready to handle everything on your own, you're not ready to handle anything at all."

Mousey flopped loose-limbed back into his chair, and now it was Mike's turn to stand and pace. He shook his head at Mousey, and a sparrow flew into the window with a hollow thud, falling either dead or stunned between the house and the rock face. The young cop flinched, reaching his arm across his body to cover his neck.

Mousey jogged his eyebrows, pointing aimlessly at the ceiling as he began talking. "Oh, you're mad at me now." Mousey held his hands up to the light, twiddled his fingers, and then lowered them to drum on the table. "You came for advice, and I'm giving it to you. I wish somebody had told me way back in the day. That feeling you had in your car, telling you to get help, it wasn't. It was telling you to quit. Just hope the whole thing blows over. Pray your name don't come up. It's your only option. Coming to me, telling a soul about this, that's a headshot mistake. Done. You're just lucky you came to me this late in life. In my prime, I'd have eaten you for a snack."

Mike stopped pacing. Eventually, for no good reason, he reached up and held one of Mousey's globes of light in his huge, flat hand, the cord slackening in the middle. He let it drop and bounce. "I'm not mad, Mousey. I just can't wait until all of you boomers fucking die."

Mousey scrunched his face, somehow managing to make it even craggier. "Boomers? How the fuck old do you think—"

Mike barrelled through. "Sure, you're right. I don't know you and you don't know me. I came to you because I was thinking—stupidly, I guess—that the saddest, most bored-seeming person I'd ever met might be up to give me a hand. Help out a young person who needs help, who you have no reason not to. But that was stupid. Because nobody your age wants to lift a finger to help anybody my age, you just want to sit on your little toilet seats made of easy cash and shit on everyone coming up. Sorry, but my bosses aren't going to have the decency to clutch their chests and keel over as they water the rose bushes, like yours did. So I'll do it alone, with no help, and no chance, and get called entitled by the most entitled generation in the history of the world. Thanks for the reminder and thanks for the drink." He turned to leave and Mousey hopped to his feet, stopping Mike before he reached the stairs. He patted Richmond sturdily on the back and chest and softened his dry, collagen-deficient face.

"Listen, Mike. Listen. I'm sorry, and I really can't get involved. I can't. But I will give you some advice. For real, I've got advice."

Mike was still pissed but wavering, so far out of his depth and just wanting to be told rather than decide what to do. "What?"

"It's by way of analogy. Just up front."

Richmond shook his head and looked over Mousey's shoulder, but eventually nodded him along.

"For real, man. For real. I don't tell this too often. But, uh, my dad was a barber. And he died before my junior year of high school, and before that I used to work in his shop. He was a very old-school barber-type guy. So he had a horsehair broom. Legit. He was that much of an Old World shit-for-brains immigrant barber. So I used to sweep up the hair he cut with this hair broom. Like an asshole. All day, I'm just sweeping up after razor-cuts, right? Sweeping away the leftovers of leftover sixties army haircuts. And then my pops died, and I became, like, a person. A person of interest in a seedy way but an important way. For a minute there. And I never thought about hair too much, because fuck hair. Right?"

Mike looked down at Mousey. Is it still called pity when you desperately need something from the guy?

Mousey continued. "So once I retired and thought back about my life as a person who had been a little important for a little while, I saw that I ended up really, really far from my dad's shitty barbershop, but that job I had when I was twelve was all I ever did. I cleaned up hair with more hair. And even as I cleaned it, it was growing back. Because that's all hair does. It grows, or it goes away because it's just tired of growing. So what I'm saying, Mike, is don't ever get too fuckin' righteous, because it's all just hair, man. The broom, the mess on the floor, it's all the same. You're the same as what you're after. It's all just hair."

Mike snorted and twirled his big, clumsy-feeling body towards the stairs then back to Mousey. "So that's your advice. Just twenty-five seconds of boring nihilism. Great. Thanks."

Mousey reached out and tapped Mike's collarbone twice, and Mike felt the hollow thud of it in his chest. "Good word, constable. *Nihilism.* Good word. Now do me a favour and spell it, you fuckin' millennial piece of shit. Run on home and jerk off to some Facebook pictures of girls you went to high school with. This business is for grown-ups. And no matter how much you hope and pray to the god of your parents' home equity, that's the only advice, help, counsel, or mentoring you're getting out of me."

Mike fished a card out of his uniform's breast pocket and flipped it onto the table. "Call me if you change your mind. And try not to commit too many felonies on my beat in the meantime."

Mousey smiled genuinely for the first time since the conversation started. He rubbed the tips of his left fingers with the pads of his right. "I won't call you. But since you're feeling strong, I'll give you one more piece of free information: if you step on my toe, I'll step on your head."

17 Campbell River, British Columbia

In the four days since Tommy had thrown away the stained bills (leaving the perfectly distinct fingerprints confirming his identity to the RCMP), he'd managed to lay out a bread-crumb trail of witnesses who remembered him clearly because he had looked homeless while dropping hundred-dollar bills at restaurants and convenience stores and chatting pleasantly but for a touch too long (as was his habit). He realized from a gaping, remote distance that he had been fortunate to avoid arrest, and he attributed his successful avoidance of the RCMP more to the hitchhiking strategy he'd come up with in the four and half hours after the girls left that it took to get a ride (only trying to get picked up within town limits, and with truckers or people with boats on top of their cars), and his willingness to resort to vagrancy in the form of sleeping in the woods behind rest areas rather than taking a bad ride.

Immediately after the creepy-but-not-in-a-directly-sexual-way crab fisherman (whose children had moved to Dubai and Arkansas and forgotten all about their old man, etc.) finally dropped Tommy off just inside the town limits of Campbell River, Tommy almost stepped straight in front of a sixteen-wheeler and decided that he would have to give in and get a hotel room for the night and sleep properly before the last leg of his journey to Quadra.

The young woman behind the counter of the Days Inn was friendly and very good at typing. She looked at the screen rather than at Tommy, and he looked at the way her tongue peeked slightly over her lip in concentration as she checked if it was possible for him to register without a credit card.

"I'm sorry, Mr. Simmons..."

"My name's Tommy."

She looked up at him, and seeing his smile, matched it.

"Tommy. I'm sorry, I just can't."

"Let's go back to Mr. Simmons, though. It's, uh, less common for people to call me that. Fancier. You seem like a unique person.'

"Mr. Simmons," she was pretty cute, now that she was smiling a little and he was actually paying attention to his surroundings. "Thanks, but I'm sorry, I can't check you in without a credit card."

"What about bitcoins, I have a bangin' bitcoin wallet, not to toot my own horn."

She stilled her hands for the first time since they'd talked. "What exactly is a bitcoin?"

"You caught me, I don't know. I just thought that was, like, a funny way to go with it."

The clerk moved from smile to smirk. "You did, huh?"

Tommy laughed and slump-turned to check the empty, fluorescent-buzzing lobby. "How about we do it this way... How much do you make a month?"

"Uh, I don't..."

"Sorry, sorry." Tommy turned to face her and held her gaze while he talked. "That was a weird and aggressive way to ask that. You seem like you work hard and, um, people don't appreciate work nowadays, right?" He cocked his head back and crumpled the skin around his eyes and mouth in a way that he hoped women still found adorable. "Actually, I have no clue what bosses like or value or whatever. I'm a bum, Stephanie." Name tags are great. Stephanie laughed. "Just a bum with $3,000 for you, and the idea that if you close off a room that nobody's going to check into anyway, and you just put, say, a maintenance flag on it that you take off when your shift's over, I'll be out before cleaning."

"And if—due respect, Mr. Simmons—if you sleep in, like a bum might?"

"Then I'm a bum who got caught in a room I snuck into after you turned me away right as we're talking on security camera right now."

She turned her head suggestively to the security camera over the desk. "I'll see you in the parking lot in twenty-five minutes. And you better have that cash, Mr. Simmons."

She had to look serious to sell it to the cameras, but Tommy got a companionable feel off her eyes, which were that shade of blue that the people they belong to will insist is grey, because most people don't feel confidently about how they look.

He thanked Stephanie, and she told him to call with any problems, before clicking her mouse six straight times and, noticing her tongue, tucking it back into her mouth.

Tommy banged the counter and tried to look mad before gliding sleepily into the parking lot.

∅

If someone had asked him, Tommy would have told them that he was going to Quadra to hole up with his mom for a few days or, if she didn't want him staying, maybe settle down in a hostel until things blew over. He definitely would not have told them that he just wanted to see his mom again, even just once, before he died, even though that was true.

Tommy had not responded to his mother's most recent letter, but he'd been glad to hear she'd moved to Quadra. He remembered their trip there so clearly, the swimming and the camping. She'd bought him a kayaking class and Tommy had learned to roll the boat. He'd seen seals from five feet away and she'd seen them from the shore. This was before Tommy had quit music classes and taken up with his friends. Before his mom had lost her temper and thrown a small plate at him. Before he'd stolen her wallet so he could go halves with his girlfriend on buying that half ounce. He knew that there'd been time after that trip, a good two years, where he'd still been, mostly, a kid, and his mom had been fine. Strict and nuts about his music classes, but for the most part fine. Those years had been a buildup, nothing had happened, but it was all snowballing. The pressure of the singing, the boredom with it. That trip was the last solid memory Tommy had of getting along with his mom, and knowing her as he no longer really did, he was pretty sure she'd remember it like that too.

After picking up the key from Stephanie and realizing he was too tired to actually make a sustained good impression on her, Tommy hustled straight to his room, dropped his bags by the door, and took a running jump face first onto the bed. He bounced pleasantly and then settled into a deep, three-minute sleep. He woke up disoriented and accidentally rolled off the bed. Sitting on the floor, he remembered the fuzzy blob of gang member he'd killed with his car. Tommy removed his glasses, placed them on the nightstand, and started hitting himself with both hands.

The slaps hurt in an irritating, skin-pulling kind of way. Tommy closed his fist and hit himself in the temple a few times, which stung his hand and rattled his head a bit. Tommy still felt poorly, so he grabbed the phone receiver and got a decently leveraged shot to his own chin. That one really rang his bell and made maintaining his basic equilibrium difficult, so he needed to focus on that instead of the gaping, spinning entrance to the vortex of his own selfishness and despair he'd opened by killing someone.

When he felt a little better, he crawled back on the bed, replaced his mangled glasses, and turned on the television. Tommy watched a man with thick sideburns eat forty-one sloppy joes in a row. When the man was done, the crowd around him cheered as he raised his hands to celebrate instead of wiping his entire face.

The man looked happy.

18 Quadra Island, British Columbia

Mike Richmond had not until fairly recently had much cause to be hatefully angry at anyone. Huge, friendly men with a decent sense of humour rarely do. People had always treated Mike with respect, and Mike had been happy to go with it. Smile, nod, don't loom over people too much, it was easy. Getting along with people was easy.

So Mike didn't really have a frame of reference from which to approach the weighty lump of rage that had been pressing itself insistently deeper into his consciousness in recent months. He'd wake up and feel fine. But every day he'd hit his front steps feeling the hate and mistaking it for anxiety. He hated old men in the grocery store who complained (or even asked) about prices, and he hated women who left dog shit on the only sidewalk in town, waiting for the old men complaining about prices. He hated bicyclists and the Jeeps that endangered bicyclists exactly equally. But he didn't say anything, didn't spread his bad mood around. He just took deep breaths, bought himself treats (suddenly he was eating Twix bars for the first time since childhood), and worried that he had an anxiety disorder.

As he drove, Richmond rested his elbow on the window and twisted the skin on his temple in a vicious swirl. He needed to do something right now, it didn't matter what. He was done waiting. Wait three years, then apply with eight hundred other people for one job, then wait five more and do it again, then wait sixteen more, then fuck off and die. That was the life path laid down for him, and he was sick of it. He didn't deserve it, and he wasn't going to take it. Mike grabbed the wheel with both hands and punched the accelerator towards Grace's house.

Mike knocked on Grace's door. Then he fiddled with his belt, hitching it up and down and hoping she wouldn't answer. The smart move was to keep some distance, watch the place, and play it cool, not spaz out like a ten-year-old on the bad end of an ADHD prescription, not go running at Grace, a move that could only really hurt her a lot and help him a little.

He was distracted with loathing himself when Grace opened the door.

"Oh shit. Sorry. Sorry, I hope I'm not bothering you."

Grace lowered an eyebrow, looked him up and down like he was a fridge full of almost-gone vegetables, probably still edible but close enough that you'd just throw them out and order Chinese food. "Easy there, Mike. My dance card is pretty clear tonight. You want to come in?"

Mike laughed and gave her a small, reflexive salute. All at once he calmed down. He was committed. "Yeah. Yes. Thank you."

Grace's living room was small and comfortable. The furniture was all old and large. There were a few certificates and prizes on the shelf over the fireplace, a music stand with a thick book propped up on it. Mike took a seat on the couch, sinking deeply into the cushion's welcoming corduroy folds. Grace dropped heavily into her chair. They looked at each other and laughed. Grace shook her head at him. "It's a bit strange to see you like this, Mike. You're halfway between cop-face and bar-face right now, it's off-putting."

Mike struggled forward on the couch. "It's a bit weird to be me right now." He paused and pointed over to the music stand. "Why is it called a Fake Book?"

"It's the book with the minimum amount of information you need for a song. Just enough notes so you can fake it, if you need to."

"Everyone has one?

"Everyone who plays gigs, lot who don't."

"Cool. Cool. I have news, Grace."

Mike thought she'd respond quicker, and then by the time he realized she wanted him to go on, he felt committed to the silence. Grace swallowed hard once. "Shit. I'm not dead, am I, Mike?"

"Not that I can tell."

Grace smiled and took to picking a cuticle on her thumb. "Way you came in here, I thought you were going to tell me I was dead, had to vacate my place for the living, something like that." She swallowed one more time. "It's about Tommy, right?"

"Yes. He's not dead, and he's not in jail."

"He's not dead that you know of. I heard about the, uh, I heard. I heard, Mike."

"I'm just here looking for background."

"Background on what? I haven't seen him...It's been a while, Mike. I don't like to get into it much."

"I understand. Totally. I just...He's on the run. They want me to talk to you and rule you out as a place he'd go. Rule your house out. You're not a place."

"Fuck. My name isn't even the same anymore. I tried pretty hard to put a bit of distance between us. On the records there."

"You bailed him out in Montreal four years ago, when he skipped. I saw your name and ran it back through records."

"I don't care, Mike. I'll talk to you this time, and then leave me out of it. I'm done with all that. What do you want to know?"

"When was the last time you saw him?"

"Years ago, like you said. I flew to Montreal. I paid his bond, sublet an apartment for three months, took custody of him. A month into that, he comes home at four o'clock in the morning, and I get really mad. He runs off as a kid because I don't like him getting high every day and stealing money out my purse. Then, fast-forward a bit, I chase his tail across the country, put everything on hold, spend...that doesn't matter. He gets home, and I go off on him, say some real mean shit that I really mean. And he says he just went home with this girl, wasn't out with his friends, he met this girl at the gym. And I just can't listen. I'm too mad. I move to Quebec, pay his bond, all of it. He isn't gonna call me? Comes home four in the morning, wants to tell his mom he was just getting laid, not knifing anyone. I really gave it to him, it got pretty bad. So I wake up the next day, and I roll over, put my tired old feet on the ground, and I laugh. I see you lookin' at me, cop-fuck, I know I laugh loud, all right? I'm bellowing for a good while. Kid's a romantic. I believe him, he met some cutie in a yoga outfit, and he talked to her for hours and hours, and then they slept together. It's sweet. It's about the best you can hope for a kid like Tom. That he's out having a nice time with some stupid girl he met at the Y. I go to his room, and he's cleared out and skipped on his bond. Which was my money. Last time I saw him. I can't tell you anything else."

"Do you know his address?"

"Christmas before last, he sent a card and gave me an address in Calgary. I wrote him a letter and told him I was moving here. He never wrote back."

"Do you know where he is?"

"No clue."

"Would you tell me if you did?"

Grace snorted softly. She rubbed the top corner of her eye, briefly exposing the red behind the white of her eye. "Not a chance. Not a rock's chance if you threw it in the sea. That's from a jazz song. Almost."

"Call me if he shows up. You know that's the best way. I'll take him in, keep him safe. It'll be better with friends."

"I'd rather stick pins in my eyes. But thanks for the offer, Mike."

"Fair enough." Richmond reached over and put his hand on hers, and they sat quietly. Mike somehow hadn't seen the huge standing clock when he came in, but it was ticking off seconds incredibly loudly then. Grace eventually pulled her hand back and nodded at the young cop. Richmond said sorry and left.

Tommy had initially been a bit skeptical about the guy with messed-up teeth and a bandana to whom he'd paid $600 for a ride to his mom's place. But the guy had turned out to be a nice man who just hadn't had dental insurance for a long time. In addition to giving Tommy a ride all the way to his mom's address, he'd given Tommy a twelver of Blue Buck and the last third of his pack of cigs. When they pulled up, the guy even offered to drive him the rest of the way down the driveway, but Tommy just hopped out of the truck, grabbed his stuff, and waved the kindness off.

"Thanks, Mark. You're really nice and you did me a big favour. For real, I appreciate it. I hope your cat's kidneys feel better."

Mark tugged on the top of his bandana like it was a hat, and then he drove away.

Tommy avoided turning to look at his mom's house for quite a while. He stood very still in the middle of the road, the cardboard handle of the box digging slowly and insistently into the meat of his fingers. Tommy stared at the opening of his mom's driveway, the gap in the treeline, and he laughed a little. It was typical. His $600 cab ride had taken him to the exact wrong place, and he'd only realized it after he got there.

Just because you do a ton of mean things doesn't make you a mean person. At least not on a given day, as you walk through it and don't think about yourself too hard. Tommy'd always felt that being nice minute to minute could make up for most—pretty much all—mistakes. But he was thinking about himself hard now and he knew. He wasn't mean enough to call on his mom again. Make her send him away, put her in the spot to be turning him down, one more time. It had to stop. Tommy wandered over to the side of the road and sat down, dropping the beer harder than he'd intended. He pulled his knees up to his chest and rested his forehead between them. With his right hand he started playing with the handle of his knife, pulled it out of its cinched-in spot on the side of his backpack. He looked for a long time at the sharp, hard gleam of the blade.

Tommy recognized abstractly that killing himself would prevent a lot of worse options: prison, torture from the club, torture from the club in prison, etc. This way would be quick, and he'd keep his feet attached to his body. But, as he pressed the dull end of the knife against his exposed arm, Tommy was impressed by the strength of his own fortitude. What Tommy realized, with the blue night bringing up a mist that could have been rain in any other light, was that you can't decide to be suicidal. You can see how others would, you can know that, probably, you're in a suicide spot, but you can't decide to feel it.

Tommy wanted to live. To watch trees, to pull fish out of the water and then to let them go back into the water, to buy a small house. Tommy wanted to send his mom $1,500 he'd earned from a job. Tommy wanted to camp, and make out with a girl from the Yukon who was rugged and strong-boned and bluntly kind.

Tommy tilted sideways into the grass and then got to his feet. He picked up his beer and walked to the top of his mom's driveway. He checked the address then walked a few more paces down the driveway, popping up onto the balls of his feet every few steps to try to see the house. Just see it. He did see the house, but he didn't get much time to think about it, distracted as he was by the huge, slumping mound of uniformed RCMP officer walking back to his truck.

As tended to be his way, Tommy froze instead of reacting immediately. He numbly watched as the cop opened the passenger door, took off his holster, fished his wallet out of his back pocket, and threw them on the passenger seat. The cop loafed in a sad-sack way around the front of his truck, as if his limbs were already bored with what his brain was telling them to do. Sensing eyes on him, the cop turned and looked directly at Tommy. Even from a distance, Tommy could tell. The cop tried to play it cool, looked back down and kept walking to his door, but he'd paused, his foot a couple inches in the air, for just a second when he saw Tommy, but it was long enough. Tommy was certain that the cop saw him, and that the cop knew exactly why he was there.

With a large backpack over one shoulder, a box of beer in the other hand, and the gravel under his feet spraying with every step, Tommy had trouble getting enough momentum to really start running. By the time he remembered the beer in his hand Tommy had turned the bend onto the road and could already hear the police truck coming up behind him. He waited another few seconds, and without turning to look he spun and threw the case with a straight arm at where he thought the car should be. The box stayed weirdly still as it moved through the air, and then struck the windshield, denting the driver's side corner inward. Tommy turned back around and took off at a good clip now, and he heard the truck swerve to a stop on the shoulder but didn't turn to look.

He weaved across the street and into the trees. He kept running, ducking between the sparse twigs among the giant trees until he lost sight of the road. He threw himself to the ground behind a bush, curled in a ball, closed his eyes tightly, and bit hard into his wrist to keep from crying or hyperventilating.

He heard the cop rustling around the bush, but it all sounded far away, and then there was no sound for a long time. Eyes still closed, Tommy released his jaw and raised his hands to cover his eyes, contenting himself with rocking back and forth gently, with the leaves of the bush brushing his forehead on the upper end of the movement.

There was no way to tell how long he had been there, but it felt like a long time.

Everything felt like such a long time.

Mousey spent the day after Richmond's visit teaching himself how to make a fancy crab frittata from a cookbook. He washed and chopped everything slowly, and triple-checked with the book before each step. As the frittata baked, Mousey stood nearby, watching his oven door and chewing his thumbnails. After he was done cleaning and eating, Mousey read an old John Grisham novel from cover to cover.

He finished the book around dinnertime, briefly considered exercising, and then ate the rest of the frittata, chased it with two Percocet and a coffee, and took a long walk along the beach towards the Heriot Bay Inn, thinking distantly about law school as he kept a lookout for the family of seals he'd been seeing around the shoreline over the last few days. He turned the corner of the bay and the bar came into view, and Mousey stopped to sleepily and intently scan the surface of the water. It didn't take long for thoughts of the seal family to be swept under the simple fact of the waves and their shifting, subtle breaks. Mousey smiled, thinking about currents that weren't visible from the surface, of bottom-feeders closing their eyes pleasurably against the invisible pressure of the sea. He closed his own eyes and pressed his fingers into them, as far as was comfortable. Reopening his eyes, Mousey felt refreshed and ready to shoot a game or two of pool.

In all the times he'd been to the HBI (it was a lot of times), Mousey had never seen another adult take much of an interest in the oversized chess set beside the parking lot. The pieces were not quite person-sized, reaching only the top of Mousey's calf (which was not a very long calf). They were bigger than normal chess pieces, sure, but not big enough to really make an impression, and it was awkward to reach down and move them. The kids young enough to like the chess set were generally just small and young enough not to be able to use it (or really understand chess). But Mousey loved how awkward and sad-looking it was. He loved how long it had stayed with nobody enjoying it, gathering cracks and stains, and just sitting like a lump. People at the bar, even those who liked him, didn't want to hear Mousey talk about the chess set anymore.

So it was a pleasant surprise that the first grown person to take a shine to the set was a beautiful twentysomething woman with tasteful glasses and a chin-length, asymmetrical hairstyle that Mousey understood to be very hip at the moment. Standing outside the old bar, sipping her drink through a straw, taking in her surroundings with a sharp, slow gaze, everything about her body language saying she was slumming it just by existing in this century with you. Her limbs loose but still compact, thick in the legs and thin in the arms, the body of a dancer who drank beer. Not wanting to betray his excitement and inherent old-man creepiness, Mousey moved towards the board slowly, as if answering a doorbell that had been rung too many times. By the time he got there, the woman with the nice haircut had moved the black pawn ahead two spaces. She spread a thin, tendony hand over the board.

"How about it, sir? I warn you, I've played a lot of strategy games with an old Russian, so I'm pretty, pretty good, but I'll go easy on you." She took a deep sip from a clear drink and narrowed her eyes at him. "If you want me to."

In sharper times, Mousey might have noticed the cold, incurious clarity of her gaze; he might have thought it odd that she was wearing a leather jacket in the summer or seen the small bulge her shoulder holster made against the front pocket. In sharper times, Mousey would certainly have noticed the flower-bulb bloom of scar across the web of her thumb, from when the slide action of her gun had caught her as she'd killed a defenceless teen. But these were not sharper times, and besides there's more than one way to be sharp.

Mousey held her gaze and didn't notice much. Finally, he broke the eye contact and picked up a rook, carried it diagonally across the board, and squeezed it onto the same square as her bishop. He opened both hands at her to show it was her turn. She nodded seriously and then looked at the board to consider her move while distractedly spinning a huge, flat ring around her middle finger. Finally, she moved her knight up to share a spot with one of his pawns, its grey, faded horse face almost reaching down to kiss the blank, tarnished nub of the pawn's head.

They went back and forth like that, each seriously considering moves that didn't exist or make any sense at all, until the pieces were spread randomly over the board, each sharing their tile with a mismatched piece of the other colour.

After placing the last piece, the woman flipped her bangs up and rested her drink upside down on top of the pointy tip of the bishop's head. Mousey kicked his king over.

"You win."

For the first time she laughed, and smiled with huge, beautiful, French-actress teeth. "Good game, sir." She threw him a wink and clicked her mouth noisily as she turned to leave.

Mousey watched her as she reached a black Lexus and pulled open the driver's side. Before she ducked in, he spoke over to her. "You want to grab a drink with me?"

She stopped moving and peered over at him quizzically. "No. That's a thing you want me to do."

Without another word she dropped into the car, peeled out of her spot wide and fast, and quickly, loosely, and dangerously swung around the corner and out of the parking lot.

In sharper times, Mousey might have been aroused.

21

Sometime in the last few years, Glass Jar's body weight had dropped to a point where it became insignificant in comparison with the musculature of his upper body. This change had come upon him suddenly, and seemingly in an instant, Glass Jar had gone from being a feeble man to—in his estimation—a strong, wiry specimen capable of doing forty-five kipping pull-ups no problem. The reality was that he was still a feeble man, now simply lighter than he was weak.

But as usual, the harsh reality of his situation had no effect on Glass Jar. The perception of strength had emboldened him in his physical endeavours, which were now more impressive than they'd ever been.

He'd climbed to his favourite spot, straight up the tree beside his shack, and was still resting there, looking only a little ways up at the hawks spreading their wings with effortless softness, allowing themselves to be blown to their tree homes. Glass Jar maintained as firm a grip as the weathered nerves of his fingers could maintain on the branch above him, careful to keep some of his always limited balance.

He took pride in the fact that he hadn't had the flu since he was thirteen. It was one of the things he bragged about sometimes at a bar, or a trap house, or a buy in someone's car; the person he was speaking to would shift a little to miss his gaze and tepidly agree that it was impressive. People he talked to always seemed like they knew something that made what he was saying sad or wrong, but never just came out and said it. That look was one of the main reasons Glass Jar had taken to solitude in the last few years.

What everyone but Glass Jar knew is that fever is relative, it requires context. In order to feel like you have the flu, your body temperature has to, at some point, drop below that fever level. And so, as Glass Jar sat and bragged about his health, his interlocutors would disappear quietly into their own discomfort, trying to avoid looking at his red, sweating face, and his bluish, quivering half lips.

Sitting in his precarious and lovely tree seat, Glass Jar was beginning to wonder if that boast might, finally, have to be put to rest. It was just possible, even though his head still felt the same temperature, that given the shivering, dizziness, and even more intense congestion than usual, he was finally getting sick again.

Glass Jar didn't know how much phlegm a normal person made, but he was sure he had the world record for the last decade. Lately it seemed like every breath was just one more mouthful of snot, or throat junk, or the deeper, darker lung stuff. It made him sad in an unusually abstract way, how much of life was just lubing up. Spit, wax, pus, snot, tears, pre-cum, actual cum, grease, sweat, blood. All of it trying to keep you wet, frictionless. To keep your joints smooth, able to touch each other without rubbing, to keep your mouth wet to soften everything coming in. Always, your body was trying to smooth it out with slime, and always there was too much of it. You coughed, spit, drained, wiped it away. You built it up and got rid of it and still felt dry. At the end of the day, it's always bone on bone, smoke on lung, food on throat, germs on blood, but your body will go on tricking itself until it can't anymore. Until you've worn down all the cartilage, all the enamel, until you've hacked out all the phlegm, cum, piss, sweat, snot, and you're finally you, the raw dog, the real deal. Bone on bone on bone on concrete. Dry enough to rub together, make a fire.

Glass Jar had been in a lot of intense kinds of physical discomfort—withdrawals and toxicities, seizures and tiny comas and trench foot—but this was a new one. He was so dry and he wanted to drink so badly, but he just couldn't make himself down a glass of water somehow.

It was unusual for Glass Jar to even think about drinking water; usually he let himself naturally get hydrated over the day, with showers and sodas and the rain and so forth, but in the last day his throat had started bothering him, thirst making itself heard even in the din of his lifelong thrash-metal concert of dehydration. He'd been worrying about being sick, and because he still remembered the news report he'd seen a while back, he'd been worrying that it was the worrying making him sick. A symptom of our fast-paced modern society.

For just a second, Glass Jar let his tingling hands release their tenuous grip on the branch, and he let himself relax into the emptiness of the air behind him, let his head tip back and the top section of his spine unfurl to join it. Glass Jar felt the wind, and the pull of the ground, and with his eyes closed he saw the ground speed up to meet him, all in that little half a second of space before he caught the branch again, pulled himself back up, straight and steady. Glass Jar took a deep, calming breath, which went just that little bit too far and caught in one of his beleaguered bronchi and caused him to launch one more ball of waste into the still, open sky then down onto the bare, stripped mud of his lawn.

22

"So explain to me, exactly explain to me"—Reubens craned forward in his chair, across the edge of the desk, looming into Mike's space, the corner of the desk pressing graphically into a section of exposed belly skin between his shirt buttons—"how, exactly, a branch can fall off a tree."

Mike waited for Reubens to relax back into his seat. "With all due respect, sir, what aspect of that would you like me to explain? What was wrong with the tree? Gravity?"

"Listen, Mike, there's no need for you to be disrespectful to a senior officer, I could write that, remember, I can write you. No, what I want you to explain to me, exactly, is how I have gone fifty-one years as a man and twenty-three years as a police officer and have never, not once, seen a branch fall off a tree onto a moving car, and you, who has been a person for a second and a half, have not only seen a branch fall off a tree but have had it fall right on your vehicle. How exactly do you account for that?

"It was an accident. That's all I can say."

Reubens nodded like a dog nods at its own vomit, with the comfort of knowing where the next meal is and where last one came from. "Exactly. That's exactly what I'm saying."

"So you're saying it's okay?"

"When has an accident ever been okay, Mike? That's, that's the problem, kids your age, Mike, no. You're responsible, and there's going to have be paper on this. There's going to be some paper, I'm afraid. I mean, I know you have your ambitions, you've made that clear, but there's going to be some paper. It's…windshields aren't cheap, Mike. And the taxpayers are paying, in case you forgot. In case you forgot the taxpayers."

"But you just said it was an accident."

"Exactly. An accident you are solely responsible for. Who do you want to write up, Mike? The tree? You want me to put some paper on the tree? I can't do that, Mike. I'm not the sergeant of the forest, am I?"

Mike stayed quiet but Reubens bulged his eyes out, demanding an answer. "No, sir, you aren't the sergeant of the forest."

"Exactly."

"So do you want me to file the report?"

Reubens stood laboriously and patted Mike on the shoulder. "Nah, you go home, I'd better write this one up myself, get it…"

Sometimes, as it road-tripped across the desert of expression, the engine of Reubens's thought would seize up, dying and burning the whole car down, leaving nothing but a dark patch of asphalt beside the road. Mike couldn't let these pauses play themselves out. He always had to finish the sentence, which was another thing Reubens hated about him, and another thing he absolutely couldn't help. "Get it right."

"Exactly. Exactly right."

23

Weather permitting, a couple mornings a week Mousey would head to Morte Lake to run the trail. He would scramble at top speed up the hills and over the rocks, jumping over tree roots, slowing to a brisk, cautious walk in the pricklier sections. He believed it to be a better workout than either traditional jogging or hiking.

Three-quarters of the way through, he would peel off the trail to change into his bathing suit, smoke a small joint, and swim in the lake. Every time he would move smoothly through the water until he got to the deepest section, and then he would swim straight down as far as he could and stop. He'd open his eyes and look at the murky bottom, the forgotten, algae-covered wood that used to be trees, and he would go totally slack, just let the water take him back to the surface. Once there he would hack for air and float in the early-morning sun until he'd regained enough breath to return to shore.

He'd been restless in the days since the whistling lesson. He didn't mind giving away the money, not at all, but he did mind a little how Grace might have felt about taking it. There's a certain amount of money that's wrong to just give to someone, an amount that implies a debt even if you don't mean it to, and Mousey knew he'd exceeded it. On top of that, he had Mike Richmond on him now, looking to be a hero.

Mousey knew the type, not a bad kid, but annoying, a self-serving young man in what ought to be the most servile business in the world. Mike was ambitious and weak. He would be persistent, as long as persistence wasn't too uncomfortable.

Mousey was troubled. The chess girl and her cool jacket and exit line should really have lifted his spirits, but she wouldn't stay in his mind. He kept going back to his awkward misstep with Grace, and Richmond's millennial death rattle.

Ultimately Mousey was a practical man, or at least a man who'd had practicality beaten into him for a couple straight decades, and he figured his malaise out: he needed a hard run. Get the blood moving. So, having spent most of the last couple days cooking weird meals and smoking joints in his window nook, desultorily playing Open-Face Chinese Poker on his iPad in view of the resplendent Pacific panorama, Mousey hit the trail at a speed and intensity that was unusual for him, at an exact time when his body was least prepared for it. Less than halfway along the trail he had to stop and rest. He keeled over against a huge, mossy rock, looking up at the fractured sunshine through the canopy of leaves and needles. He covered the sun with his thumb and breathed, took a water bottle out of his backpack.

A tiny bright yellow bird flitted into the tree a foot to his left. It stayed there a minute then jumped to the branches across the path. The bird rested for a while, its head twitching complacently from side to side. Mousey dared not move in case he upset the bird, which seemed skittish, if temporarily unaware of its surroundings. Eventually, after a long, pleasant time watching the bird innocently peck at the leaves, Mousey shattered the relative peace of the forest trail with a long, shouted cough. The bird flitted instantly away, and the detective was left to stare glumly at his lungs' waste trickling slowly, frothily down a series of fern leaves.

Every state of being, no matter how transient or undesirable, has some legitimate and unique benefits. One of the chief advantages of being temporarily depressed and grossed out by your own wretched, aged, and abused body is that it allows you to hear the movements of others very clearly and to disguise your knowledge in the show of staring blankly. Mousey had always been able to find and exploit advantages where they presented themselves. After hearing the twig snap behind him, he kept staring ahead, pretending to be zoned out, and as the person sneaking up on him continued walking, *trudging* may be the better word for it, the detective reached subtly to his side and wrapped his fingers around a thick stick.

He waited, listening to the sound of dirt being stepped on by an idiot.

Tommy had been hiding in the bushes around Morte Lake for just over twenty-six hours, but the long, cold night beside the groomed trail had already exhausted the full extent of his outdoor survival skills.

His hopes for his Quadra Island time had not included mugging a hiker for trail mix and stealing his or her car, but real life had so rarely matched up to Tommy's hopes that he was less discouraged than others might have been.

At the heart of Tommy's failure as an outdoorsperson were three assumptions he'd been super-sure about, which had each turned out to be exactly wrong. The first was that there would be tons of cookable animals to hunt, the second was that he would be able to start a fire on which to cook the hunted animals with no lighter or matches, the third was that even if he did finally happen to see a deer blinking at him aimlessly and unafraid not six feet away (for instance) he would be able to actually catch and kill it with just his legs and hands and knife. Tommy had spent much of the sleepless, buggy night cursing the misnomer of his "hunting knife."

The hiking trail was so beautiful and inspiring and made-up-magical-kingdom-seeming that Tommy was surprised no hikers had come by since he'd returned to the groomed path, not fully realizing how early the sun rose on Quadra in August, or how long the night seems when you sleep for zero hours, or how slowly the morning passes when you've eaten two meals in three days. Tommy was unaware that it was only a few minutes after seven.

The guy he saw coming up the path wasn't Tommy's idea of an ideal mugging victim. For starters, he was an adult man. Just right off the bat, a bad start. Worse still, the adult man seemed a little bit insane, sprinting and scrambling up the trail like he was being chased. The crazed hiker seemed small, smaller than Tommy at least, but not tiny or skinny, reasonably broad across the shoulders, and probably in good shape, the way he was hustling. Abruptly the man stopped his psycho-run and leaned against a rock, wheezing, sweating, and fishing around in his bag for something, hopefully water. Tommy felt that things were looking up. As he inched closer, Tommy could see that the guy was staring at something in the trees; then the guy let out a real champion effort of a smoker's cough. Tommy sprinted ahead as the adult man hacked, taking the opportunity to close the distance. Then the hiker settled down and got really still, just staring into space. Tommy withdrew his knife and silently wished for a protein bar, maybe a Vitamin Water. He hoped hard enough to disperse his attention from the task at hand, and he stepped on a thick, dry twig, snapping it loudly.

He froze in place for at least a hundred heartbeats. Being neither a trained nor an intuitively acute strategist, Tommy closed his eyes to hope harder that he wouldn't be seen.

Then he opened them and watched the trees sway hard in the wind, threatening to kiss at their tops. His hoping successful, he looked back at the hiker still staring into space, water bottle dangling by his side. Tommy needed to get to him before he drained it. He removed his glasses and kept walking, faster than he had before, even; if the guy didn't notice the twig, he must be dead to the world.

Tommy was now exultant in his relief. This guy was practically already robbed; he might be so easy Tommy could kidnap him, as long as he was careful not to kill him. If the guy needed to get away so badly that he'd make Tommy kill him, Tommy would just let him go, simple as that. As long as he got some food and a car and some water right now, he'd be fine. But Tommy felt confident about the kidnapping, sure in his logic and abilities. He felt it now as a certainty: he and this crazed hiker would hole up in the hiker's hotel room or house, eating fresh seafood together and becoming friends, even after their rough start. The man would give him money.

This hazy, hunger- and insomnia-influenced thought process led to Tommy walking up in a much too upright and relaxed posture. His voice came out chipper and out of line with his words: "Hey, shit-fucker, gimme your..." Tommy barely saw the hiker spring off the rock, barely had time to process the thick, knotty piece of tree branch as it swung swiftly into his crotch. Instantly blinded by the pain, Tommy dropped his knife and staggered face first into an ivy bush. Disoriented by the bush and the intense, visceral worry about and pain in his testicles, he was doubly hurt by the second stick-strike to the sternum, which dropped him and turned his blinded vision from an angry red to a blanketing, vacant white. Tommy dropped to his hands and knees, feeling paralyzed from the waist down, and was unable to move or defend himself as the hiker stomped viciously on his kidney, dropping him all the way to the dirt. After that, the entire forest went silent for a long time.

Eventually, Tommy curled sideways into a fetal position and vomited the contents of his empty stomach into the soft, nutrient-rich soil. Then he whimpered inconsolably and drooled bile for several minutes. Finally, when he recovered a couple of his senses, he opened his eyes and saw the shape of the hiker leaning back against his rock, unlit joint dangling from his lips, Tommy's own knife pointed casually at him.

"Now." His voice sounding like he had a napkin stuffed in his mouth, the hiker wagged the knife at Tommy like an impolite finger. "Nobody says 'gimme' and nobody fucks anyone else's shit…" Tommy just looked up at the blurry man, confused and not remembering what he'd said. "And we can be hiking friends. Not going for coffee, talking about the bone spurs in my ankle and how it's weird that Fiona got married like four months after we broke up, capital *F* capital *R* capital *I* capital *E* and so forth friends. But, maybe, grab a hike, watch baseball, whack a tennis ball around and shoot the shit type pals. That's better, anyway. I'm sort of done with depth, y'know? Depth as an important thing."

Tommy croaked out a vague, affirmative sound and fumbled his dinged-up glasses back on.

The hiker got this weird smile on his face, placed the knife on the mossy rock beside him, and tossed his water bottle to Tommy. He wiggled the joint up and down in his mouth for a second, watching Tommy pull himself painfully up to a seated position and drain the water. "You look drawn. That's, in my experience anyhow, that's a sign of a silly diet or a guilty conscience" — the hiker smiled at Tommy as if Tommy were a funny joke the hiker'd heard a hundred times — "or both."

Tommy was still struggling too much to follow. He dropped his head and looked at the ground, trying to gather the courage to touch his testicles.

The hiker went on: "What do we have here, then? Is it an either, or is it an all kind of a thing?"

Mousey hadn't met a person like Tommy Marlo in a long time, and he hadn't realized how much he'd missed people exactly like Tommy Marlo until he did.

It had taken less than three minutes of conversation for Mousey to confirm his file-read on Tommy, and less than fifteen to elicit a confession for the money-stash robbery. The kid was a small-time street mugger with about a half a lobe more than most of his contemporaries and a lobe and a half less than a modestly talented sixth-grade debater. Mousey liked him, he was a nice kid, all armed robberies aside.

Even his last decade in Chicago, working SIU and Internal Affairs, running bag for the DA, he'd been operating at too high a level to meet many Marlos. Sketchy, dumb, funny, reckless, and sweet small-time street criminals. Tommy was exactly the kind of person Mousey had always used and sometimes helped and usually made friends with working vice, when Mousey had been a young guy who was having fun doing his job.

Talking to Tommy, even just looking him in the eye, Mousey knew him to an acute degree. Knew how to play him, knew how well Marlo meant, knew how dangerous he really was and really wasn't. On the street, guys like Marlo were victims who just got out in front of it and did their victimizing first. It reminded Mousey not just of people he'd known but of a time, and of himself. When he'd loved it. When he'd been having the time of his life, working crazy shifts, riding obscene, joyful amphetamine rushes, playing a quick, scary, hilarious game every second of his life.

Tommy had finally gotten up to stand, pacing gingerly with his hands consciously elevated, as if maintaining an imaginary force field over his lower body. He stilled himself, caught Mousey's eye. "You're a cop. Right, Mousey? You're a cop."

Mousey held Marlo's gaze, took a sip of his water, and then set to staring at the thick, layered spread of forest leading up the hill. "Not at this moment, no."

Mousey stayed staring off, but he heard Marlo start moving around again, kicking sticks as he paced. "That's a thing you're saying to fuck with me. Right? I mean, you're not a cop at this moment means you're a cop sometime. And for the fucking police, that time is anytime. So tell me, I'm ready to go, man."

"Go where?" Mousey looked over at Marlo, half a smile peeking through his grimace like sun through an eyelid. "Well, Tommy, you're going wherever you want. I used to be a cop, as in I'm not anymore, and I wasn't exactly a stickler even when I was. So you're going wherever you want to go, Tommy. That's your business."

"Why'd you pump me for all the details, then?"

"I was a cop. I'm nosy as fuck, that part stays with you. Even if you're not a stickler."

Tommy seemed to accept that, moved over to an adjacent rock, and started to sit down with extreme care. It took him at least twenty seconds, which is one of those amounts of time that seems long when all you're doing is watching another person sit down.

Looking at Marlo, Mousey remembered being twenty-four years old, two weeks out of uniform, running an errand for his new senior partner, picking up a brick of coke that Kenny (the partner) was planning to chop up and split among the squad to make up for the money everybody'd dropped on the Bears that year.

Mousey, the low man on the pole in the vice squad, waiting out on a street corner for a drug dealer, feeling small in his jacket. Showing up five minutes early and pacing, checking his watch for fifteen, seventeen, twenty minutes. Finally, a beat-up old Cutlass rolled up, a dealer named Rob at the wheel, scar across his face, girlfriend in the back seat, looking about fifteen years old. And Mousey remembered how nervous, how scared he'd been. How much he'd cared about all the consequences, and he remembered feeling that there were so many. He remembered gulping and getting in and barely croaking out a hello. The scar on Rob's face running from eyebrow to lower lip, thin and discontinuous and spaced out into skipping stones of raised tissue, like it'd been done with a coat hanger, which, Mousey would find out later, it had.

And they were both really nice. The girl in the back looked fifteen but was really twenty; she offered him half of her orange and asked if he'd seen a brand-new show about this bruiser of a chick who swordfights with gods and snakes and shit, and he'd said no, and Rob had crinkled his scar by winking, patting him on the leg and saying, "You'll love it." They'd sped to the apartment, which was a huge, horrifying tenement with a coat of paint on it, hustled past the crackheads, and gotten to the TV just in time to catch the third episode of *Xena: Warrior Princess*.

That was really a moment. One of those days that you can actually and accurately point to as a day that started a whole series of years, and as having everything those years had in them: surprise, relief, dread, fun, genuine interest, all permeated with straight-up human misery and humour, in not quite equal measure.

Mousey left his would-be mugger alone for a while longer. The young man had had a rough morning. The detective strolled up the path a few paces and climbed onto one of the taller rocks. He looked across the surface of the lake as it rippled and moved with the shifts of the wind, and he thought one thing: fuck Mike Richmond. Fuck him forever.

If Mike wanted to catch this kid, he was going to have to catch him solo, Mousey wasn't going to help him. He was sick of weak, ambitious men. He'd been an ambitious man for a good stretch in his late twenties to mid-thirties, and it made him feel strange and distant from himself to think of that time, like the three-week summer camp he'd been to as a kid where he told everyone a bunch of lies about how many girls he'd kissed and how much he drank and how many cigarettes he smoked on his way home from school.

Mousey was going to help Tommy the only real way he could, right that second: give him some food and go swimming with him.

Ø

Having smoked half the joint and run harder than usual, Mousey found himself not without regrets about giving away his protein bar as he and Tommy sat on a log, waiting it out so Tommy could swim without a cramp. The young man was still recovering from the beating Mousey'd given him and had his head craned down, looking at the sand, his hand rubbing repeatedly over the stubble of his shaved head, making a brisk scraping sound, clearly audible in the early-morning silence.

A stern rumble emanated from Mousey's stomach as he stood and stripped to his swimming clothes. He hooked a thumb towards the lake. "How're your balls?"

Tommy smiled and popped off the log, placed his mangled glasses carefully down, and started peeling off his shirt. He spoke with the stretched fabric pulled tight over his face. "Good enough to wade. I'm not a big backstroker or whatever."

Tommy got the shirt over his head and Mousey considered him carefully for a few seconds. The knife was about five steps closer to Tommy. It was sitting on the log, the blade still, redirecting light onto one small spot in the sand.

An eagle glided soundlessly a hundred feet over their heads, and the two men watched the bird as it smoothly drifted over the lake, sliding across in a casual semicircle, then moving its wings twice and disappearing over the opposite treeline. They looked back at each other, and Tommy smiled in a way that suggested crying. Mousey turned his back and walked into the lake until he was underwater.

It was a sunny but windy day, and after a little convincing, Tommy agreed that he'd be better off with more of his body under the surface, warming himself by treading water. The two men splashed around aimlessly for a while, and then Tommy decided he'd have more fun and be less worried with something floating to hang onto, so he dog-paddled over and pulled a log to Mousey.

"It's big enough for both of us."

Mousey tested the log's buoyancy by pressing it below the surface. "This side's heavier, I'll take this one. You take the other to balance."

Tommy nodded seriously and took his station at the other end, holding onto it with white knuckles and using his legs as an engine for the craft. Mousey balanced on the other side of the log, alternating between straddling the log and pinching it with his knees, paddling with his arms to help Tommy, trying to stay balanced on the log as Tommy powered it forward. After a while, they saw a big log that was also a floating greenhouse, three different kinds of fern growing out of the top. They communicated wordlessly and floated smoothly towards it.

Mousey almost fell as he tried to pull the two logs together, hanging stretched between them, one toe fiercely gripping their first log, his hand anchoring them to the fern log. Tommy had little actual depth perception, so his efforts to move the logs closer together mostly resulted in random, lurchy parallel shoves. Eventually, after a minute's silent labour, they had the two logs firmly anchored, the tip of their first tucked securely under the new fern log. They sat together and breathed.

Tommy's mood seemed to have brightened. "We've brought them together."

Mousey nodded, glanced briefly over the sun-soaked fern leaves. "What do we do now? We didn't really think this one through."

Tommy closed his eyes and turned his face to the sun. Mousey stayed quiet for an uncomfortably long time. The water on his legs was starting to separate into drops. "I think I might leave you now, Tommy. Are you going to be all right?"

Tommy didn't turn his head or open his eyes. He smiled and nodded.

"How about I'll get you some groceries, I'll leave them in the parking lot. Before dinner tonight."

Tommy opened his eyes and looked at Mousey. "Thank you. I appreciate it."

Mousey nodded. It was time. "Tommy, I knew about the, uh, the money. The gas station job. You didn't kill anyone."

Tommy looked like he was swallowing something about the size of his throat. "What?"

This, right here, was why Mousey had always preferred the Tommys of the world to the Mike Richmonds. Tommy, a lifelong fuck up, would torture himself forever over the idea, the possibility that he'd accidentally run over a guy who was actively trying to shoot him in head. Tommy would never even check, see if he was right; he'd just suffer. Mike Richmond would let a homeless kid choke to death on her own vomit and torture himself with the worry that he'd get a bad fitness report that quarter. Mike Richmond would Google comparable situations in which officers had escaped punishment, print them off, and present them at his hearing. "I heard about that thing, the Victoria deal. Nobody died. You were talking about people dying, but you've been in the news. Nobody got run over. You, uh, I don't know, man. You didn't hit anyone with your car."

Tommy stared at the space between them on the log. Then he closed his eyes again, angling his head back up. Mousey slid off the log and swam to shore. He got dressed and looked back, Tommy still cross-legged on the fern log, looking straight at the sun with his eyes closed.

Tommy wasn't really sure how long he spent on the log, but he stayed there with his eyes closed, sort of dreaming, for long enough that his thoughts turned fuzzily sexual (as they will), and in spite of or maybe a little bit as a reaction to his recent groin injury, he became almost fully aroused. Eventually, he noticed how chilly he was. He rolled off the log and paddled back to shore. He didn't put his glasses on for a second, just looked at the smudgy black patch of them on the driftwood beside his pants as he reflected sadly on the fact that he didn't have a towel. As he slipped the glasses on, Mousey slid into focus, leaning heavily on a tree, looking like somebody was forcing him to grin.

"Hi."

"Did you forget something?" Tommy twisted his hips slightly, trying to disguise his spongily engorged penis. He was trying to get the bulk of it down a leg of his shorts, which it was just barely pliable enough to do.

"See, I'm going to tell you something, Tommy. I find myself doing it a lot lately, telling people things, and I think, y'know, when did I become such a tool? It's an impossible question."

"You seem nice to me."

"I've been nice to you, that might be why." Mousey pushed himself off the tree, and all of sudden, Tommy started to wonder who should feel sorry for whom. "Aside from the beating. What I'm saying: you'd believe me if I told you I'd done some pretty horrible things in my life."

Tommy gingerly fingered the rising swelling and raw skin on his lower chest. "I'd believe you."

"You put down two serial rapists...maybe not serial. Multiple rapists, anyhow. You do that thing just two times, and it is such a good, necessary thing you did that it gets really hard to find one bad thing you could do to compete with it. And you look around, you look at all these people with all this money, and you look at yourself, and you realize that it cost you. It cost you a lot. And every good thing you ever did was a little bit horrible to somebody."

Tommy had literally no idea what he was talking about. When had rape come into the picture? "Sure."

"I mean, everything we eat was living at one time."

It had been a long time since Tommy had considered the fact that plants, even though they don't move, are still alive. "Not processed cheese."

"Not any kind of cheese."

"Yeah. Yeah, man, no kinds of cheese."

"Do you think dolphins have better lives than people?"

Tommy was openly shivering now. Mousey was still looking at him with these faraway eyes. Tommy felt the familiar ice-drip of something big about to happen, like Mousey was either going to give Tommy a million dollars or kill him. He was too scared to talk, and Mousey let the pause go on way too long.

"Me, personally, I think there was probably a good couple million years where it was better to be a dolphin. Back in the day, y'know, people barely have fire. Wolves are a legit enemy to mankind. Like, it's a world war against wolves and starving to death and cutting your foot and getting a staph infection, all the time. Dolphins, they're just fucking each other's brains out. They're playing and swimming in pods, carousing. We're still not that much smarter than dolphins. They just don't have these." He wiggled both his thumbs. "Without these, you're in a spot where you wait a few million years, and the animals with thumbs will build a bunch of shit that can kill you. And they can dump poison into your whole paradigm. The ocean's a paradigm. So are thumbs."

Tommy relaxed a little. The guy wasn't going to kill him, he was just zombie-eye stoned. The guy kept rambling.

"And you can't do anything about it, because it's just you and your fins and your dick that you use for fun. You're a dolphin. You're a dolphin in this version."

Tommy wiped the back of his neck nervously and reached for his pants. The water had soaked through Mousey's shirt in odd patches, sticking to him in four spots. "Yeah, man, I see that." Tommy saw just about nothing, in either a literal or a figurative sense.

"Put your clothes on, Tommy. I'm getting you a tent."

"Wait, seriously?"

Mousey pulled his shirt off his chest then let it fall back to where it'd just been stuck. "I get you some groceries, I leave you here, and I do it knowing the kind of trouble you're in? That's amateur, sleep-at-night, Good Samaritan bullshit. And one thing I'll never be is a Good Samaritan. You and me, Tommy, we're low-lifes. Two different kinds, but kinds of the same thing. Nobody looks out for low-lifes but other low-lifes."

Tommy started nodding several seconds before he understood what the guy was saying, then he kept nodding. "It's like how everybody hates smokers but smokers always let you bum one. Smokers share more than anybody."

"We can pull this one off, Tommy. You come with me, you trust me a little bit, we can pull this one off."

For the last minute or so, Tommy's dick hadn't been stiff at all and had really wanted to go back to the middle of his shorts, but it was caught in a fold. It was time. Tommy reached down and moved his dick back to its proper, neutral spot, ready to go.

Wherever.

Tommy showed Mousey the patch of grass where he'd slept and left his bag, and Mousey told him to gather it all up. The kid had pretty much submitted to him now, he was going to take whatever Mousey gave. He patted the kid on the shoulder and pointed at the bag, at the shape of the bag. "You're going to throw out that skillet."

"It's seasoned, man." Marlo moved over to the bag and carried the skillet over, his arms bowing shiftily under the weight of the iron and his own exhaustion.

"That's not seasoning. That's a rusted skillet."

"No, Mousey, no. It's, like, if you cook a steak on it, right? then the steak juice and the salt and everything like that stays and makes the pan tastier and thicker and whatnot. I'm not really sure. My buddy Scotty was a chef at Earls for a while."

"Yeah, but you're supposed…Were you washing this with soap? And the ravages of time…"

Tommy dropped the skillet to the grass, settled over it and looked at it closely. "I really was taking Scotty's word on this. He's got his Red Seal, but, yeah, yes, that's rust. I see that's rust now. That's not good, is it?"

"Eating rust? No. It isn't."

"Fuck yeah, man. I've eaten a *lot* of rust; I'm seeing that now. What is rust, exactly? Never mind, don't answer that."

"Sometimes it's better not to know."

"Yeah, you have to be specific about when you think not knowing is better, or you're an ignorant person, but yeah, as a general thing you're right." Marlo stood up with the pan in his hand, swung around in a circle and sent the pan sailing into a rotted tree stump, which disintegrated on impact. The two men stared contemplatively at the loose pile of rot on the ground. Tommy broke the silence as he went to pick up his bag, "Same thing with rotten wood. Like, what is *rot*, y'know? As an object? Is that one of those things where it's just the word *is* that thing. That's just rot, there's no, like, science description of that, I think. Sorry, I'm really tired and stoned. Where are we going?"

Mousey stayed silent.

The detective had a lot of thoughts about power. The main one was that most people didn't get much choice over how they used it. Most people, they have power over another person, real power, maybe once or twice in their lives. And the first time you have someone in your control, where they need you and can't hurt you back, nobody's a good enough person to respond totally ethically to that. It feels too good and too wrong.

The way Mousey thought about things (and he'd been thinking about evolution lately), people aren't that much better than monkeys. As far as animals go, monkeys are close. But there's a lot of emotional stimulus a monkey can't handle. Monkeys can be in captivity for years, their whole lives. And they'll be fun, they'll love people, but the second they hit sexual maturity it's over. It's just too much for them. They go into such a mania they start humping human legs. That's not the right body part or species, but they will just openly try to mate with it. There's not even a hole. They go so crazy they can't even see what's in front of them; they just want to fuck it to death, whatever it is. These monkeys will attack people. If a monkey attacks a person, they've lost sight of self-preservation. They don't care if they live or die, because sexual urges are too emotionally complex for them to handle. Complex urges, complex feelings, there are plenty of them for people too. Someone gives it up to you. When they confess to a crime, or beg for protective custody, or offer to blow you if you let them keep their heroin. Those are complex moments, with complex feelings attached to them.

Mousey had stopped being a scared errand boy picking up small-time bricks of coke a very long time ago. Scarface Rob hadn't stayed scary and Mousey hadn't stayed nice. There was another little moment he could remember with Scarface Rob, and in that moment nobody offered anybody half of their orange, in *that* moment Scarface Rob was doing the kind of crying that only comes out after someone's finished begging, and that moment, although Mousey remembered it just as clearly, wasn't the start of a whole series of anything, it was the dead middle of nothing. Just another thing he remembered doing, as opposed to a thing he remembered feeling.

Mousey had been in this spot many times. Deciding if he'd ruin someone's life or spare it. Power didn't overwhelm him anymore. He could just take it as it came, think things through, and make a choice. Tommy Marlo wasn't going to die in the woods, and he wasn't going to get kidnapped and tortured and killed somewhere else, and he wasn't going to get arrested and killed in prison. Mousey had decided.

"I'll tell you, Mousey, man, it doesn't get enough play, but being tired is the drinking-on-an-empty-stomach of smoking weed. And people just don't talk about that, because there's people who are tired all the time. We all know those. What're you gonna tell them, the always-tireds? So we all let it slide, as a people, we let it slide."

Mousey got the look he got on his face whenever he liked a funny thing too much to laugh at it. "Gather your stuff Tommy. Throw a bunch out, keep what you need, we'll roll the rest into this ravine. That's why you have all those bug bites, by the way. You camped beside a ravine."

"We're throwing out stuff for fingerprints and shit? I haven't been worried about that so far. I mean, fuck it, right?"

"No, that's the exact opposite of how we're going to be approaching things from now on."

"Gotcha. Let's burn the stuff I'm throwing out, for the fingerprints."

"We're in a..."

"Forest. Yep, gotcha. I'm telling you, man, toking on an empty REM bank, or whatever. However you keep REMs. Sorry, sorry, I'm...I'm tired and silly."

In sharper times, Mousey would have used this moment to give Marlo a hard check, probably verbal, maybe a quick throat grab. Herd him a little bit towards seriousness, but keep him nodding along and following what he said.

Instead Mousey walked over laughing and hugged the kid, giving him that creepy grab behind the neck that men sometimes do when they're too emotional to think about the person they're hugging as a sentient being who would like to control the movement of their own head.

After they finished rolling Marlo's tent and most of his (oddly heavy and bulky) supplies into the ravine, Mousey drove them to the hardware store and made Tommy lie down in the back seat as he bought a pop-up tent. On the way to the campsite Mousey patiently explained the situation and the plan. They stopped again and Mousey picked up some groceries and clothes, and also a phone card for Tommy.

Mousey paid for the campsite, booking an isolated spot up at the top of the road that overlooked but did not touch the ocean, and then the two men ineffectually tried to build the tent for a very long time. Eventually, it was close enough that they stopped, built a fire, and enjoyed the rustling silence of the forest and watched the wood burn, passing a two-litre of cider back and forth. Mousey stood up before talking, wanting to make sure the kid listened, make sure the kid remembered that Mousey was only a nice boss, not a nice man.

"You chill out here. You don't leave the tent much, and you never leave this campsite. See no people. Call me if you run low on food or booze or whatever. Do not spend money. I can get you out of here soon. It's just maybe a bit hot to do it right now. You got it?"

Tommy was mid-swig on the cider. Mousey was starting to think ADD wasn't just a myth he and a bunch of people like him had made up in the nineties to get legal speed.

"Tommy! Do you get it?"

Marlo looked up at him. "I get it, man. And holy fuck, nobody has ever stepped up like this for me. I appreciate it, and I won't let you down."

The campsite was close enough to the beach that every wave was audible, but the only things visible were trees. "No problem, Tommy. No problem, we're working on this thing together. I'll need your help, and I'll need you to stop being such a fuckin' floating blimp-head of a guy for me pretty soon."

They both laughed. Marlo looked back to the ground. "I'm...I'm what to you? Why are you doing this? Like, why bother? For real." Marlo's voice came out rubber-band tight. "What's in it for you? You're risking...you're risking the same thing as me if you help. What you're telling me, fine, I get it. It makes sense, but like you said, man, that's all Good Samaritan shit. And like you also said, you're not that."

Mousey skipped over, snatched the two-litre off the hood of his car, and drained the backwash. He leaned back over the car and laughed. Tommy Marlo was about half as smart as would be helpful in this very grave situation, but it was the half Mousey liked. "All right, you got me. I used to do this kind of thing. This exact kind of thing. It's pretty much the only thing I'm really good at. I got run out of Chicago, and at the time I thought great, sure, whatever, I'm burned out. I'm done. But, it's been a minute, and Netflix, internet Scrabble, and my weekly poker game aren't really cutting it.

And I know. I know what happens to you if I let you be. So I'm going to try to get you out of a really, really bad spot. I'm going to do that and ask you, after it's over, to try to be happy and be a nice person. Is that all okay with you?"

Marlo finally let go of the moss. "Yeah, I can see that, I can see all that." Tommy rubbed both eyes for an indulgently long time with the back of his fists, like a tired anime toddler. As he finished and looked back at Mousey, his eyes were watering so much that his body probably thought he was crying. "That's some thrill-seeking shit, though, man. Just helping me out because you're bored."

"Not just, Tommy, not even mostly. I miss it. I miss this, and I think I've got another one in me. I think I can pull this off. I've got about a gram and a quarter of moral fibre in my diet, and I like you a fuck-ton better than any of the people coming for you. So add it all up. Some combination of all that."

"Fair enough. I believe you. But you got the jump on me, man. I told you everything, I told you all my shit, and I don't know anything about you. You're from Chicago?"

"Yeah."

"Is it nice there? You like it?"

"It's my favourite place in the world. I love it. You've never been?"

"Nah, man, I never been out of Canada. Kicked out of school, right?, ran off, didn't take my passport, and then I had a warrant, so...Why're you here?"

Mousey looked up at the sky, bruising to purple, framed by the tall trees. "I told you, I got run off."

"You married? Divorced?"

"Neither." Mousey's neck was starting to hurt from the angle, but he didn't want to look at Tommy yet. "I was, uh, I was with a woman for seven years, though."

"Ah, yeah, man, don't have to marry 'em to count for something, for sure"

"Well, she was married."

"Oh shit, you dog."

"She was married to the head of the Illinois Liquor Control Commission."

"Damn, Mousey, seven, that's . . . you were a full-time mistress. Respect. What happened, she, uh, she stayed with the liquor man?"

"Nope. She did a speedball with way more heroin in it than either of us realized there'd be."

"Fuuuuck. She died?"

"Yep. I fell asleep for about twelve hours and she died in less than one." Mousey finally looked down. Who needs a therapist when you've got a sympathetic dirtbag the quality of Tommy Marlo around? "There's a saying in cut-your-throat municipal politics: better to be caught with a dead girl than a live boy . . ."

"That's pretty homophobic, dude."

"It's a pretty homophobic world out there, Tommy, but, uh, turns out it's also really, really bad to get caught with a dead girl if you're an ex-cop with a fixer job at the biggest law firm not on either coast and you've never loved anybody else more in your whole, fucked-up life than that dead girl. Woman. Dead woman."

"Jesus, I'm sorry, man. I'm so sorry. That's awful. That's . . . I'm sorry I even asked, man. That's awful."

Mousey launched himself off the truck. "So that's one way to get run out of a nice town, Tommy."

"Yeah, I've been run out of, fuck, twenty towns? Never heard of that way." Tommy bit his lip and paused, finally spoke, looking at the ground. "Well, glass half-full, this way you got to meet me." He peeled back into a Japanese-soap-commercial pose, his smile showing all of his dirty teeth. Tommy Marlo: earning it.

Mousey didn't say anything back. He just laughed for about ten seconds longer than was comfortable, then coughed for another ten past that. Finally, he reached down and ran his hand over Tommy's shaved head. That pleasant, wrong-way scrape barely reaching his ears above the sound of the empty forest.

Greta spent the next morning driving from one end of the island to the other, stopping occasionally to poke her head into the bushes and identify hiking trails she'd assessed as reasonable Marlo hideouts. She was gradually and uncomfortably settling into the mindset of an upwardly mobile professional and was therefore always thinking vaguely about real estate. Quadra wasn't a bad place to have a place, it seemed to her. If you picked off one of the residential lots near a ferry, it would gain value, especially as prices pushed everyone further from Vancouver.

Around eleven thirty she did a second pass in front of Grace Simmons's property, a nice, mostly wooded lot. Less cultivated than Greta was looking to buy (she was a move-in-ready kind of gal), but respectable. She parked on the shoulder a few yards down the road and hiked back up to the house. She ducked down along the stand of trees lining Grace's driveway, irritably swiping at branches and pausing occasionally to orient herself. As she got closer to the house Greta could swear she heard singing. She pulled her Glock and dropped into an athletic crouch. She moved swiftly towards the sound, emerging into a small clearing where there was a squat tree with a sprawling mushroom cloud of leaves branching out. It was one of those trees that gives the impression of whole insect lives lived under its branches. A tree that makes you think, for once, about ants. The forest was very quiet, and Greta tucked the gun into her ankle holster and approached the tree. She turned her back and let herself fall loosely into it. The hitman rolled around the tree to see the house from cover.

Grace was standing at a music stand, belting a song with her eyes closed. The music coming out loud enough for Greta to barely make out. She brought one hand up to rest on the tree, draped it at the height of a person's hip, adjusting the pressure of her fingers as she swayed in time to Grace's voice, enjoying the still, resolute lead of the tree's dancing.

After Grace finished her practice, Greta cased around the other side, confirmed the absence of cars other than Grace's, and formed a solid read that Marlo wasn't staying with his mother, not yet, anyway. No signs of shithead.

She returned to her car and ate a flavourless cup of Greek yogourt. The phone on her hip began buzzing insistently, and Greta let it ring through as she painstakingly scraped the sides of the yogourt cup. Finally, she pulled the phone out and returned Sergei's call.

"Hey, big cat, what's the good word?"

She heard Sergei pulling the phone away from his face to cough twice. "Dearest girl, I have often requested that you call me anything besides this 'big cat' you so insist upon. A big cat is Garfield, he is the only big cat I know. How he disgusts me. A fat lump, eating lasagna and emotionally abusing a lonely, loyal office worker. Tell me, is this the way you see me?"

Greta's sustained laugh was her only response.

Sergei expelled the weight of years through one sigh. "How goes your quest?"

"Mmmm, I'm on a quest. That's a nice way to think, Serge. But yeah, nowhere fast. I'm pretty sure he's not with the mom. I just finished checking her place. Anything on your end?"

"Do you have a pen and paper?"

"You always ask me that. No. I don't take notes, never have never will. Tellllll meeeee."

"Very well. First off, an impressive number of official record searches were traced to the RCMP office on Quadra Island."

Greta bonked her head against the window. "So it's off. I'm rabbiting if we have heat."

"Calm yourself. There has been absolutely no other indication of RCMP involvement on the island. The searches were conducted after hours, so we are assuming, you and I, that the two RCMP officers on the island know about Tommy's plans but are not confident enough to alert their superiors. A text message is forthcoming with details; you should proceed cautiously but swiftly, use your judgment, and be as thorough as you need to be. I will alert you of any activity from the police, whose cyber-security in this instance is deplorable. As I'm given to understand he has informed you, the aggrieved father is waiting just over the water. He is waiting for your failure. Should he need to scorch the earth behind you, you may be allowed to burn as well. Remember, at last, that. Have a wonderful and positive day."

"Are you forgetting something?"

"I am not an elephant, so perhaps. They are vile, stupid creatures, those elephants."

"If I have to do what I'm going to have to do, you need to double my cash."

"Obviously. Your money will be doubled but still contingent on your initial task, the Marlo fellow. If you cannot find him, the rest of your services are, as we say at the Spaghetti Factory, on the house." He sighed directly into the phone. "I have never been proud of being a man, only ever of not being an elephant."

"Deal."

"Deals cannot be made more than once, my darling, or they have not been made at all."

Greta turned off the screen of her phone, waited for a minute, and let the phone buzz once without looking. Seven minutes after Sergei sent a text, Darillo sent a wordless one that was just a string of emojis: Knife, Gun, Knife, Gun, Gun, Shotgun, Rain Cloud, Shotgun, Ambulance, Gun, Gun, Knife, Pickup Truck, Thumbs-Up, Stormcloud, Sucked-In Cheeks Smiley, Rain Cloud, Stormcloud, Knife, Small Patch of Grass in an Implied Wind, Gun, Clock, Shotgun, Clock, Brick of Money, Thumbs-Up, Clock, Knife, Gun, Knife, Gun, Old Hindu Man, Old Hindu Man, Old Hindu Man, Money Bag with Wings.

Sergei had included the names and addresses of the two RCMP guys, and their probable snitch, some meth cook named Glass Jar. Apparently Darillo, not knowing his ass from a hole in the ground, had put out the word to this character to keep his head down, thereby telling him, for no useful reason, that there was something going down. Tic-tac-toe, Glass Jar had figured it out, snitched to the locals, and she'd gotten incredibly lucky that they'd kept it to themselves and hadn't beat her to Marlo yet.

Greta's plan was to talk to Glass Jar, confirm that he'd been the leak, and if she didn't have any leads after that, follow the cops to Marlo, kill the cops and Marlo, and then hit Glass Jar on the way out of town. She should have asked for more money.

She pulled up to the shack already pissed off, and more than a little grossed out. Somehow the nice, glowy green of the air and trees around Glass Jar's place just made the trickling lines of rust, the dirty window, the soaked patches of oily dirt he used as a driveway all seem meaner and sadder and more disgusting.

Before she got out of the car she checked her gun and flicked off the safety, then she took a switchblade out of her glove compartment, fitting it loosely into her palm. She wasn't even out of the car yet, and Glass Jar was already waiting for her, his arms suspended against the top of his door frame, his hips cocked back, torso canted like a compound fracture. Greta wondered, abstractly, if Glass Jar thought he looked good, or thought he looked any way at all. There was one dark speck on his white T-shirt, the exact size, shape, and colour of a one-month-old piece of canned tomato.

"Hi there."

Greta nodded up at him. "Hi to you too."

Glass Jar let go of the door frame and stood up straight. He raised a finger to his chin, coquettishly. "If you'll sorry me, I don't remember making a date with you."

Greta walked up beside him. Glass Jar went to scratch his left arm, and she grabbed his right firmly by the ulnar nerve. "Hey. Uh, Glass Jar...It's Glass Jar, right?"

He swallowed a chunk of dry air.

"Yeah. Glass Jar. I'm here to talk to you. And I'm sent by people who won't forgive you unless I give them the good word. So what we're going to do, Glass Jar, is we're going to go inside, and you're going to tell me who you snitched to and how you did it, and if I get in a good mood I'll give the people who sent me one good word." She let go of his arm, stood on her tiptoes and peeked over his shoulder into the kitchen/living room. "You strike me as a microwave kind of guy. A man who's cracked the odd mini-pizza. I'll bet your freezer works. I bet that one could fit an entire dead thing in your freezer, in pieces, maybe, but it'd fit, and nobody would smell the pieces of that dead thing for miles and years. I'll just bet your freezer works." Greta put one arm forward and stiff armed Glass Jar backwards into his shack. He tripped over his feet and landed square on the twin sticks of his tailbones. "I'll bet your freezer is running right now."

Glass Jar sucked what was left of his teeth, turned his head to the side, and spit foamily on his own carpet. "I guess I better go and catch it, right boss lady?"

With everything else around them completely still, the

blade of Greta's knife sprung out. They waited in stillness for a second, and then she jutted out her bottom lip and blew her bangs up in the air. "Ba-dum-bum."

Glass Jar loosened up a little when Greta let him have some (more) of whatever clear, weirdly viscous liquor he was drinking. Too stupid to realize he was already dead, Glass Jar relaxed into his story, telling Greta about the big young cop who'd caught him dirty with meth and stolen scripts, open booze in the car, and a bag of stolen scallops.

In Greta's experience, the things that people got contract-murdered over were usually on the sadder end of cheap and the cheaper end of sad, but a bag of scallops had to be the lowest price she'd seen yet.

Greta stood beside the door, leaning on the frame because she was a bit too sleepy to stand upright but also a bit too germ-conscious to sit on any of the furniture. Glass Jar was rambling now. With his wrist flopped downwards at a sickening angle, exposing dirty bandages stained by blood from the inside and dirt from the outside, Glass Jar let his head droop to meet the wrist and stared at his disgusting, cigarette-butted carpet. "Do you...You from around here? West Coast, I mean by that."

Greta almost didn't answer, as she was busy figuring out whether to kill him now or wait until after she'd done Marlo and the young cop. Waiting was the smart play, the only play, really. It was crazy risky and unnecessary to do it now, but she really, really wanted to. Just from looking at his neck tendons. "Nope."

Glass Jar seemed to wake up a little and swung his head up at her swiftly, broke into this weird half-ass snarl. "I am. I grew up here. I grew up down in Sidney when they still had the wood boat races." He smeared his arm across his nose, his snot across a razor wire tattoo that didn't go around his arm, just down it in a random straight line for about four inches. "These boats, they were like, whatzaface, replicas. Remakes of old boats. The race went right by my house. And this is the first thing I remember in my whole life. I'm, like, eleven or twelve years old and I'm at the beach, and I'm lying down because my friends buried me in the sand. You ever been buried in the sand, boss lady? When you were young? Young as you still are."

Greta didn't respond. She had been buried in the sand by her friends at the beach as recently as a couple years ago, but she wasn't going to tell Glass Jar that. She just looked out his stained window and reached around her back to put her palm against the butt of her gun. It soothed her.

"Anyhow, since I'm talking to myself, I'll keep on it, there's this small wood sailboat with a round bottom, looks sort of like a bath toy but real-boat-sized. It's called a caravel." He looked up at her, the corners of his mouth pulling back in a vaguely human way. "That's a thing I still remember. I'm lying in the sand, I'm packed in, and I'm warm all over, and all of a sudden this caravel comes up over the horizon, I'm serious as a ball cancer right now..."

"Wow, that is serious."

"The tip of this boat, it's purple, like bright-ass purple, and the bottom of it is a mirror, showing me the sea under it, only a little more red and a little more blue than usual.

And this huge boat, it just floats over everyone, and I look around and nobody's looking but me, and I just think: they're here to fetch me. I think the word *fetch*. Have you ever thought the word *fetch*? Because I haven't, before or since. And then I fall asleep. And that's all I remember. True story. That's a thing happened to me."

"Cool story, bro." Greta turned to go, then, against her better judgment, she turned around. "You don't remember anything before you were twelve."

Glass Jar was back to just staring at her breasts now. "No. Not…Whatzit? Clearly. Not clearly. I worked in this dry cleaner's in high school. You ever heard of carbon tetrachloride?" He waited two seconds then plowed ahead again. "Don't matter, because I huffed it either way. Just a whole strong hootful of it. Almost died. Did me a shred of damage."

"You were getting high?"

"Nope. It's toxic. Don't get you high, though."

"Then why'd you do it?"

Glass Jar actually took a second to think about it, or at least to think about thinking. "Just to see."

"Explains a lot. It's been a slice. But I have to get going now."

Glass Jar squinted at her, hatefully. "Yeah? You're busy?"

Did he think they were going to hang out now? Greta turned to leave. Her hand on the door, she heard Glass Jar, back to his baby-bear snarl now.

"Hey, girly, before you go, you know what a hole is?"

Greta stopped another second, took three deep breaths, and once again did not spin around and shoot the junkie eleven times.

"A hole is a while of nothing with a circle of shit around it. That's what a hole is. So if anybody called you one, a hole, that's what they were sayin'."

Mousey had called Grace six times and left two messages before he decided to bring her one of the breakfast muffins that she liked from the Cafe Aroma.

In sharper times, Mousey would certainly have noticed some of the hard skid marks in the gravel of the driveway or the dented case of beer in the ditch.

He hopped out of his car, leaving the door open, and tried to make his body language chipper and pleasant as he approached Grace's porch. He knocked as loudly as he usually did, and then winced. Mousey had a really good cop-knock, but he'd never quite figured out the friend-knock.

Grace appeared at the door, her eyes hooded with sleep, squinting disdainfully at him. He made a sheepish face, gave a thumbs-up with one hand, and held up the muffin bag with the other.

"Motherfucker."

"Too early?"

"Motherfucker, *yes*. I got your messages. I was going to ring you up, I was going to spend your money, and I was going to do it on nine fuckin' hours of sleep, son, come on!"

"I can see where I misplayed this. Want a delicious muffin?"

"I love that muffin, I want that muffin, and I know you're bullshitting me right now. You're a tofu-eating drunk who's afraid of carbs. I don't understand it, and I don't like it. I know you don't love that muffin the way you should. Love it the way it's normal to love a muffin."

Mousey handed her the bag and she took it. "Gracey, I'm sorry. I could have done that a bunch of different ways, with the money and all, and I meant it nicely, and it came out fucked up. I don't have much family. And I have hardly any friends, and you mean a lot to me. And I'm a middle-class white man of a certain age, so I bottled a bunch of shit up and then just shoved my smelly feelings all up in your face all at once in the form of cash. And that's what happened back there."

Grace laughed and shook the muffin bag at him. "You're a good apologizer, Mouse-Man. Good apologizer. Awww, come here." They hugged, and Grace spoke into his shoulder. "It's all good, now lemme go. And lemme go to sleep." They released each other and Mousey stepped back and took a deep breath. Grace peeked in the bag. "These have bacon in them, and sausage, and green onions, and bits of egg." Everybody took two breaths. "Ah, it's all good. I've been a little out of it myself. I'm not shoving anything in anyone's face, but…yeah."

"What's going on? I'm available to listen sensitively to your problems." Mousey made a small sidelong shift towards the open door.

Grace hit him with a dose of side-eye cold enough to freeze smoke. "I'm not worried about how you're going to listen, okay? I'm worried about how you're going to respond.

Is that going to be sensitively? Because that's the only part that affects me. You listen to whatever you want, cry on your wounded man-insides. I don't care. How are you going to respond to my problems?"

Mousey stopped, stood up straight, and stilled all the irony-muscles in his face. "Sensitively."

Grace smiled, shook the bag at him. "Tonight, around suppertime, go to the HBI, sit on the patio and order yourself some dinner, and I will join you. Might even ask you for some advice about something. Now scram. Some of us are sleeping. Some of us are sleeping right now."

Mousey rocked back on his heels, let the lack of balance carry him to the steps. He skipped off the porch, light-stepping back to his car.

After he got home from Grace's, Mousey considered going to visit Tommy, then thought better of it, smoked a relief joint, drank a very poorly blended fruit smoothie, and accidentally passed out while watching an episode of *Catfish: The TV Show* where nobody actually got catfished, the couple just hadn't bothered to meet in person for eight years.

Glass Jar usually liked to get really, really tweaked before he watched the local news, inevitably staying tuned when it switched over into the Mandarin news. Typically, these sessions would switch seamlessly between his harsh cursing of ethnic minorities; vicious, unavailing masturbation to the female anchors; and loud, vicious, oddly bird-themed commentary on the physical appearances of interview subjects. And today was no different.

Glass Jar was rummaging aimlessly around the front of his sweatpants when Tommy Marlo's face appeared in the air beside the comely Chinese anchor's beautiful, round, but somehow also thin face, instantly redirecting Glass Jar's erotic reverie on a long, violent detour. Marlo's face onscreen was close enough to smell the gorgeous tiny Asian hairs of her cheek. Glass Jar spoke to Tommy's image on the television, slowly at first, stretching his vowels out like they were rubber bands he was shooting at the ceiling. "Everybody knows. Like your half-a-shade-past-white-Arab face is fooling anyone. We all know. You ain't Turkish."

Glass Jar jumped to his feet and began pacing, kicking old beer cans and candy wrappers out of his path with his eyes still fixed on the screen. Picking up steam.

"This fuckin', this fuckin', this fuckin'...I'm...I'm stuck now. Boss lady up my ass now, fuckin', I need business. I need business. I need to work. This guy, this fuckin' guy, MOTHER BIRDS COULD MAKE A HOME FOR THEIR BABIES BETWEEN HIS LIPS. I'm ready. I'm ready to make money and touch every cheek hair of every fullmoon-skinnycheek around, and this fuckin' half-a-nigger twists my shit all up, robbin' a fuckin' money stash, moron half-a..." Glass Jar stopped his path and raised his hand to his chin thoughtfully. "Yes!" He ran across the room, swept his arm through a mound of the garbage on his kitchen counter, did several unintentional jump squats, punched his fridge, and threw three beer bottles into the wall across the room before dropping to his haunches and pumping his fist sixty times. "The black lady from the bar. It's her. She's his mom. He's at her place." He jumped up and ran out his door, leaving it open behind him, he went straight to the truck, fumbling for his keys. Glass Jar was ready to break this thing wide open.

"Niggers, niggers, niggers; I'm a goddamn genius!"

31

Tommy knew that it would be smart to follow Mousey's advice, and more importantly he really did want to, but he ended up leaving the campsite and finding a nice group of surfy-seeming people on the beach nearby. He did it a little bit because he had the start of a cider buzz on and he smelled their pot and heard their shitty acoustic guitar and the sound of pretty girls laughing, pretty girls who were also willing to hang out and pitch tents and get sand in their clothes. And he did it a bigger bit because sitting alone in the campsite with nothing but nature around him gave him a horrible feeling in the bottom of his chest, like people he couldn't see were thinking about stepping on it.

The beach party was inclusive and a bit fluid, and after passing around a few cigarettes, Tommy found himself comfortably situated, talking to a small group of well-groomed hippies about jobs. Three of them worked in Victoria, one at the Ministry of Agriculture, the other two at an organic bakery down the street from the ministry.

Joey was the least hippyish of the bunch, wearing a maroon sweater cut to look like a rich woman's winter coat. She'd said her name, and it was the only one he remembered, but she hadn't said what she did for a living. She was sitting on the far log, drawing heavily on a cigarette with her head turned away from the circle, checked out of the conversation, but in a calm, easy way rather than a stuck-up way.

After he'd listened to the others talk a minute Tommy got up and walked across the circle. He almost managed to disguise losing his balance as his foot moved around a large rock and he landed heavily on the log next to her.

Joey pulled her head around then, slow but not lazy. Her hair was a little too short to get in her eyes, but she gestured at pushing it aside anyway.

"Howdy, leadfoot." She waved her cigarette at him, and for the first time Tommy realized she wasn't just too cool for hippies, she was a few bong hits deep, and a few hours deep into the session. "I didn't forget your name. I just didn't listen when you said it." She let the silence ride a minute, then she poked him once on the elbow, laughing in that way where the laugh stays halfway inside your mouth. "Did you have a plan when you launched yourself over here?"

Tommy ran his hand across his shaved scalp, stopping to brush back and forth with and against the grain for a second, then he dropped the hand to his side. "A plan. Those are things you make right before you almost dome yourself on a log, right?"

The sun was finally starting to dip below the horizon, the light orange and drained out. She laughed. Tommy took a little pause, and he thought for a second about what he'd say next. Joey filled the pause, reaching over and touching him briefly on the forearm. "Are you from here?"

"BC yes, this sweet island no."

"I grew up in Kingston, Ontario. This is a very sweet island."

Tommy sucked in a breath and shook his head sympathetically. "Ooof. Sorry. Man, that's bad."

She laughed again, flicked her cigarette into the sand, and waved a loose, goofy fist at him. "If you say 'Onterrible,' I will..." She paused to think but kept her fist waving in front of him. Their bloodshot eyes met.

"It's tough, it's tough to think of a good threat. I see your struggle. On the spot, it's tough. I get it."

She moved her fist to knock twice on the top of her head. "You're right. How do the threateners do it? All the threateners out there."

"It's like anything else, they think it up in advance. But that option's passed you by. So get that fist back out. I'll show you." She shot her fist back in front of his face, started another playful wobble. "Great. You've got that hammer ready..."

"It is a hammer, yes. I am a hammer woman."

"Totally, totally, the hammer is solid. Now, all you've got to do is show me that I'm the nail. Right? So just go for it. From the heart. I just said Onterrible. What are you going to do to me?"

She stopped the fist and held it an inch from his nose. She wiped the smile off her face and narrowed her eyes at him. "I will...beat you."

"How bad?"

She lost the straight-face game, dropped the fist, and snorted involuntarily. "Bad. Really bad."

"To death?"

Joey sat up straight, turning to look at him out of one eye. "No, just short of that. So you learn."

Tommy laughed, waved his arms like a linesman waving off an offside goal. "Wow, that's hard as fuck. You got it. You're ready. You're a threatener now. I won't say...that word. Out of respect."

"Respect for these hammers." She made two fists, then broke one to wipe at her hair again.

Tommy said, "I lived in Kingston for a couple months."

"Really?"

"A hundred per cent. And I'm thinking, we're two people ten feet from the ocean who have both shopped at the President's Choice in Kingston. We can't afford another second not looking at this water. This natural-beauty shit."

Tommy immediately lifted his legs up and spun around. A sharp, residual pain shot across his bruised sternum. He sucked in a little breath, then he offered his arm to her, which she ignored as she cautiously stood, walked around, and reseated herself. The waves were breaking gently over the rocks.

Joey started speaking a beat before she'd finished pulling a loose strand of hair out of her mouth. "Did you give yourself a splinter?"

"No. I gave myself three splinters."

She supported her chin with her hand and her hand with her knee. "And you didn't even cry. You must be tough."

"You must really know what you're talking about." He stretched his legs out and crossed them at the ankle. He tilted his head back and looked up at the trees overhanging the beach behind them, now starting to get framed by the darkness. Joey reached over and gently placed a joint between his thumb and forefinger. The pad of her finger brushed against the knuckle of his thumb. It was a calm night and only the very tops of the trees moved and only slightly.

He thanked her using his eyes and the angle of his head. Tommy lit the joint, held the smoke for as long as he could, and passed the joint back before exhaling in the general direction of Alberta. At some point the joint appeared back in his hand and they sent it back and forth for a while before it went out. Instead of relighting it, Joey stuffed the roach into a pocket of her coat-sweater, situated oddly somewhere in the middle of her ribs.

The two of them sat there quietly together, not holding hands but with their hands close together. It was dark enough now that the ocean and the sky were indistinct, both just a stretching, softly audible darkness. And they continued not to talk, and their hands stayed a small distance apart, and their legs brushed only on the downswing of Joey's kicks, and Tommy so, so did not want to get tortured to death by a motorcycle club.

As bad as his fact-, word-, name-, and number-retention was, Glass Jar had a freakishly mimetic spatial memory. Given any amount of time, he would not recall the name of the current Canadian prime minister, but he could remember in an instant how to reach houses in cities he'd visited once, years prior. Glass Jar was always aware of the cardinal directions and saw an expanding spiderweb of interconnecting routes to and from where he was, or wanted to go.

Once, after a few drinks at the HBI, Glass Jar had followed the large black woman who lived on Quadra back to her house. He did it in the same way he did many things, thoughtlessly and fully assured, something unspoken and unspeakable pulling his head along, the rest of him only following. If at the end of the trip he'd ended up helping her take out the garbage and making best friends, or killed her and stolen her jewellery and microwave, he would have felt equally that it wasn't what he'd been planning to do. That night she'd driven herself slowly home, in a legally-over-the-limit-but-not-drunk way, as Glass Jar barely contained his urge to drive his truck so fast that it merged into her car and they became one thing and their new onething drove until the horizon met the sea and they felt hugged by the cold, everywhere touch of water. He maintained a tight follow on her bumper. By the time they got to her house she'd already tried to wave him around and was shoulder-checking him constantly, definitely aware and afraid of him, and Glass Jar had enough of a sick-belly feeling that he simply sped off after she turned into her driveway.

That night had been over a year ago, and he'd spent less than four seconds outside her house. But, in the thin, squeezing focus of his crank fix, he plotted the most efficient possible route back there, occasionally banging the fuzzy, pilled ceiling of his truck with his fist. As he went to make a slight right turn, his left arm lost motor function, he felt the wheel pulling through his loose, slipping fingers, and he let the truck inch itself slowly to the shoulder before he yanked the parking brake. He dove out of the car, shook his arm wildly from the shoulder, rolled sideways across the gravel, and ended up on his back, dragging the limp arm through the pebbles and the dirt, leaving a vague trail of blood as he reopened his dog bites.

"Come on, wing. I need this wing, I need two wings. I need two wings to be me. To be who I am, in the sky. Who I really am in the sky, I need the wing. I need you, wing, to work."

He took two good hammer-fists to the arm, scraped it in the dirt a little more, and then gradually got to feeling as if the feeling was coming back. Glass Jar stood, gingerly made a fist, and kept the wing moving as he walked back to the truck, trying to remember where he'd put his pipe.

Constable Mike Richmond had already spent a pretty decent portion of the time he had left to pursue Marlo pulled over to the side of the road, digging the heels of his hands between his eyes and crying. It was the weeping of a person unused to tears: a hard, eye-swelling sob, born more out of frustration and the pre-emptive knowledge of rejection than actual sadness. It was self-pity, tempered in no degree whatsoever with irony.

There was no part of Mike that could laugh his failure off, no part of him that could rationalize the ways in which, at least, he would have avoided hurting others or himself, no part of him able to open the umbrella of perspective against the steady downpour of his anticipated disappointment.

Richmond came out of his crying spell feeling soothed, purged at the very least, and he started the car back up. The calm, sonorous voice of Buddhist stock tips boomed immediately from the speakers behind him.

"There is no safe ground on the path to enlightenment. The path *is* the taking away of ground. That's all the path ever was: a slow, hard losing. A losing, not a loss. Thinking there was a you and being wrong, if wrong were a thing you could be if you tried. If you tried. If there was a you. If, if, if, if. Ffffffffffffffffffffffff. Now, let's turn this perspective to currency trading in the smaller Eastern markets…"

Once he thought of it, Mike immediately began beating himself up for not thinking of it earlier. The key was Glass Jar. It had started, for Mike, with Glass Jar, and one way or another it would end with Glass Jar. He'd gotten the information from Glass Jar and immediately run from and ignored him. Glass Jar had talked, he'd talked to Mike, and he'd probably talked to someone else. It stood to reason that if he kept an eye on Glass Jar, he'd get something out of it. A club member, maybe the hitter. If anyone was coming to the island, they'd check in on Glass Jar, make sure he didn't get out of line, maybe have him run an errand. It was a long shot, but it was also his best shot. The only problem was the one Mousey had told him about: he was alone. He couldn't waste time watching the shack just in case some club-hired hitter stopped by for a chat, and he couldn't watch the shack for that long at a time anyway.

And of course, the answer had also been given to him, accidentally, by Mousey. Mike was, as Mousey had pointed out, a cop without anyone's help, trying to mess around with a life-and-death situation in his spare time. But he was a cop with access to equipment, and without the supervision of a competent, engaged, or in any way organized superior. Reubens had literally no idea how to use the digital surveillance equipment they had at the station. They'd never had to break it out, and if they ever did, Mike could wipe it or postdate a formal requisition, no problem.

The only thing that didn't go smoothly about putting the camera in Glass Jar's house was that Mike stepped ankle-deep in a puddle of spilled oil in Glass Jar's driveway/lawn. As a result, Mike'd had to sit down, take off his shoes, and roll the slick pant-leg up against and into his considerable leg hair. He'd had to watch his step very carefully after that; there was a weird amount of broken glass on Glass Jar's front lawn.

But Mike was growing better at managing his expectations and disappointments, and he couldn't really have asked for better: Glass Jar was out of the house, and there was a perfect, vaguely inconspicuous tree from which the front door, living room window, and driveway were all in range of the camera.

Mike drove home barefoot but proud of himself, proud of the chances he was starting to take, the things he was starting to realize. He was giving in to the fluidity of the situation, and he was doing all he could: taking away a little bit of ground at a time.

How weak and slow and sad.

Greta watched the huge, clumsy, incompetent rookie cop place surveillance equipment on his snitch's property. She had suspected he wouldn't be a problem when she'd first seen him slumping around the police station, taking ages to get the equipment ready, and he'd confirmed his utter floundering with this move. Glass Jar had told him more than he even knew, and the kid's only move was to double back and watch Glass Jar. Weak, sad, not a problem. He even looked like he'd been crying, but it was possible that was just the general puffiness that so often accompanies mediocrity.

The rookie even walked back to his car without shoes on, because real, actual, watching-a-person-through-your-windshield-and-planning-or-at-least-deeply-considering-their-death life has nothing but disdain for subtle imagery. *Barefoot Baby Cop Slumps Home to Wait for Irrelevant Surveillance Footage* was not a great, nor even a passable painting; it wouldn't hang in a gallery, but it sure was realist.

So on the one hand, she knew that the Quadra cops were, after all, no threat, which was a weight off her mind. On the other hand, she had wasted her entire first day on the island and was no closer to Marlo. Her plans were, as yet, vague but would probably involve staking out the Simmons house. She would sit outside a retired singing teacher's cabin, working the job her career was riding on (and, with Darillo waiting and hating and being a psycho in the wings, maybe her life more than her career), depending only on chance. Greta sneered once more at the young cop as he drove away to go twiddle his thumbs somewhere.

Having just thought about the move in such derisive terms, she resisted the urge to twiddle her own thumbs as she thought about what to do next. The hitman liked it best when a decisive action was available to her. That decisive action could be a subtle thing, to wait or to flee, or to take a minute and get more details, but she would do it steadily and confidently and smoothly, because that's who she was now. A person who did real things in the real world to real people, as if life itself were a sport for which she had trained. But there was no decisive action here, no matter how subtle or how guns-blazingly overt. She thought about calling Sergei then flipped her head down and sent him an upbeat, if somewhat terse, text. She thought about heading to the Simmons house, staking it out for the night, but she hadn't brought her night vision stuff with her, and the chances of Marlo rolling over at dusk, carless, felt small.

The smart play was to go back to her hotel, drink a valerian root tea, and sleep the sleep of surgeons. She would wake up steady-handed and steady-headed and ready to pull a forty-eight-hour stakeout and triple banger if need be. That was the smart play, and now, with Darillo on her and Sergei already losing confidence, was the time for smart plays, more than it had maybe ever been.

The hitman stayed an extra while in her car, staring at the forest through the shabby windows that went right through Glass Jar's shack, which was a bit like staring at a beautiful statue that somebody had framed with rubble.

Her pensive moment was interrupted when she ran her knuckle down the outside of her throat and sensed rather than felt the long, oddly dark hair that had, like a shocking number had recently, somehow sprouted all alone in the middle of her neck. She barely even grew arm hair; now this? One dark hair at a time, always on her throat; this was life now? With her right hand, Greta twisted the hair out and drummed a jerky, nervous tune on her steering wheel, then her thigh, and then her left hand. And then she started the car.

The hitman was going to get very drunk.

3⟨

There was a thin slice of the spectrum between sobriety and full-on amphetamine toxicity in which Glass Jar felt confident enough to approach another person while he was carrying a gun. Sitting with his car door open, staring at a small bald patch of forest a few feet away, Glass Jar reached his sweet spot. This pipe was just about done, but there was no reason not to blow it out and get one last good smoke out of it.

From somewhere, Glass Jar heard beautiful singing that he couldn't imagine imagining. He closed his eyes and listened to the tiny, dissipating pieces of song his ears could catch. Glass Jar wrapped his sickly, trembling fingers around the gun's barrel, pointing it, as one unschooled in the basics of firearm safety, at his chest.

"Money. Money. Get the money. Keep the wing moving. Soar. Get to Argentina alone. Spit on a rain cloud. Money. You are grown. And you handle yourself, no matter what." He opened his eyes so wide that the lids became forget-table. He spoke into the canted rear-view cutting diagonally through his image. "All you need to handle is you, every-thing else is just pebbles on the road. They go where they go. You handle you."

He lost his balance getting out of the truck. As he moved to stand straight, he caught himself wishing for his plan to work. He smacked himself abruptly in the forehead with the gun, opening a small, instantly swollen cut. A thin line of blood ran down his face and off the tip of his nose. "If wishes were fishes, they'd live in the sky. And they'd die real fast there."

Incautiously dropping the gun at his feet, Glass Jar removed his shirt, throwing it to the side. He picked the gun back up, and on legs that felt like bubbles of air he ran to the door, threw it open and entered the house. The Marlo mom stopped singing as soon as he was in, but she didn't move from the music stand. She put a hand up, like she wanted to use a crosswalk. Glass Jar charged towards her and skidded as he tried to stop; the mud caked into his boots had filled the tread flat, and he tripped over the ottoman. He looked up at the woman, and quakingly levelled the gun at her stomach.

Then there was just fast breathing for a long time that was really just a few seconds. Glass Jar hoisted himself up, walked towards her, and slammed his gun hand into her belly. The other wing had gone sleepy again. She dropped to the ground and, he was pretty sure, pissed herself. He loomed in close to her.

"You want to know what I'm thinking, right? You want my brain. You want it. I'll tell you if you ask me, but I won't ask you to ask." Glass Jar slanted his face into a harsh, Juvenalian satire of a wink. He pressed the barrel of the gun as deeply into her arm as he could, until she yelped a little. He felt sad that the barrel wasn't cold steel anymore, that he'd handled it too much, that he never got to make anyone feel the exact way he wanted them to feel.

"What are you thinking? What do you want?" She spewed snot and barely got the sound out. But Glass Jar was feeling generous and answered anyway.

"Goldfish." His mouth felt heavy and uncoordinated. He leapt back from her and slapped his own face quite hard. "Final answer, Alex Trebek. What is Goldfish? It's not a real *Jeopardy!* answer, though, because nobody asked by telling me the answer."

"I don't have any goldfish."

She started to go a bit slack and looked straight out in front of her, and Glass Jar stood back up and kicked her in the shin. "Wake up. I want the money." Glass Jar saw her eyes panic as the rest of her slumped further towards the ground. "Yeah, yeah, yeah, yeah. Tell me. Tell me. Tell me."

He wasn't even looking at the woman anymore, waving the gun where he thought she was, and he imagined her not moving.

"I don't. I don't know. I don't know. I don't know."

Good cop/bad cop is not a made-up thing. It had been tried, and had worked, on Glass Jar himself. And in this world, Glass Jar knew, sometimes you have to be both. Like water. Freeze cold, thaw into someone's desperate and thirsty mouth. All that. "You think I don't like you, but I do. I like you fine. Lots of things. Your hair is too tough to care about the wind. I like that. I should tell you. I should tell you that your voice sounds just like the radio, in the same kinda way the ocean sounds like a glass of water. Glug. Glug. I should tell you now."

She was staring straight at the ground, or maybe at her own fat legs. Glass Jar spun his limp arm in a wide arc, hitting her across the face with the tips of his fingers, which for the first time in a few minutes felt something, even if it was only the pinchy sting of numbness. He grabbed her by the top of the hair and tried to drag her to the kitchen, but she was too heavy and he only toppled her over, like a traffic cone grazed by a tire. "Crawl! Crawl! Crawl! Crawl!" She listened, which made Glass Jar feel pretty good and like he was in charge.

Her crawl was like none he'd ever seen. She didn't seem to want to put her knees straight on the ground, her legs spread a bit apart, and she just pulled herself along, the fleshy inside part of her knees moving like a cloth over the clean hardwood floor. It made Glass Jar sad again. She reached the kitchen, and collapsed in the middle of the floor. He thought he'd give her a minute.

Over the course of the half hour it had taken him to get from his television to Grace's house, the lines Glass Jar had drawn between the money-stash robbery and Grace as Tommy Marlo's mother had frayed. He'd mostly forgotten about Marlo, but he'd kept securely in his mind the idea that there was a lot of money in the house. He went straight for the freezer, using his already numb hand to roughly dump the contents on the floor.

Instead of looking through the boxes individually, he just stepped on them, hoping to feel cash through his boot. An overwhelming rage took him over after he tried to stomp a frozen salmon fillet and he fell, firing the fish across the floor. He scrambled across the ground, falling in place next to the fat woman, pointing the gun for the first time at her head.

"I can see the line of your neck move with blood and your eyes look three-quarters full of water and it kind of makes me want to crush you to death with a rock. No disrespect. No disrespect, just, just that's how I feel is all." She was swallowing at the kind of weird jerky pace that people about to tweak right off this earth did sometimes, and he knew he had to calm her down. "It's okay. It's okay. It's so okay you don't know it." He slumped back and rested his back against the kitchen cabinet, waved the gun around like he imagined a professor talking about the environment would, and forgot to speak out loud. He looked at his wing, and he smiled like boxers do when they're cut and they can't feel it yet. He fell into a long, brutal cough. Blood splattered out of his mouth, catching her in the face. She spazzed to the side like it was buckshot.

"You think I'm greedy but I'm not." Sometimes the things that run down your face could be blood or tears or both, and you can't tell. "It's not greed, is what I'm saying.

"My high school girlfriend, greasy little slut named Taryn, greasy fuckin' little whore, lovely cheek hairs on her. Like, denser cheek hair than you might think was sexy on a girl, but I liked it. You can like almost anything if you're right up close to it and smelling it and all that. And she was good to go, right? The last time I saw her, I'd just fucked her and we were getting post-fucky and all that little boygirl shit like that there. And she's lying on the pillow, talking about moving out of town, being gone, talking about being gone. And she did an impression of a kite, right? Leaned over and kissed me, and then pulled her head up and away, like a gust of wind came, picked it up." Glass Jar had started crying a while ago. "And it was a good impression, a really good impression. But she forgot the grass and the string and the running and the sun and the flying and the wind, and that tug in your hand. The tug of something weighing nothing. Do you get it? Those are all the good parts of kites." She was just staring at one spot. Glass Jar smiled benevolently, went to touch her cheek, and she moved away. For the first time in a while, he smelled the piss. Glass Jar patted her leg. "It's okay. I'll just go look now. I'll just look myself."

For a little while, the house settled into a calm, buzzy place for Glass Jar. He gathered himself enough to close the front door. His system of searching consisted of violently throwing the large objects around and slowly sorting and finicking with smaller objects. He made a large, pretty pile of different-coloured coffee mugs.

Glass Jar would never have thought to look in the piano bench, for a number of very good reasons. The first was that he did not actually know what a piano bench was; the second was that even if he had known, there was no piano in the house; the third was that, all pianos aside, the idea of a seat opening itself up was too much for the lead-legged vertical leap of Glass Jar's imagination to even allow him to graze with the end of a fingernail. So it was fortunate for him that the bench had popped open when he'd tossed it against the fireplace, and even more fortunate that he'd happened to spot it while spinning around in a circle and casting a wild eye over the room.

Glass Jar dug his hands into the fireplace, ashes floating

into his face and eyes, attaching themselves weightlessly to the sticky surfaces of dried blood and tears and snot. He picked up the three red packets of money and almost instantly began crying again. Hard, heaving sobs that racked his body from his weak, febrile chest down to his rancid, fungal feet.

He wanted water so badly.

Grace began crawling towards her bedroom, and Glass Jar spun around firing, blowing three holes into the ceiling between the living room and kitchen.

"I will kill your arms and legs! I will splinter your bones if you move them again."

She went flat and stiff. Glass Jar sprawled to his feet, ran towards her and took her cheeks in his hands, roughly torquing her eyes to touch his eyes. He'd intended to ask her for the rest of the money, but once he got there he forgot about it.

Glass Jar screamed into her face about ravens and magpies and ice and darkness and grass and gin and ice and darkness and tonsils and ice and darkness and the way your fingertips feel after you've just picked flowers.

The idea of flowers, the image of grabbing one forming in his mind, caused Glass Jar to curl the fingers of his right hand tight, squeezing one shot off into the ceiling. A thin spurt of blood exploded out her ear, and she rolled out of his hands to the ground, screaming into the tiles. Glass Jar let himself reel back a little, lost his balance, and slammed his head into the door frame. He spun around, and as the room shrank down to the soundless space of his vision, he drifted over to the money, grabbed it, and walked into the darkness towards his truck, which was splayed sideways across the driveway. It felt like there was a tiny, beautiful pillow under each of his feet, moving with him as he walked.

The list of things that could make Mousey feel sad in a weak and authentic way, rather than an amused-quickly-turning-to-vicious way, had been steadily whittled down over the years. It's never worth tallying up these sorts of lists, subjective as they are; what's important is really just the losing. The slow paring down of possibilities. Two of the few that remained were: being abandoned by a friend, and too much red meat. Mousey'd had plenty of both for the night.

He was far from drunk, but he did have a pretty solid rear-wheel skid of a buzz on. The sense of a deeper intoxication than he was feeling, held back by the heavy meal draped across the bottom of his belly. Finally admitting that Grace wasn't going to show up, Mousey fished some money out of his pocket, briefly considered jumping the fence of the patio, then changed his mind and took the long way back through the bar.

Inside, the HBI was full and buzzing. Some surprisingly talented old men were playing blues at the front; the pool table and darts (slightly to his disappointment) were both in use. It didn't take much looking for Mousey to spot the young woman from the chess board.

She'd seemed so calm when he'd met her, cool, but she'd had a lot more to drink now. Looked like she was stretched a bit thin. She was randomly surveying the room, one arm loosely draped across the bar to protect her empty glass, peering disdainfully at every other person around. Mousey stopped walking, started waving with both hands. Her drunk scanning was pretty much random, so it took her an awkwardly long time to spot him. He kept the hands waving, thinking that her flush drunkface looked a little warmer, a little more receptive and like a person who might cuddle, than she'd looked outside the other day. When she saw him, she popped her head up, covered one eye with her hand.

"Chessdude! What's up? Come and sit down. Or sit down and come, it's a free country!"

Mousey ambled over and plunked down on the stool next to her. He tipped a hat that didn't exist. "My name's Alan. People call me Mousey."

She did not touch any imaginary clothing. "Mousey. Jesus, what is up with people on this island and the novelty names. My name's normal. Greta. Starts with a *g*, ends with an *a*, normal, everyday stuff. See, that was a show of trust right there, the real name I just gave you. I'll make you a deal."

"Already we're making deals. I'm just here to relax."

"By relax you mean get stood up? Haw haw. I saw you outside earlier."

"I missed you coming in."

"You were occupied, looking like your mom was too busy getting furtively drilled by her office manager to pick you up at the soccer field. You tell the coach that it's okay and he can leave, your little head poppin' up every time a green

Chrysler minivan drives past...which they pretty much always do."

"We just walked home when I was a kid. Nobody played soccer either."

Greta wobbled slightly away from him. "You're old."

Mousey grabbed her by the wrist and pulled her up to sit steady. "You can't prove that."

She shook her hand free, then she ran the hand through her hair. "Let me tell you one thing, bro. One thing. We played floaty chess. We did that thing. So you can stay and hang out with me, but we have to skip the get-to-know-yous. I'm saying we played floaty chess. That's a bond tighter than knowing where you're from. I'm saying you can stay, but you've gotta interest me a little. Do some being interesting at me."

"Sure. Goes like this. This is how it goes."

"Ooooh. Tell me how it goes. Old-ass men telling me how it goes, that's a thing I don't get enough of in my normal life."

Mousey winked and carried on. "I was under a tree, this was a while ago, beautiful day, breezy and sunny. Sky all blue and shit. I was standing for a long time in one spot under this tree, and it was windy, and the wind was blowing yesterday's rain off the branches, and for a couple minutes I was sure it was raining only on me. I could have sworn I was standing under the only rain cloud in the world."

"I bet you used to be really observant. You're dull now. That's what I'm saying. A dullard, if dullards are a word or a thing. A thing a word talks about."

"Good. I like dull, I'll take it."

"Was that supposed to imply that you're actually super-exciting? Like you're so exciting you like to be called boring? Because that's subtle."

"Hey." He spread his arms wide in a way that should have seemed like something a fun and outgoing person would do just because they were fun and outgoing. "I'm a salesman. It's what we do, imply shit."

"You're a salesman?"

"I was."

"Of what?"

"Garage-door openers."

"People sell those? I thought they were just a thing at hardware stores."

"Jesus, you're young. Your skin looks like it feels like the top of a milk pudding."

"What's a milk pudding?"

"Jesus." Mousey motioned for two drinks, peeled a twenty out and left it on the counter in front of him, and turned to face her again. "You're young."

"Repeating yourself ain't makin' ya less dull, gramps."

"You're too young to say ain't."

"I'm not young."

He took an awkwardly long enough pause that the drinks had time to get there in the middle of it. "Well." Mousey smiled the bartender away and nudged one of the drinks towards her. "That's about the most youthful thing I've heard a body say."

"If you want me to finish this drink anywhere near you, you need to tell me one exciting thing that's happened to you, ever."

"Ever, huh?"

"Ever ever ever ever."

"So, like, if I shot a pimp in the knee one time?"

"So, like, if you did, yeah."

"Oh. I didn't. But I did get in a fight the other day."

"You did?"

"Yeah, first one in a while. I was running, keeping in shape, obviously," he patted his stomach with both hands, "and I almost got mugged at knife point." He said knife with an audible *k*.

In sharper times, Mousey might have noticed her eyes dart quickly at him and then back to her drink. "At Knife Point? I didn't even know that was a place."

"It's more of a state of mind."

"Where was the real place?"

"Ever been to Morte Lake?

"No."

"Yeah, so at that place you've never been. It happened, for real."

"I believe you." He might have seen how suddenly and quickly she was bringing herself to focus, might have read the name fixing itself in her mind. "What happened?"

"I was running on the hiking trail, and a young man came up with a knife," he said it without the hard *k* this time, already a bit embarrassed to be this deep into it. "And he asked me for my shit."

"Did you give it to him?"

"Nope, I, uh, tuned him up a bit with a nearby stick, took the knife off him. Then we talked it over and went swimming. I gave him his blade back. We had a good time."

"At Morte Lake."

"At Morte Lake."

"On the hiking trail."

"On the hiking trail."

"What happened after?"

"I bought him a tent and some hard cider. We didn't hug, but we looked at each other's chests and hugging came to mind."

Greta nodded, cocked a finger-gun towards him. "You said you were what? A garage-door salesman?"

"Something like that, yeah."

The thumb-hammer fired, then she let her hand drop to the side and the whole thing was just fingers again. She let her head hang back, let that neck expose itself a while. Her long, lined throat bobbed with the words: "I'm drunk."

"That's not good strategy. Announcing it like that."

"There's different kinds of strategy. There's defensive short-term strategies—for example, a person with apparently desirable holes announcing her drunkenness in a bar. But then there's longer-range, equity-based decision making, wherein one must factor in and show awareness of a greater quantity of complex variables. For instance, keeping in mind the paradox of being a straight man in this century, if one is, in fact, living in this century, that showing an awareness of, or merely a vague, implied sensitivity about, rape culture to a drunk-announcing woman in a bar actually sort of makes one seem like one is a wee bit of a rapist that should be factored into one's approach to the aforementioned drunk-announcing hole-haver." She straightened suddenly and placed a hand on her upper chest, as if hoping to hold the burp down with her hand. "I think I might have gotten lost halfway through that sentence. You get the idea. I gave it to you."

"Honey, I've been approaching drunk-announcing hole-havers since you were just a thought in your father's nutsack."

Greta looked up at him impassively. "Leaning into it, as a macro-strategy, not so bad. Mentioning my dad's balls is questionable."

Mousey slapped her heartily on the back. "Well, kiddo, since you seem to find me about as appealing as a sensitive toddler finds three dead rabbits stacked on top of each other, we might as well have some yuks."

"That was an oddly detailed image."

From looking at her eyes, Mousey could tell he looked blurry. He'd looked blurry plenty.

They went back and forth, throwing bits at each other as Greta drank water and Mousey drank cider, trying to catch up. Eventually, they decided they were even and each ordered a double gin and tonic. Mousey took a deep slurp and grinned into the citrus pucker.

"So whyya here?"

Greta rolled her left eye over her nose and just let her right drift a bit to look at him. "A vacation."

Mousey nodded and considered his drink for a second. Then he dipped his fingers in the empty glass he had left over and flicked a good slop of watery gin at Greta. She recoiled and slammed a bony, muscle-deadening fist into his arm. Turned the knuckles over and everything.

"Ow. Good slug. So you're on one of those twenty-six-year-old-woman solo vacations? That's what you're doing here?"

Greta sluggishly let her chin droop down to her collarbones, then she rolled her head back around and spoke to the ceiling, her long, lined throat bobbing with the words. "Twenty-six? Oh gee, thanks, Mr. Subtle Creeps."

"Always guess low, as my uncle, Dr. Lecherous Overture, taught me."

"Haw haw." She said the laugh like it was two words each filled with lead. "But to answer your suspicion, I'm not on vacation. I came for work, writing my thesis. Need some alone time."

"That explains the weeknight drunk."

"Haw haw haw. Because academics drink a lot, I get it."

"What's your thesis about?"

"Hieronymus Bosch, the greatest religious painter of the Renaissance, and the forever king of the triptych."

"Follow-up question."

"Shoot."

"What's an academic?"

Greta made an actual laughing sound, swivelled in her stool, and closed one eye thickly, looking him over. "You're a little bit less dumb than I thought you were."

"Right back under ya."

She tilted her head to the side.

"Instead of right back at you."

"Who says 'right back at you'? Are you selling me a used car in the early eighties?"

"What do you know about the early eighties?"

"Bitch, please. I'm an historian."

"You're not curious about garage-door openers? Sales? I asked you about your triplitch thing."

"Dude, no. I'm a little curious how you came to be beating muggers up and buying them tents. Like, what life led to that? But I'm not curious enough to ask."

"You're not curious enough to ask directly." They passed each other a smile that wasn't really a smile. Mousey lurched regrettably towards her. He clapped a hold of the young woman's leg just above the knee. "I can answer that question. Just not in public."

Greta cocked an eyebrow at him like he was the random sexist subplot in an otherwise decent romantic comedy. Something caught her eye and she reached out and snatched his hand, dragging it into the light. "Can I bite your fingernails?"

"Bite your own."

She dropped his hand and raised her own, twirling her fingers sadly. "They're gone. I spit them out on the ground or else they might be in my belly, I'm not sure how it works with fingernails if you accidentally swallow a couple while you're driving. If they're like hairballs or not. Probs you just pass them."

"Charming."

"You're charmed. Gimme your girly fingernails, I'ma bite 'em."

"First off" — he slapped her hand sharply away from his — "they're not girly, they're princely. Princes are men... or boys. Secondly, you can't bite my fingernails until you tell me why you want to bite my fingernails."

"So you're saying I can bite your fingernails?"

"And you're saying you'll tell."

She pointed at him with one finger and touched her nose with a finger on the other hand in a show of coordination Mousey would have thought impossible for her at that particular moment. "Okay. You'll be disappointed, it's not a story. I just like the feeling of it, especially other people's nails. I'll bite my own, but a foreign nail has this sweet, chunky quality to it. Three other people have let me do it."

Mousey nodded evenly then raised his fingers to her mouth and waited patiently, occasionally looking out the window or shrugging at passersby as Greta bit off each of his fingernails in turn.

When she was done, she drained her drink and looked at the nails she'd lined up on the bar. She was still holding his hand firmly, a proper Korean-nail-salon grip, and for the first time, Mousey looked at her hand. It was a nice hand: short, clipped, polished nails; slim, dexterous-looking fingers; and that lonely, lovely bloom of a slide-action scar on the webbing of her thumb, like a hitman sent to a Gulf Island might have.

"Thanks, Mousey. That did me good. That was perfect. I'm gonna call it a night. I got a crash room at this hotel before I even started drinking, because I'm a genius. And you live in some other place, and you'll sleep there tonight. Sincerely, though"—she reached over and put her hand on top of his—"thanks for the nails. They were wonderful. Catch you on the flip." Then she hopped off the barstool and walked down the corridor to the guest rooms. Shoulder holster subtle but bulging like crazy once you thought to look for it.

Mousey examined his somewhat raw and tingly fingertips. The bartender used his eyebrows and the angle of his head to ask if Mousey needed a refill, and Mousey dropped a hand to cover the glass.

"That was a new one for me, Joe."

"My name's Keith, Mousey." The bartender snatched the glass out from under his hand. "And that was a new one for all of us."

As he often did after having had too much to drink, Mousey woke up early, feeling alert and ready for the day. He popped up almost spryly before realizing that his feet were sore and maybe even a little swollen from his long, rocky beach walk home the night before. Mousey floated through his clear, almost colourless house, made some coffee, drank it, grabbed his gun and spare ammo from the safe, and wobbled to the door. He walked to his car, stopping briefly to watch the small family of deer who inhabited his property hop on seeming straight legs in seemingly perfect unison into the trees.

Driving over to Grace's, he muttered, still in a floating state that moved between half-drunk and wholly hungover, about how much smoother things would be going if he'd just figured everything out when he was supposed to. If he'd cased the hitman the first time she had been standing two feet away from him, strapped with two guns. If he'd thought, as he had arriving home blind-tired-drunk, to follow up on that one random thing Tommy and Mike and Tommy's file had all specifically mentioned, with one very simple records search. That thing being Tommy skipping bail on his mother—G., as in Grace, Marlo, née Simmons.

How easy his life would still be right this second if he'd only been paying attention, or working, or putting anything at all together when it would have been useful.

Seeing the splintered door frame of Grace's cottage from the top of the driveway, Mousey reversed immediately and parked his car beside the road. He pulled his gun, checked the mechanism, and took one of those very deep, very measured breaths that are never quite deep enough.

On his way down the driveway, moving in short, sprinted increments between cover, he thought about nothing other than the layout of Grace's house and the order in which it would be safest to clear the rooms. When he was within sight, he angled himself towards the far side of the house. He splayed backwards against the wall then moved in a slow crouch to the window. He did a quick check of the bathroom, which was empty with the door closed. He moved swiftly to the kitchen, but the window was too high for him, so he hurried around, hopped the porch as quietly as he could, and once more flattened himself against the wall to look through the living room window.

The place was trashed, the couch flipped over, piano bench having spewed its contents onto the floor. He took three deep breaths and made a preliminary plan. The living room was empty, so the first priority was to clear the other rooms. Fortunately, there was only the first floor (including closets), and the basement. While clearing, he knew he would also be checking the places where (if she was still there and alive) Grace would be sitting or lying. Because he was alone, he would have to finish clearing the house before helping her or checking her vitals if he found her incapacitated.

Mousey moved through the front door silently, checking the far-right corner of the room before swinging around into it and doing a visual survey of the living room. He peeked through to the kitchen and saw Grace lying face down on the floor. He had a few seconds' indecision about whether to head left to her or right to clear the bedroom.

He broke right, opening the door, scanning the room, and clearing the closet. He kicked the bed askance and ran back to the living room. He flattened against the door frame before moving quickly to the kitchen, grabbing a kitchen chair off the floor and jamming it under the door handle to the basement, and running to Grace's body on the floor.

The first thing he saw was the small pool of blood under her head. It wasn't enough blood. He knelt next to her, and as he went to check her pulse, she stirred slightly and started to roll over.

In sharper times, Mousey almost certainly would have left her to check the basement. In the present, he stopped her rolling, dropped his gun to the floor and tried to reassure her as he asked her a series of basic diagnostic questions. After she'd answered enough for him to be confident it was safe, he pulled a chair up for her to sit in, and then helped pull her to sit. He hugged her very hard and emitted one loud sob. She didn't hug back.

Tommy had awoken that morning disoriented by the tent but feeling, for the first time since he'd seen Bitch Face and her easy laptop, blank in a pleasant and actually neutral sort of way, rather than blank-in-an-absence-of-what-should-make-people-happy-or-sad-or-a-part-of-the-world-at-all sort of way.

He was standing on one of the rocks he'd used as a seat the night before, sipping a Pepsi and looking over the tops of the trees in the distance and admiring a little bit of the Pacific Ocean, when he heard what he hoped was Mousey's car pulling up. For the first time since he'd opened Bitch Face's easy laptop, Tommy wasn't terrified by a sound he couldn't see but curious to see what the sound was. He'd hoped correctly, and he waved at Mousey's car with one hand and toasted with the can in the other.

Generally, Tommy's grip on reality stayed pretty relaxed until the early afternoon. He'd never had a straight job, and none of the crooked ones start on the right side of lunch. So when Mousey grabbed Tommy around the waist, hustled him into the car, and threw his bag and anything that wasn't in the bag loose into the back seat and peeled backwards out of the spot, these events all seemed, just as many things that had happened to Tommy at ten a.m., like things that might or might not be happening.

He hadn't even seen his mom sitting in the front seat, shaking and rocking back and forth and holding a bloody hand over her ear. Tommy went to speak and didn't make a sound. He reached over the seat and got as close to hugging his mom as he could, putting a hand on each of her shoulders, and she used the hand that wasn't bloody and holding her ear to squeeze Tommy's, and she even leaned her head over to try to kiss his hand, missing and getting her own instead.

Mousey, who usually looked a little sleepy and a little stoned and a little bored and a little amused, was gripping the wheel so hard his forearms quivered, his face looking bloodless and drained, shoulder-checking obsessively, speeding and taking every weird side road until Tommy lost track of where they were. And the more things that only might be happening to him happened, the more Tommy relaxed back into the smooth shove of time going just one way.

Greta woke up groaning. She raised herself immediately to her knees before sagging forward and allowing her face to mush itself pleasantly into the give of the too-soft bed.

Her phone had stayed on the pillow next to her head, so she was able to reach it without moving anything other than her arm. She stopped the brutal assault of her ironic-favourite Tyga song by answering. Darillo didn't say hello, he just started talking.

"Mistakes. I'm about a half a foot from sea level, and the sun's about a half a minute from coming over a mountain with more trees on it than I have hairs on my head, and I'm sober, and I have a daughter who teaches me about emojis and memes and climate change, and if you'd asked me twenty-one years ago if my life could ever be this good, I would have shit in your mouth on purpose. And all I'm thinking about is pliers and fingers and broken teeth. Clocks that tick your sneaky cunt-time down in mistakes instead of minutes." He took a psychopathically long pause. "The sun just came over the top of the mountain, and even though I've lived with this sun and these mountains a few feet above the water on ground that's ready to split apart any second my whole life, I can still tell it's beautiful. And what am I thinking about? Tick, tock, grow a cock. Why so slow? You should have been sprinting for three days, and you've been jogging for two. Mistakes. I am coming as soon as they let me loose, and when I'm loose, honey, I am *loose*. Better finesse this thing fast."

He hung up, which saved Greta from having to look at the screen of her phone to hang it up. She threw the phone blindly towards the top of the bed, where it made two thick, wooden bounces. She did not look up to see what it had hit.

Greta allowed her weight to fall backwards and pulled herself (and her reluctant, reluctant eyes) painfully into the morning light, which blasted unfettered through her windows.

The hitman limped (in the way one limps when any part of one's body other than a leg hurts) to the bathroom, took a white-knuckle hold of the sides of her sink, and looked at herself reversed.

"Listen, Drunkself. I've given you a lot of shit. Over the years, a lot of shit. And I hate you a little bit even right now, I do." She released her hold on the sink and stood straight. "But no matter how much I hate you right now, I have to thank you, Drunkself. Thank you for existing and, in your own crazy way, getting me out of this. Thank you, Drunkself, for all the money you found me last night, and all the time you saved me. Thank you Drunkself, for trading tons of really bad real headaches for this one shitty headache right now. Thank you, Drunkself, for how scared you are of hot showers and sleep and Aspirin and how good you are at happening upon random idiots sitting all alone in random tents in the middle of bunches of giant trees on a rock in the ocean. Thank you, Drunkself, for being a good-time drunkself, and not a crying drunkself. Thank you, Drunkself, for always leaving, and always coming back."

Having scared the last of her drunkself away with a shower, a change of clothes, and a scalding black coffee, Greta drove to the large beachside campground at Rebecca Spit slightly less recklessly than was her usual style.

Sometimes Greta liked to pretend that her body had no perceptible shape, that she was really just eyeballs and eardrums perceiving their way across the ground. When these moods struck her, she made use of a large, somewhat sack-like beige shirt with an image of a man and a dog hunting ducks on it. Greta stopped the car and pulled the shirt out from her body to look at it. The man was not definitely hunting ducks, the ducks were a thing she'd always assumed. Looking at it now, given the colour scheme and all, it occurred to her that even the sky, on this shirt, was assumed.

Greta spoke to the man at the campground's check-in and did a good job of letting him explain to her where Mousey had set Marlo up in the campground and how important it was for her to remember these sorts of details, without gutting him or reacting any way at all aside from smiling and thanking him and calling herself stupid. On the way back to her car she cracked eight knuckles in two vicious motions.

From Greta's very limited viewing experience, hitmen in movies usually cracked their necks from side to side to show that they were pent up and not to be messed with and barely containing their rage and so forth. She'd seen it a few times in the few times she'd watched her profession represented onscreen. She liked the move and had decided to pick it up for herself. Unfortunately for Greta, the hitmen in movies, and probably in real life too, hadn't obsessively read dozens of articles about how sitting will one day melt our spines and turn us into bulging, hunchy monsters and stayed on an intense Pilates Reformer kick for the last year and a half, as she had. So the tough-looking neck snap was just not there for her, as compact and pliable as all the discs in her spine still were, so she was stuck with the full-hand finger pop, which wouldn't intimidate anyone, but felt crunchy and relaxing. She shook both hands out, first as a group and then individually, then she closed both hands theatrically and mentally prepared herself to kill Marlo, Mousey, and anyone who might see her do those things.

Greta did not even have to get out of her car to see the empty two-litre of cider beside the sloppily assembled tent. She walked straightforwardly up to the site, her handgun dangling in a relaxed fashion behind her right knee-pit. She toed open the tent and swiftly brought her gun to bear on a little bit of empty space, coloured blue by the sun through the tent walls. The hitman smiled in a not strictly disappointed way as she ducked smoothly into the tent and took a quick look around. Then she dropped to sit on the empty, unzipped sleeping bag. She smiled in a directly excited way as she used the barrel of her gun to pick up the empty cigarette pack and toss it back to sit on the top of her head, then she picked up the matchbox that had been next to it.

She sparked a match and blew it out, for the smell.

As often happens when everyone has many important and sad and useful and loving things to say, Mousey, Grace, and Tommy rode in complete silence to the mouth of the Heriot Ridge hiking trail. Every gentle but outsized bump of rock had its full impact as the small wheezes and jolts of Mousey's suspension echoed through the quiet car.

They had stayed, Tommy with his face mashed into the back of the headrest, Grace death-gripping his hand and her ear, which was definitely blown out. Reaching the beach entrance, Mousey stopped short, lurching everyone forward and back. As he'd so often had to and hoped never to do again, Mousey broke the silence and imposed some firmly worded conditions on the traumatized single-parent family riding in his car. "Okay. I'm going to give you guys a minute, but then I have to take Grace to the ferry. Tommy, I'm going to leave you here, give you a place to go, and you're going to wait for me there. You're really going to wait, and stay the whole time. Okay?" Nobody moved or said anything. "All right, just get out of the car when you're ready."

Mousey was not a person who generally respected privacy. It was, after a life of witnessing, enacting, and being subject to thousands of harsher and deeper violations, not a concept for which he could muster much energy. So it wasn't out of respect or friendship or obligation that he spent the length of Tommy and Grace's conversation sitting by the side of the road, staring at the flat grass that would soon collect enough water to be a ditch, instead of watching the car and trying to pick up whatever information he could about Grace and Tommy's relationship.

The detective didn't really have time to think about what the young man he'd brutalized with a tree branch would say about him to his mother, who had herself been assaulted by the detective's drug dealer, or what his friend, who knew him only as a burnout, would say to her son, who knew him as a person he needed to trust to live. He didn't have the time, because once again, there were too many practicalities to think about. Too many plans to make and too many pieces, who were also full, entire human beings, to move around the giant, petty game board of a life-and-death situation that boiled down, finally, to nothing more than a little money and some bad reputations that could only really get a little worse. The grass just sitting there, green and living and still always growing, without even trying. Without even knowing what trying was.

Mousey enjoyed the familiar, cracky-paranoid buzz of thinking, of focusing wholly on just the facts that came from short, terrifying seconds, the facts that came from quick decisions that nobody really felt they'd made. He didn't think it had been that long when he heard the back door of his car open and close, and he waited through each of Tommy's slow, ginger steps on the gravel of the road.

"Has anyone ever told you how loud your footsteps are, Tommy?"

Marlo's throat caught like a jailhouse door. "Never told me, no, but people have let me know. You're going to get my mom out of town."

"Yessir."

"This is my fault, right? This has got something to do with me."

"Nope. Not at all. Nothing on you. This was about some money I gave your mom. A robbery."

"I don't believe you, Mousey. This is about my money."

"That is a thing that you are entitled to think. But I'm only going to say the one thing. Meth-head robberies, they happen. I'm saying that one thing, and I'm your only real shot to get out of here alive. As long as you believe that, we'll be all right."

Mousey rolled onto a knee, looked up at Marlo's appropriately cry-swollen eyes, and without standing all the way up gave Tommy thorough instructions about how far down the beach to wait for him, and how silently to walk.

Mousey was more likely to use the word *awkward* to describe a fall or a running gait than a social interaction. This was a little bit because of his age and a big bit because awkwardness was too weak a concept to describe the kinds of silences he had sat in so many times, in so many cars.

It's not awkward when you and a beautiful singer whose perfectly tuned eardrum has just been shattered can't find the next thing to say to each other. And it's not awkward when your only real friend within 2,300 miles thinks you almost got her killed, and you can't correct her. Those are both whole other things. Two more things too horrible and too common to have picked up a name.

"This the part where I make a joke about turning on the radio. My radio doesn't work, though."

Grace's hand was fastened to her ear, still. "No, Mouse, this is the part where you shut the fuck up and give me a ride in your car and I hold what's left of my ear to my head and try to forget about your crackhead drug dealer who punched me in my belly to steal shitty, dirty money that I didn't want and that wasn't even mine and that I didn't even need to know existed. No. This isn't the part where you make any joke to me. This isn't a *part* where you anything about anything."

They missed the ferry by less than two minutes, which meant they had about fifty-eight minutes to wait for the next one. After Mousey parked in the overflow lot, Grace stayed sitting and holding her ear and clenching her other hand in a fist so tight her palm probably wasn't even sweaty. It took Mousey way, way too long to ask.

"Would you like a hand out of the car?"

Grace laughed just a little bit. "I don't know if I'd like it. But I do need it."

Mousey helped her by grabbing her hand and guiding her by the other elbow, which was still bent to help grasp the ear. Not having the purchase, and feeling about six different kinds of shaky, he dropped half her weight at the worst possible time, and her knee buckled and she fell flat to the pavement.

She kept her hand clenched post-trauma-tight over the ear, but as he helped her up, he saw three dark red drops of blood escape, dribbling down her shirt in long, stretched-out drops, each of them spreading out into nothing before any blood hit the pavement, like a waterfall so high it's nothing but a mist by the time it reaches the bottom.

They stayed away from the walk-on waiting area, worried that staff would ask questions. Grace sat on a concrete barrier and Mousey paced in a way that he could tell was impossibly annoying. A half dozen sailboats bobbed in tiny, tethered rhythms a few feet away.

Mousey let almost the whole hour pass before he tried again. "Okay, sorry, but practical thing: I have to get back to Tommy, but you've got cab fare?"

Grace didn't look up from her feet. "I have my wallet."

Mousey stilled himself and spoke a bit louder than he'd intended. "Listen, a lot got really fucked up and I'm not, not even going to apologize, because I can't. But I want to tell you that you mean…"

Grace finally looked at him, and it was not a good look. "Don't you try to tell me anything about what I mean to anyone, least of all you. Even past whatever the fuck just happened, you are trash. Serious trash. You're a white cop who shot poor black kids and ended up with a beautiful house in the Gulf Islands, that's who you are."

In sharper times, Mousey might have been able to hold his temper around someone he cared for very much and whose life and well-being he'd accidentally altered in the last few hours and who was right this second bleeding from a precious organ. "It was one, all right? And he sure as shit wasn't a kid. He was a three-hundred-pound pimp who was strangling me to death." Mousey pulled his lips back into a sneer he knew was far uglier than he'd be comfortable seeing in the mirror. "Anything else you say, I'm probably that thing, but I'm not some dumb, racist cop. I'm just not. That's...that's about the only thing I'll stand up for."

"Mooo-thurr-fucker. Who says you know what you are? You're the last person. I'm a singer who just had my fucking eardrum blown out. I can barely even hear you, and when I do it hurts. And you're still talking. You have no idea what the fuck you are, and you sure as shit don't get to tell me. It doesn't matter what's in your heart. Nobody cares how you feel. You're a white man living in a glass house on a Gulf Island who fucked over a city full of poor people to get there. Maybe you don't think dumb, racist thoughts to yourself. Sure. Good for you. But, at a certain point, it really doesn't matter how you feel. Because you are what you are, and everywhere you go, people get hurt. You don't think I realize that crazy asshole who did this to me was your drug dealer? Dealt you your pocket-rattling little pills that you're whacked out on three-quarters of the time? You don't think I know that? You think you're the only one thinking, looking around. Everyone does that. That's what being a person is. You like to talk, so you rambled about giving the cash away, and your maniac drug dealer listened and came to my house and fucked me up, really bad. That's what happened."

When it was time, Mousey could sit and take it. And so he did. This wasn't a misunderstanding that needed to be corrected, just in case. Just in case Tommy somehow lived, and Grace somehow saw him again, and Tommy somehow kept his mouth shut. Just in case of all of those combined.

Grace started up again, steaming along in full stride. "You think this is my problem with you? Your lazy, reckless shit happening, this time, to blow up on me? That's not my problem with you, that's just the shit you took on my dinner plate as a bonus. My problem with you is that you're a terrible person. You're a good drunk and a fun guy. That's all. There's no feelings here. If we lived in a place big enough to have a mailman, we wouldn't talk. Because you are everything bad but boring, and even that I'm sure you'll get quick. I don't know how you got in with Tom. And he's, God knows, he's a grown man who can choose, and he did choose, and that was a long time ago. But, I don't know how he found you, what you're doing...He thinks you're helping him, but if anything happens to Tom...I will do whatever it takes to fuck you over. Believe it." She finally let go of her ear, flexed a cramp out of her hand. "All this shit you brought. You tell me you blew up someone's leg, like that's a story. A person's knee. What was it worth to you?"

Mousey didn't so much cry as leak from one eye and snort a large, solid chunk of mucus down his throat. "What was it *worth*?" He pulled his shitty gaunt neck even tighter. "What's a web worth to a spider?"

Grace turned her head all the way away, and Mousey shifted his unfocused eyes to follow, watching the ferry slowly careen, almost sidelong, into the bay.

Grace stood, took two hobbling steps towards the dock, and then turned back. "I'll thank you for some good times, Mousey. I'll thank you for the drinks, and I'll even thank you on spec that you help Tom, and then I'll say goodbye for fucking ever. That's it."

Mousey nodded and whistled three tone-deaf bars of a song from a Sergio Leone movie, the name of which still escaped them both.

11

Greta was a woman of many talents: drawing, cooking, arm knitting, marksmanship, photography, always knowing where the best cheap pho joints and Korean booth-style karaoke places were, close-quarters knife-work, interior decorating, Zumba dancing, and garrote, to name just a few. One talent she'd never possessed, however, was managing her expectations.

As a child, Greta had been exceptionally small and even more exceptionally emotionally sensitive. She often, for example, buried her face in the couch rather than having to speak or make eye contact with her regular babysitter. The problem was not that she was embarrassed but rather that she had developed, in her mind and from books, an ideal of how she wanted to be with other people—what they would think of her, how perfectly they would understand her—and something always went wrong. After however many thousands of tiny disappointments, Greta eventually found herself expecting nothing of people. Taking what was useful, and letting the rest hang. Like basketball, or any sport your hands are too small to play properly: just don't play. For Greta, to expect even a little was to hope for that thing to be perfect, and even after all the years she'd spent consciously hopeless, and even after all those corpses and all that yoga, all those breaths gathered at heart centre, she'd still get caught wanting sometimes.

As she sat, lazily alert in Tommy's tent, she began to realize he wasn't coming, and she began to realize how perfect she'd planned the whole thing to be. Marlo comes back in from buying cigarettes, goes down smooth, practically puts himself, still alive, into the trunk, and she speeds over to Glass Jar's and finishes him (maybe with a knife, just because), and she makes the ferry, drops off the car and the still-alive mugger in the trunk, then chain-watches *Gilmore Girls* episodes on Netflix until she falls asleep and wakes up with more money than she thought she'd ever make in a year in a Cayman bank account. The exact perfect way it could happen.

The longer she sat, the more palpably she felt that vision creeping away, and she was forced, once more, to rage silently and adjust to the day as it would really go. Finding the old drunk guy from the bar, maybe having to cut a finger off to get him to give up Marlo, then the kid going down sad and bloody and slow and begging. Greta not even trying to make the ferry; one more night on the road, six too many drinks, one more time.

Greta bought a few feet of plastic sheeting, a staple gun, plastic bags, duct tape, and a litre of bleach. One more time. There was a tall, square, breathing callus behind the counter, and when he rang her goods through, he laughed. "A suspicious person would think you were looking to dispose of a body or two, sweetie." He had the voice of a seventies rock DJ who'd had his throat run over by a lawn-mower.

Greta sneered in the way men always mistake for an embarrassed grin. "A suspicious and a cautious person would think that, be glad it wasn't his body, and let me walk out of the store."

The callus laughed uproariously. Greta cracked the ghost of smiles past.

Having composed himself a little emotionally and having popped a steadying Percocet and a half and a zooming four Dexedrine, Mousey finally felt ready to sit Tommy down and give him the facts.

Mousey had always been disgusted by the assholes, and there are many, who drop news like it's theirs to drop, apologizing all over themselves, as if the tragedy is their having to tell the family, not the whole rest of that family being dead or raped or never getting out of jail.

Mousey's knees cracked worryingly as he sat down, and Tommy didn't even look up, just kept staring gormlessly at the gaps between the rocks. Mousey reached over and gently pushed the kid's shoulder, and Marlo didn't move even a little; instead, he started talking.

"Why did you come here?"

Mousey was there because he wanted to be, because it had become important to him, and because Grace wanted him to be. That and never talk to her again. So Mousey knew the answer to Tommy's question, but somewhere between being caught off guard and a bit freaked out by Tommy's new-found twenty-thousand-leagues-under-the-sea stare and his mouth being dry from the Dexies, Mousey flubbed on answering. His tongue covered with spit balled up like pills on a sweater, and his whole mouth tasting like sharp metal covered in bile.

Tommy continued, "I came here because I'd been here before and it's where my mom lives now." Tommy wiped the middle of his face with his hand, twisting the skin of his cheeks a little then letting go. "I've got a really good throat. That's what my mom told me once. She told me that when I was twelve, I think, she was, uh, she takes music serious, man. She's a mean music teacher. She was, anyway, I don't know what she's like now. I got a little older, I realized my mom did everything she did because everything I did made her sad. Just sad. That's it. Anyhow, I did my recital and it was an embarrassment, to her anyway. So we're talking about it, and I didn't think I did that bad. I hit all the notes, my voice sounded good. And she looked at me like I was retarded. She's like, 'Yeah, if the conservatory ever does a karaoke night, I'll be sure to bring you.'"

Mousey let the kid stare at the rocks some more, then he started whistling. The kid let him whistle, looked at him sidelong, and even smiled a little. "What I'm saying, Tommy: you're not a bad singer."

"Nah, man. She was right. Put the words up, and I can sing along, sound good. Singalong. That's what I'm good for, following the bouncing ball. Hitting notes isn't talent, it's *a* talent." Tommy whistled a few bars of a beautiful song. "So, Mousey, is this where you kill me? I'm not that dumb, I can see the ball bouncing." Tommy nodded limply at the gun in Mousey's waistband.

Without feeling himself do it, Mousey slapped Tommy

hard enough to knock his head to the side, then he reached out with both hands, stopping them before they touched the kid's face. "Gah. No, no. Sorry, Tommy. Shit on a stick. Sorry." Mousey took a breath and noticed that he was bouncing his leg manically up and down. He made a buzzy mental note to watch the Dexies. "Okay. No, sir. I'm not killing you. If I was going to, it would have happened already. That's straight up. Does that make sense to you?"

Marlo nodded, not even looking spacey anymore, looking like actual, empty-forever-and-a-day outer space.

"I have this gun, Tommy, because you've got a hit on you, and there's a hotshot hot-chick hitman here to kill you. That's why we had to move you from the campground. So what I need you to do is grab me that cash, okay, and the computer. Those are our chips here."

Tommy nodded his head and puffed his lips, stood and loped to his bag with all the urgency of a bear with a salmon in its mouth walking up to a garbage bin. Mousey put his head in his hands and listened to his bullet-train blood whip around the corners of his eyes.

He waited until what felt like a very long time after Tommy should have found a thing as large and important as $51,000 in cash. Three small black dots appeared on the edge of his vision when he looked up. When he finally did meet Mousey's gaze, Tommy had already given up and was sitting cross-legged on the ground beside his pulled-out bag.

"Hey, Mousey, remember when we threw out that frying pan? And that tarp."

Mousey hopped up on one leg and bounced aimlessly a few feet over. He took a giant breath of clean air and cast a suddenly exultant gaze over the midday sky, sitting there wide and hot and open, a window kicked out from the inside. "We tossed away the money."

"Um, yes. Yeah, I think it was, like, tucked in the tarp when we threw that down in the what's it…"

"Ravine."

"Yeah, when we rolled all that shit into the ravine and felt good. Yeah, that was the money. Fuck. I'm sorry, man, I was so tired and wired, and…Just fuck. Fuck."

Mousey laughed and doubled over and for some reason got on a jag of saying "hee" over and over through the laughing, which was off-putting and not how he usually laughed.

"Maybe we can go back? Like, I know roughly where it was."

Mousey gathered himself, stood back up, and waited for the painful, glowing cramp in his abs to ease. "It's a rainforest, Tommy. That money is mould."

"Fuck."

Mousey's giddiness settled down as he slowly and abstractly became aware of how large and widespread his numb dehydration cramp had become. He bent over slightly and looked up at Tommy. "That about sums it up, yeah."

"What are we going to do?"

Mousey exhaled through his already thin lips, which he'd pulled tight and bloodless. "That's the computer?" He was careful to put the hand back in his pocket after they both saw how much it was trembling.

"Yeah. You want to look in it? It's password-cracked, so you can."

"Tommy, my man, there's nothing I'm less curious about in this world than that. No, but that's our last chip. I'm going to try to get you out of here, but if you get caught, you need that computer."

"Okay. I'm going to keep it."

"For real, Tommy. Actually, you know what, let's, uh, yeah, I'm going to straight-up duct tape that computer to your chest. I think that's the right thing to do."

"Did you bring tape?"

"No."

"We don't have tape."

"Then I'm going to trust you. Please don't lose that computer."

"I won't, man, I won't. What are we going to do, like now? About the money."

"We. Us. You and me, Tommy. We're going to go rob my drug dealer to get you a stake and a boat off the island. Does that make sense to you? Because we need to be clear, and we need to be efficient now. This is it. There's no pressure, there's no regret, there's just things we need to do safely and quickly. If that is clear to you, we're going to start going over some details about how we're going to do the things we need to do. So how about it?"

Mousey, on principle, believed in full, honest disclosure in situations like this. But he believed in morality triage in all situations. Tommy was barely hanging on, and telling him it was Glass Jar who'd busted up Grace would be way more than the guy could handle.

Tommy moved his head in a way that convinced Mousey that he was trying to bear down and think about it, his eyes still a bit vacant, posture still slumped and sad and soft. "Wait. So the hitman's a chick?"

"Yeah, man, she's a real cutie patootie, too. I accidentally got drunk with her and told her where you were last night. Sorry."

Marlo nodded and shrugged a bit. "That makes sense."

"Does it?"

Tommy shrugged again, a little more decisively. "Is she a problem for us?"

Mousey waited for the kid to look back up at him. "Cutting odds, I'd say she's probably about a four-to-one favourite to kill me in a fight. Yes, that is a problem. A pretty big problem."

"What about me? What're the odds on me?"

Mousey laughed a bit too hard at that one. He couldn't stop shaking his leg, so he stood up. "That's a bet you might have trouble getting action on."

They separated to climb the rocks, and Mousey's legs felt thin and weak. Tommy helped him the last step up, and Mousey held his hand a second, gave it a short, hard squeeze. "We got this, Tommy. Trust me, sometimes you're the bottle, sometimes you're the fridge, and all anyone cares about is hops. Y'know what I'm saying?"

"No. I don't think that makes sense, man." Tommy sucked his teeth, letting out a wet, muted screech. "Robbing your drug dealer, shit. I fucked up. Why? Why did I do this? Like, for what reason?"

"You sure did. But take it from someone who's fucked up big and fucked up plenty: when you fuck up, all reasons become excuses."

"And when you're a full-time fuck-up?"

"Same applies, but for longer."

Tommy laughed again, with a lot of breath in it this time. "That doesn't make me feel better, Mousey. You're a trash motivational speaker, man. For real, watch a TED Talk."

Mousey's laugh got stranded somewhere in the desert of his throat, so he slapped his knee with his tingling hand. "Get it together."

Tommy looked over to the sea. "Man, seeing my mom, it makes me think, you know. What would've happened? I don't skip my bond in Montreal, I plead out, I get six months inside and five years' probation, which is..."

"Shittier than it sounds."

"Yep. And I move in with my mom when I get out. I work part time and get my GED, then I go to community college, and by now I'm, what, doing an apprenticeship? Making eleven bucks an hour learning how to install air conditioners? I've gotten super-into, like, NBA 2K or something. I'm just working, coming home, drinking six beers, and playing 2K until I go to sleep. Getting clowned on by Korean preteens. Then what? Two years from now, I get my certification, and I'm making twenty-eight an hour, get my own place, and I can actually get some dates, and everything is..."

"Fine."

"Yeah, everything is fine. It's fine. It's fine, but it's pretty fucking grim too, isn't it?"

"Most things are."

"Yeah, I guess so. I had a run, dude. I had a good time. I had, like, a hundred real friends I could party with, any weekend I wanted. Never had to wake up, never had to clean for anybody. Cute girls who like to dance, right? I had all that."

"I hear you."

"Only real regret I have is that I didn't go pick herb at my guy's farm in Penticton. Buddy offered me fifteen an hour cash to stay in his bunkhouse, pick weed ten hours a day. I'd be there right now. Right now, my back would hurt, I would not really care because I'd be high as fuck, and I'd have, like, four grand in cash, because what am I spending it on in fuckin' Penticton?"

Tommy hung his head, looking into the middle distance, flicking the index finger of his left hand with the middle finger of his right. A butterfly with wings the colour and pattern of very beautiful old wallpaper landed on his shoulder, and without turning his head or moving at all, Tommy raised his eyes to meet Mousey's. They waited an amount of time that Mousey knew better than to guess at. They waited through five of Tommy's still, quiet breaths, and about a hundred of Mousey's knee bounces, and then the butterfly flew away.

Mousey balled his fist hard, hoping to would stop the tremor. "Why didn't you go?"

"My guy pitches the job to me, tells me to think about it. I go out that night to the Edgewater, that's…"

"The casino."

"Right, yeah, so I go there, blow off a little steam, play a little twenty-one, and upstairs in the poker room, this guy wins a twenty-two-K pot in the Pot Limit Omaha game."

"The one-two-five game?"

"Yeah."

Mousey whistled.

"I know, man, I know. Bunch of people came up to sweat the action. Took like ten minutes to deal the turn and river, count up all the money. It was a crazy pot. So I hang out upstairs awhile, and I watch the guy who won the pot. He's an anywhere from sixty- to ninety-five-year-old Chinese man. He's got on, like, a Cultural Revolution sweater with all these holes in it, and I'm looking at the guy, and I just know in my soul this motherfucker did not pay for parking. End of the night, he goes to the cage, cashes in his chips, takes a cheque and a bunch in cash. I tail him outside, and I'm right, follow him onto the street. I roll the guy, and he's got $5,800 in his fanny pack. And that's a lot of fifteen-buck-an-hour shitdays. Enough to get me to Victoria, get an apartment." He made the sound of a very bad commercial actor drinking a Sprite. "Get totally fucked over."

"Good catch on the parking. Smart."

Tommy shook his head slowly. "Nah, man, nah. I'm not smart"—he did a very slow and sad version of jazz hands—"I'm just lucky."

Mousey looked at Tommy adjusting his huge, bent glasses, the frames canted around his nose like an unfinished roundabout. Mousey thought about whistling and ears and how many friends he'd ever made sober. And he so, so did not want to see Tommy get tortured to death by a motorcycle club.

Ø

Tommy was halfway back to his usual halfway-there self, but Mousey was still a good deal more than halfway worried about what was about to go down at Glass Jar's place. His plan was to break in, zip-tie Glass Jar, and toss the place for the cash, maybe put the boots to Glass Jar if it wasn't turning up quickly enough. Once they had the money in hand, he'd send Tommy back to the car and give Glass Jar an accidental overdose. Easy. It should be easy.

The shack only had one window, so sneaking up wasn't too much of a problem, even with zombie-legs Tommy tripping on every pebble between the car and the wall. Mousey pulled his weapon and took a second to compose himself. Tommy moved in front of the door and lifted his leg to kick it. Mousey reached out and gently stopped him, put a finger to his lips, and turned the doorknob.

Glass Jar was, as expected, passed out. Less expectedly, he was lying face down on the floor, foamy spit bubbling out from the side of his mouth in time with his breath. His pants were halfway down his legs and shit-stained from the waistband down. There was a dark brown puddle under his crotch that could equally have been disturbingly solid urine or disturbingly liquid feces.

"Holy shit, is he dead?

Mousey walked over to the body, kneeling beside it and holstering his piece at the same time. "Would you ever call a jellyfish dead?" He briefly considered feeling for a pulse but thought better of it, then he patted his pocket and realized he'd forgotten the zip-ties in the car.

Mousey figured that Tommy was probably more used to watching the door than he was effectively searching a very messy and broken-glass-filled home, so he left Tommy in the living room with his knife, and told him not to let Glass Jar move. Not that Glass Jar looked ready to earn a participation ribbon in any kind of track meet right then.

The search went slower than he expected, mostly because Mousey really didn't want to cut himself, or get stuck with anything, or maybe just catch straight-up hepatitis C by osmosis.

Then there was the shit.

It didn't so much seem that Glass Jar had shit his pants a time or two around the house, but rather that he'd been spinning in a circle spraying relatively small portions of feces out of his fingertips, like an industrial sprinkler head on a high school football field. There wasn't any consistent pattern, smell, or colour to the flecks. It was a collage of overwhelming diversity, the distinctness of the excrement coalescing into a unit more powerful than the sum of its parts.

By the time he finally got up the nerve to search the bathroom, it occurred to Mousey that it was probably where he ought to have started. He'd searched the house the way he would have searched the house of a sentient human being, which, to be fair, Glass Jar had at one time been, but Mousey had wilfully blinded himself to the current reality of Glass Jar.

Guys like Glass Jar, the one-percenters of addiction, are easy to imagine as conscienceless monsters. The truth of them is, as it always seems to be, sadder and far less easy.

The Glass Jars of the world do horrible things, and they never get better, and they never stop until they die. But for however long they last, they do the things they do, always aware of the world's pressures and codes and consequences. And the more they do the worse they feel, and the worse they feel the worse they do. The Glass Jars of the world feel pressure, feel the firm, choking grip of morality around their throats, but they are too weak to handle it. They want to do better, and they know what better is, they just can't manage it. That's not how it is with monsters. Monsters don't understand pressure. Monsters take care of themselves. Monsters love life.

Mousey saw it clearly in his mind, as he toed the bathroom door open and steeled himself against a new wave of smell: Glass Jar had gone to Grace's, gotten what he wanted, and gone completely bugfuck body-included insane with guilt. He'd driven straight home, probably still feeling good, and then he'd lost it. Smoking six hits too many, crying, puking, shitting himself, probably started in the driveway and continued into the living room, sputtering out tears and weeks-old opiate-constipation shit, smashing bottles. He'd gone to the bathroom, tried to clean himself up, shit in the toilet awhile, and he'd gone back out to the living room and given up. Too bereft to even take the money with him. He'd left it there on the sink, untouched. Sat in the living room drooling and blubbering and inhaling whatever downers he had around as fast as he could swallow them.

Gingerly lifting the money off the counter between his index finger and thumb, Mousey began searching the cabinets for drugs. Mousey had rarely failed to steal drugs from a house he was searching, and he was conscious that he would have trouble getting his hands on the stuff for at least a little while. He found the pill stash pretty quickly. Glass Jar, original as always, kept it in the cabinet above the sink. As he was filling his pockets, Mousey heard Tommy shout out in pain from the living room.

He ran back into the living room and saw Glass Jar with a firm bite-hold on Tommy's ankle. Tommy was slamming the handle of his knife into the back of Glass Jar's head, but Glass Jar was holding on with his teeth, his arms limply hanging at his side, his legs twitching only slightly. Mousey took a steadying breath and fired two bullets into the wall adjacent Glass Jar, the third hitting him high on the right side of his chest, bluntly jolting the junkie's long, bird-bone-light frame back into the wall, somehow propping him upright. Tommy sprawled sidelong across the room into the opposite wall and almost stabbed himself in the chest. Mousey ran across the room and grabbed the knife, shoved Tommy to sit on the floor. Tommy grabbed his ankle, the hand coming away bloody. The pills rattled jauntily in Mousey's pocket.

Mousey moved over to Glass Jar, dropped down to his haunches. Glass Jar, steadily foaming blood out of his mouth, spoke softly, air moving out as if through a pinhole in an empty balloon. "I died. I died. I died. I died."

Glass Jar's blood was so dark. Mousey gripped the back of the junkie's neck, as if beginning the world's most pointless massage, holding the head steady and angling it away as he put one more bullet through the temple.

Two questions at the bar and three hits on Google were all it took for Greta to find out who the old drunk was, and how close she'd been to going down. Alan Mouse, retired Chicago Detective Bureau legend. She shook ice cubes around in her glass and thought about it. Seeing him now, half of you would never guess; the other half would have a tickling suspicion too gentle to mind.

Greta was a bit better with large-scale disappointment than she was with in-the-moment flubs. Since the mid-morning, she'd gone from being minutes away from the biggest score of her life to coming home empty-handed, having cost Sergei a five-figure hit in expenses. Sergei liked her, but he was a cautious guy. Probably she'd be riding the bench, picking up odd jobs until he felt like she'd learned her lesson. One more old man getting one more chance to teach her one more lesson. Like she didn't know. Like she didn't know it would have been preferable to find the kid in a day and come home, like she hadn't tried and done better than he would have done in the same spot. Like everything all the time.

She wasn't even thinking about Darillo. Not even ever bothering or daring or caring to think about Darillo, a six-minute boat ride away.

She wandered out of the bar without paying, Keith the bartender unreasonably pinning her as trustworthy, and found a quiet spot in the shade of a tree. Even if you're drinking in the mid-afternoon, if your shoulders are narrow enough and you're hip and stylish and white and without face piercings, you get that specific kind of trust.

The hitman sat and pulled out her phone. It was funny, of all the things that had changed since that night in the stairwell at Grumpy's Tavern, the most distinct was her relationship to telephones. She remembered all the afternoons of her childhood, sitting in bed, drawing absently on a sketch pad and talking. Just talking freely, and forever, to friends she'd been with all day. The whole wide net of words they'd spew out, catching everything. And then there was now: quick codes, clipped tones, talking about friends and dads and sons, who were always all just future dead people or the people who would kill them. Staring at the second hand of her watch as she talked and listened to Sergei. She already knew what they'd say. It was already decided, and she just had to punch in the numbers and let it ring.

The hitman looked across the water at some trees, at the deep forest, and she thought, for the first time in a long time, about Karen, and wooden dwarves, and curly hair, and listening intently to dial tones.

Because he believed himself permanently entitled to treats, Sergeant Reubens could not abide the idea of going to Cortes Island to deal with a domestic violence call without turning the trip into an unofficial mini-vacation for himself.

In the relatively short time Mike had been stationed on Quadra, there had been eight calls for them to take the boat over to Cortes — four had been car accidents, one a house fire, and three had been the same incredibly sad repeated domestic dispute. Each time — even though the calls had involved, respectively, a potentially life-altering neck injury, a third-degree burn on a child, and a chronically battered woman — Reubens had hustled through them, handling the situations in as scant and perfunctory a fashion as was legally permissible, before making Mike take the boat back and heading straight over the creepy bed and breakfast he frequented there, eating and doing whatever awful things he liked to do when alone.

Since Reubens's extracurriculars made it necessary for them to separate at the end of the day, Reubens always took the boat and made Mike drive on the ferry, but this time Mike had faked a traffic accident call on Quadra and managed to get Reubens to let him stay behind.

With Reubens off the island, Mike knew this was his chance to make some headway on finding Marlo. It took him over two hours to make his fake accident report, so by the time he really got down to work on the Marlo thing, it was already time for lunch.

Mike remembered something Mousey had told him a long time ago, when he'd first gotten to Quadra. He'd been wading through another pile of Reubens shitwork, and Mousey had squeezed his shoulder with that loose, halfway-towards-patting grip and told him about paperwork. About how everyone had paperwork wrong. Most cops think of paperwork as this artificial thing that you end up having to impose on the real shit, real life, the things you did. And they have it exactly backwards. If you think real life is this thing you have to boil down to put on paper, you're always going to be following. But if you go the other direction, if you know that the paperwork is coming, you can switch it up. Break reality down into its parts and think about them the way you'd think about writing it up. Think of the things you do as paper you'll have to file, because that's exactly what it is.

And now that he was in it, a real situation where he'd have to do real things, Mike was starting to see the mostly baked wisdom of it. Mike tried to think of all the things that might happen as things that had, things he was only now bringing hindsight to bear on. He made himself a large coffee, carefully laid out his file, and resolved to act carefully and calmly.

Less than an hour into watching Glass Jar surveillance footage on fast-forward, and less than a second after recognizing Mousey and Tommy-in-the-Actual-Fucking-Flesh Marlo as the two men walking through Glass Jar's front door, Mike bolted for the car, toppling a chair and leaving the front door to the police station wide open, peeling his car across the only two lanes of traffic on the whole island without looking, and speeding towards the shack.

Having never found a corpse before, Mike couldn't tell if the smell had more to do with Glass Jar's body or the huge amount of excrement and rot decorating the walls and floors and countertops and upholstery of his home. Mike dropped to his haunches, pressed his closed fists together, and then pressed the double fist into his forehead as he tried to think the situation through without vomiting.

Standing back up, his already seized legs revolted, and Mike fell towards the exit, steadying himself against the door hard enough to bend the hinges, then sprawled his way across the meagre grass of Glass Jar's lawn. Flat on his back, half-blinded by the sun, Mike noticed the huge, undead tree on Glass Jar's body's property for the first time, somehow its enormity being only visible to him in relief against the whole sky behind it.

Mike started laughing in a creepy, sad, inauthentic way that would have been unimaginable to him just a few days prior but which felt both comfortable and comforting to him now. Sad realizations are sad. That's the downside. But the upside is you only have them after you've seen the situation as a whole and understood it. If Mike had done it all by the book, Glass Jar'd be in lock-up, whatever scraps of drugs and cash Mousey'd killed the guy over would have been seized, and he'd be in his office, staring out his window and making plans that were slightly more likely to actualize than they'd been before.

Instead, he was at least half-responsible for Glass Jar's murder, and Glass Jar was at least half a person, and he knew, even lying on his back despair-laughing into the hot, wide open sky, that it was a thing he'd never live with, or more that he would always live with it, but never happily, or even neutrally. But he also knew what he had to do now, and there was a calmness, a coldness, that came with that knowledge. Mike stopped laughing, stood, and looked one more time at the top of the tree, then one more time back to Glass Jar's house, imagining the body behind the wall, and then he weaved back towards the shack, closed the door, and shoulder-checked carefully as he slowly pulled his car into the empty street.

According to Mousey, the beach property he was setting Tommy up on belonged to Joanne Withrow, a lovely sixty-two-year-old woman with multiple sclerosis who spent all day making unique but similar paintings of young women's faces melting into long, gentle streams. Mousey either took care of—or pretended to take care of and actually paid some local kid to work—the thirty-year-strong garden on the edge of her property, which had recently become inaccessible to Joanne. Mousey had decided to set up Tommy's tent in the garden for the night.

They'd placed the tent in the shade of a tall wooden gazebo covered with the kind of ivy that looks pretty but, once you've had someone explain it to you, is the garden equivalent of a fascist state. The ivy will just grow outwards and choke any plant nearby, and anything it can't choke it'll just surround, hug hard and without permission. Obviously it was a pretty well-planned garden, so that gazebo was separate from the perennial garden, which overflowed and bloomed in a huge, billowing corner of the yard with a view of the gap between two mountains.

About once a month, Mousey ate dinner at Joanne's

house, and he was babbling his way through a lavish description of her dinnerware when Tommy just couldn't take it anymore.

Tommy had no idea which direction the house was even in. "Wait. So is she going to come up here?"

Mousey, who'd been in some kind of amphetamine speech trance, shook his head from the side and bobbed it from front to back before gathering himself and responding. "No, well, shit. I mean she *can* get up here, if, uh, if her caretaker, I think his name's George. If George takes her, she can get up here. But, yeah, the garden here, it's sensitive to her as a symbol of the, umm, the shocking and practical and rolling-terrifyingly-downhill nature of her aging and disease, or something like that, y'know what I'm saying? Probably. I'd feel that way, I was her, I'd feel that way. I shouldn't speak for her, but I can guess. I'm a guesser, by nature."

Tommy continued to debate telling Mousey about the bloody piece of skull suspended from his hair. "Mousey, why are you talking about her if she ain't coming up here?"

"I'm saying she won't. But I'm saying, now, if she does, you need to treat her with respect and care. She's a sweet woman, and just...She deserves a certain generous and unselfconscious tenderness paid to her."

As Mousey rattled on, the gore wiggled loosely and almost pleasantly, the way a tiny toy giraffe on a mobile does.

Tommy tried to hide a deep shiver and nodded, curling back into silence as Mousey swiftly switched the topic to how he was going to get Tommy off the island. And Tommy tried to follow along, even though his head felt three-quarters full of cotton that had been pulled off cotton balls and bunched back together.

Tommy had never been particularly resilient in the face of colds or fevers. Usually, if he felt slightly off, he would stay in bed all day — probably making himself sicker by not standing to get himself water or food as much as he should have. But now, right now, was a time to grow. To really improve. So Tommy kept a firm, steadying grip on his elbows, keeping his shivers in check and trying to look attentive as Mousey explained what would happen with the boatman.

Mousey spent a weird and unnecessary amount of time trying to convince him of how cool and smart his account- ant, Mr. Wu, was. Mr. Wu didn't even really matter, as far as Tommy could tell, he'd just referred the boatman. Plus it's always pointless to try to make someone know how cool a person who's just a name to them is. You have to meet people to know if they're cool. Tommy thought that was pretty basic, and Mousey probably knew it, but he was zoom- ing: dry-mouthed, twitchy, sweating profusely as he talked. Dude needed to chill out on the pill-popping.

So, combined with the fever, the accountant ramble had completely exhausted Tommy's ability to pay real attention by the time Mousey got around to actual logistics. Tommy looked out at the water and let the fever drift over him for a second, and an image came into his mind of Joey, the girl from the beach, bobbing in the water behind a canoe. She was bobbing in the water, her hair wet against her head, holding a rope in her mouth and smiling around it. And even imagining it, Tommy could tell that if someone saw a picture, a still picture of it, they might think she was in trouble, or that it was disturbing somehow, but he knew, being there and breathing the air and seeing it, that she was happy, that it was fun.

The whole daydream probably took a second or two total, Tommy couldn't be sure, but however long it lasted was just long enough for Mousey to notice and slap Tommy across the face again, the pain radiating feverishly across all of Tommy's nerves this time. Tommy curled in on himself.

"Ah, shitshit. Okay, I'm going to stop doing that, Tommy. It's not fair, and when you do stuff that isn't fair, you've got to... Sorry, I'm off. Are you sick? Are you all right? What's going on? Are you sick, man?"

Tommy exhaled a jagged, shivering breath, and reached his hand out to stop Mousey's babbling. "Hey. Stop. Sorry, I've been trying to be cool, but yeah I'm sick, and you're talking really fast." Tommy looked dreamily over Mousey's shoulder at the skyline and the slightly separated mountains. He thought of the phrase "sky cleavage" and laughed a bit to himself.

Mousey took a deep breath and tented his hands over his nose. "Yes. Good, this is...this is communication, Tommy. Right? Not like radios or Oprah and therapists and whateverwhatever, but communication between people in a tough spot. The thing. The real thing. This is what we need. So here's what's what: tonight, you cover yourself up, just go right to sleep, sleep until I get here. Chill. All right?"

Tommy was done with the sky cleavage, so he looked back to Mousey and gave a small, sincere nod.

"Then, tomorrow, I show up and I take you to the boat.

I take you to the boatman, you give him one envelope; I'll mark it so you know. You give him one envelope *after* you get to Campbell River, and he puts you in the car. You drive the car as far as you can, all right? Then you pull into the cheapest hotel in whatever town you're in, and you pay the clerk $500 to let you take a room without registering a name. Follow me?"

"I follow you. I'm with it."

"You sleep, you take some Aspirin, you watch some TV, whatever. As soon as you can, you get back in the car and drive until you hit the prairies. Then you do what we talked about before. Under-the-table job, all that. But that's later. Right now it's about envelopes, cars, and riding out this fever, yeah?"

Tommy smiled the weak, brave smile of a sick adult who feels really, really sorry for himself. "Yeah."

Mousey went back to his dry-mouthed pace. "Tonight, you wrap yourself in every fucking blanket and sleeping bag I gave you. You drink all the water I brought you. And I go home and pack you your bag. I'll put everything in it. Tylenol, some food, plenty of water. What you're going to need. I'll get that ready for you, then I'll come pick you up in the morning, drive you to the boatman. That's the whole plan."

This time Mousey didn't bother demanding any active listening cues from Tommy but rather took him around the shoulders and helped him stand and walk over to the supplies. Tommy tried hard to remember the plan before he fell asleep. Tommy felt Mousey pulling the sleeping bag around his shoulders. Then he saw the water being put beside him on the rock and he knew he should say thank you, so he did. Mousey snugged up the sleeping bag and rubbed Tommy's head, which was a thing Tommy really wished he'd stop doing.

Mousey was almost off the property by the time Tommy remembered. "Hey. Mousey, wait." Mousey turned around and held his hands out inquisitively. The piece of skull had fallen. Probably during the slap. Tommy might have asked or said something about his mother or explained about the piece of skull and what it had looked like and how distracting it had been, he might have told Mousey that he'd never seen someone die before, but he chose instead to breathe quietly and lift his arm to wave and hope that some of it was clear just from the angle of his arm against the giant sky, or the way he held his body, not quite upright on the rocks.

A thing Greta really liked about her entire professional life being totally separate from the rest of her life was that her good friends would seek out counsel at scary or sad times, without even an inkling that she might be, say, planning a murder or three. Or feeling herself botching those murders. Or fearing her own murder at the hands of a crazed motorcycle-gang father. Or some combination of all those things.

She told Charlotte to wait a couple minutes, and she hustled up to her room, genuinely excited to FaceTime with her friend for a bit and talk about something that seemed, and therefore was, important to someone else.

Charlotte's pretty, clean, in-for-the-night-face popped up and took over the whole phone. Greta slid to her back and held the phone above her head.

"Hey!"

Charlotte waved several times. "I got your out-of-town message. But, do you happen to have a minute—"

"To talk about the minivan commercial? Of course I do."

"Okay, great, so I have the mom-in-minivan-commercial crisis. That's one thing we have to cover. Where are you, by the way?"

"Work. They made me run out last minute to assess a piece in the Temple University archive."

"You're somehow always away for work and usually available to hang out at like one p.m. on weekdays. It's very weird. You're an odd duck. Hey, where's Temple?"

"Philly."

"I thought so. Why are you in a log cabin hotel in Philadelphia?"

Greta laughed and glanced around her room. "Airbnb, son. So what's your beef?" Greta asked to get the conversation rolling, but she knew the beef. Charlotte Li had been offered a great paycheque to be the mom in a series of car commercials about how it's possible for moms to successfully disassociate from their awful children while driving if what they're driving is a Kia. The problem with this being that just two years prior, when she had been thirty-one with great skin, Charlotte had done another commercial, this one for a piss-water beer, in which she had played the ambiguously young adulty party girl at the most racially diverse frat party in history. The sudden transition was leaving Charlotte with a lot of questions and rage and urges to die/disappear.

"Okay, this isn't a beef. You know my beefs. I'ma take the cheque, try to get my one-woman show on, do more writing, and so on and so on. But I might have to take the paycheque and move towards actually quitting acting entirely, totally entirely. That's the new thing."

"That's not a new thing."

"But with a new vigour behind it." Charlotte waved her hands into the picture, as if they were very fast-growing vines. "And I have to confess one thing that happened that helps to explain why, before I actually do that vigour."

"I love confessions. Priest me, Char. Priest me."

Charlotte giggled and kicked her desk, knocking her phone askance in its stand. "Okay, so, oh this is bad, this is bad. I went out, this is the week before they wanted to mom me, I went to an audition for an oily-skin-cleanser commercial. And I get there, and it's me and seven hundred pounds of white girl in eight very similar shapes, and I was just... I felt like I was looking down a well. Straight down the top of a well. That was the feeling. So—oh, Greta—so it turns out that it's a group audition, which I fuckin' told my agent I wasn't... Whatever, whatever, me and these girls all line up, we all have perfect skin, and they tell us about how to wash our faces. And, just, rage. So when the time came for us to wash our faces for the imaginary future camera, I started scrubbing super-viciously between my eyebrows and shouting, for real shouting, 'T-ZONE! TEEEE ZONE...' over and over until they asked me to leave."

The two women laughed hard into each other's digitized faces and gradually settled into the comfortable and separate silences of their rooms. Greta stroked the screen where Charlotte's cheek was. "It's time to quit acting. Or, like, shitmoneyacting. That's as clear a sign as you're going to get. Or give yourself, as the case may be."

Charlotte nodded then turned to look out a window that Greta couldn't see. "Yes. It is. I feel a lot better now that I told someone that. That was eating at me."

Greta nodded and smiled and thought about consciences.

Charlotte took a long exhale and set her shoulders. "I might become a model for hairdresser pictures. Like, on the walls there."

"That could really work for you. You looked great with that undercut."

"I did. I so did. That haircut might have cost me a part in *Speed-the-Plow* and definitely got me a non-speaking in a Future video. God. Acting is the worst. I'm so done."

"And you were the worst of the worst! Wait, that's not what I meant."

They laughed again, and Charlotte waved dismissively at the screen. "At least you didn't call me a moon-face again."

"HEY! I totally meant that nicely, and you know that. I just didn't know what 'moon face' actually meant. I thought it was, like, nicely round in the face in a beautiful way like you are."

"You thought it was a generic compliment you could give to Asians. It's okay. We're past it."

Greta brought the screen of her phone closer to her face. "Hey. I'm getting crazy pings on my phone here. I'll take you out when I get back—say, next Thursday? You are great, and you will be fine. You don't need this acting shit."

Charlotte winked. "I'll pick you up in my minivan . . . hon." She said it like "hung," and the two women chuckled, reached towards their phones, and made each other's faces disappear.

Greta had a series of texts from Darillo waiting for her.

U R on FaceTime!?!?!!!?

Why are you FaceTiming? Should n't you be working. I am waiting here. Gun, Gun, Storm Cloud, Waves.

Sergei has not been in touch

I need details

hey accept my facetime

Hey, I am facetiming you I am not your boss but answer or I might Kill you one day for fun haha

Lols

You are a stupid bitch and i am a angry experienced man

tick tock

Cutn

Stupid spoiled cutn

Autocorrect my phone remembers

accept my facetime its important about your job

Do you say accept for Facetime? ISt wrong?

Take my facetime its important for your job

Stupid lazy bitch its important about your job

Greta was just too profoundly tired to even think a murderous thought. She tapped her screen and a disturbingly clear image of Darillo sitting straight up on a couch masturbating through his fly, his gross old dick, that kind of hard gross old dicks only ever seem to get when and where they're not wanted. Beside him on the couch was a partially open butterfly knife; on the other side was the most overfull keychain she'd ever seen. She could see one corner of that *Easy Rider* poster that everyone who has ever died on a motorcycle has owned.

Mostly it was just the gross old dick, and Darillo's sudden, sad transition from slow maintenance strokes to that desperate, is he angry at it? pounding motion. Often, a gross old dick is all there is to it, at the end of a bad day.

Because things exactly like that were not the kind of

things she could afford to lose sleep or words or thought over any longer, Greta just turned her phone off and went to sit at the desk. She poured a moderate amount of GHB into a glass of water and drank it and stared at a Gustave Caillebotte painting on her computer that she could remember having cared about a very huge and very naive and very beautiful amount a very long time ago.

Had Mousey's hands not been quaking so hard on their own, they just might have started when he saw Richmond's truck, dented-in windshield and all, parked in front of his house, Richmond pushing himself off his perch on the bumper.

Mike Richmond was getting to be a real nuisance. Someone Mousey would still have minded in the best of moods and someone he hated a whole lot right now.

If he'd had the time and the patience, he could have dealt with the kid properly and easily, plant some of Glass Jar's stash in his car and dime him out to Reubens, something like that. Mousey made that plan, and a couple others, as he sloppily parked the car then backed it out and re-parked it. He swung out onto the gravel and pushed the door closed with his foot.

Mousey started out by talking significantly louder than he needed to or thought was reasonable. "Next time let's do this somewhere else. How about that? Shit's getting re-re-re-repetitive. Y'know what I'm saying?" Mousey moved to walk past Richmond without looking at him, but the big, dumb sweetie-pie found it within himself to stop him with a firm hand across the chest.

"The last thing I want from you is more advice, Mousey. I know you have Marlo. And you're going to tell me where he is."

Mousey gently pushed Richmond's arm off him and walked to the front of the police truck. As he went to rest his weight on the hood, Mousey lost his balance, misjudging the distance and landing harder and with his legs further out than he'd intended. He adjusted himself a little, got comfortable. "I'm not going to bullshit and bore you here, Mike. Cut to the chase: I just don't want to give you this Marlo collar. I don't feel like it. And you don't have any way to make me do anything I don't feel like doing."

Richmond smiled wide then, and Mousey knew that he was wrong. That the young cop had the goods. Richmond standing there looking like a sad, sweet black bear who'd accidentally wandered into a blueberry jam factory. Mousey decided to poke the black bear, see if he could knock him off stride a little.

"So how long do you want to feel pleased with yourself before you tell me what it is you've got? What you think you've got, anyway."

The smile went away, and the young cop reached into his pants pocket, fished out a crumpled .38-calibre bullet, and tossed it into Mousey's chest. The kind of crumpled only bullets thinking about trees can get.

"I *think* I've got about six more of those, Lieutenant Mouse, so you can keep that one. I dug 'em all out of that nice big tree in your yard. I *think* I've got a half-dozen noise complaints from your neighbours to explain how I got 'em.

And I'm *sure* I've got two more I can pull out of Glass Jar just like 'em."

Mousey used a cheap smirk to buy a very small amount of time. "I guess you're getting invited inside after all."

At a certain time of night, a time that changed by just a little each day, a light would fill Mousey's house that made everything look different from reality and nothing like a dream. Dreams, for Mousey, were always tilting and swirling around in a long, slow forgetting, even as he had them, or grasped at them in the morning. This light, for a few minutes at some point in the evening moving to night, bathed his glass house, his small, sad life, in illusory clarity, a layer of what dreams could be if they were real. Mousey didn't like to waste this light, especially not when he had the back end of a come-down opiate buzz gliding gently out from behind his eyes. So he didn't look at Richmond as the young cop exulted, pathetically, with his half-baked, half-smart boy-detective story. Mousey looked instead through the window at the rocks he hadn't paid to have destroyed to make his view better. Rocks covered in a moss that had the decency to stay the exact depth and thickness of a haircut the day you get it.

Finally, a slightly suspenseful interval after Richmond finished talking, Mousey turned his stare, lazily, to a small acne divot between the young cop's eyes, to give that slim impression of straightforwardness so valuable to small-timers like Richmond. He spoke slowly and reluctantly, as if spitting out a mouthful of particularly well-flavoured toothpaste. "You didn't call in the body. Good for you. Good for you, Mike. Didn't think you had that in you." Mike just smiling, eyeballing him back, knowing he had it regardless, knowing that the murder beef might hold, and if it didn't there'd be an audit and they'd seize the house, just to start. Mousey held Mike's stare, not moving his hands at all. "What's to stop me from maybe plugging you a few times, dumping your body in a deep grave, take my time taking care of Glass Jar? A little something like that."

Richmond went to his magic evidence pocket, dug out his cellphone, and slid it across the table. Mousey turned on the screen, and the video was already teed up. Glass Jar's shack in higher definition than seemed right to film the place, like watching a toe amputation through very expensive opera glasses. A camera right on the entrance. Mousey moved his face around a little without finding a definite expression.

"Yeah, that'll do it. How's that going to hold up in court, though, warrant-wise? I'm not sure how it works up here."

Richmond motioned for the phone back; Mousey wiped a fingerprint off the screen with his pant leg, then accommodated. "Yes, you are. And it absolutely would not hold up. But that won't really matter to a retired public official living about half a million dollars over his means who happens to be on tape at a murder scene, will it? Maybe the charge sticks, maybe it doesn't; either way, they find my body, Reubens gets these bullets…"

"I guess you've got it all figured out."

"See, all that stuff you've got. The career to look back on, the house, the law-enforcement carry permit, the pension. All that Freedom 55 loveliness that just up and evaporated in time for me, it ties you down. Gives you a lot to lose..."

Mousey would ruin this kid. Kill him maybe, wreck him for sure. He already had a pretty good idea how too. A little finesse, and it could be done. Mike Richmond would get got. "Sure. Bullets for the Marlo collar, easy peasy. You cross me, I drop the dime on *your* procedural fuckery, Mike, and maybe that sticks to *you*, maybe it doesn't."

"Fair deal."

Mousey stood briskly, motioned to his car through the windows. "Good. Let's go get him."

Richmond stood up just to look down at him, coming on subtle as a spin-class playlist. "You think I'm stupid. You drive me out to the woods, you know where we're going, and I'm along for the ride. Nope. I might be a rookie, Mousey, but I'm not stupid. I'll follow in my car."

"No go. I set him up in a spot with a vantage on the road. He sees two cars, he's gone. Into the forever of the forest. Like a sasquatch."

"So I guess it's on you, then. Isn't it?"

Mousey slumped silently back into his chair. "Mike. Mike. For a long time, like everybody else stupid, I thought that expression 'have your cake and eat it too' was redundant. Like, having cake, that's eating cake, y'know? But then I came to understand it. You want the cake, you want to gobble it into your greedy mouth, to taste it and shit it and wipe it off yourself. But you still want to *have* it. Want it to be there for you, so you can know it's around. Use it, but never use it up. And you don't even realize how disgusting that is to someone like me. Someone used up. You know what they say, Mike: sometimes you're the cake, and sometimes you're the fork. And either way, all anyone cares about is..." Mousey didn't even have to sell looking defeated. The bonus to being a burnout. "Cute sayings."

Because Mike was a man with an undergraduate social sciences degree who'd gotten mostly B-pluses he had, until pretty recently, known but not quite understood the meaning of the word *ambivalence*. What Mike thought was that the word referred to a kind of medium-negative feeling. Like you had misgivings. What he'd learned recently was its real meaning: you feel many ways. Like feeling you're a terrified rookie staring down a smart and dangerous and dirty operator. Like feeling you're a smart, brave, ambitious person staring down a dead-eyed burnout zombie you're just about to put back in the ground. Like both of you are all of those people and zombies, and all of those things are happening, and you couldn't be happier or more confident, and your foot is vibrating so hard you have to squeeze your thigh painfully just to keep up appearances. That's what ambivalence really is: being totally sure, every way the wind blows.

Mike's voice came out a bit shaky, but still almost as low and slow as he'd hoped. "So lay it out for me, Mousey. Tell me how you're going to save yourself."

The tumbleweed shrugged, snorted, and stretched his arms towards the ceiling. His voice coming out clear and firm and only as muffled as the harsh realities of time and his horrible accent mandated. "See, that's a sad thing, Mike. At your age, at this moment, that you just want it to be over. That's what you want, right, Mike? You want me to give you the answer, and you want to write that answer down and get your pat on the head, and you want to go home and dream of a slightly more comfortable life. And that's sad, Mike. In your line of work, that's sad. To want time to pass over you like that. Take a breath, my man. Take this time, these next few hours, own them. Learn something."

Richmond had learned, finally, that going back and forth with Mousey was no way to handle him. "I'm pretty sure I'm the least sad thing that's ever been in this house. And I'm not the one that needs anything right now. I'm the one sitting in my chair, counting options. Last chance: when and where can I pick Marlo up?"

Mousey hauled a notebook wearily out of his pocket and wrote a very short note. He tore the page out in one violent motion, folded the paper and held it aloft; then Mousey closed his eyes, and spoke suddenly clearly. "He will be here, on this piece of paper. Nine a.m. He won't be there before then, and I doubt he'll stay much after. He thinks he's meeting his ride off the island. I'll make sure he isn't armed. As long as you show up on time and with your cuffs ready, it'll be easy as pie. I don't think the kid has much fight in him. Door won't even be closed. You can walk right in."

Mike grinned. "That wasn't so hard, was it?"

Mousey opened his eyes again. He wasn't crying, but his eyes had more water in them than was standard. "I've got one more cop story for you, Mike. One more that you should probably hear, that I can tell you without that fat idiot around. You want to hear it?"

Mike almost felt sorry for the guy. Almost sorry enough not to hate him. "Sure. If it's short."

"I'll be concise. I had a snitch, name of Darnell Revis. Slung a little rock, knocked off the odd white kid came down to buy drugs. Nice guy, funny. I liked him. So, early November, and this is Chicago November, Darnell's just hanging out on his corner, drinking a Colt, holding down his spot. This Narco cop, Roberts, rolls past. Old-school, beet-red, dad-was-a-mill-worker-so-he-knows-struggle, shit-kicker-with-a-sap-in-his-front-pocket type, he drives by. Roberts is one of those fire-hose racists, the real deal. Everybody knew — shit, I knew it — that Roberts'll make a few good collars, but you gotta put a leash on him where the blacks are concerned.

"So he drives by Darnell, no reason to stop, he's headed somewhere else, he has shit to do. But he doesn't like the way Darnell's standing, spitting on the street. So he pulls over. It's cold, so his partner stays in the car while Roberts rousts Darnell. Darnell was wearing his winter coat, which, just for context here, had this, like, Christmas-card-type picture of a kitten on the front. Darnell thought it was funny. And Roberts walks up on Darnell, and he starts, he *starts* to say: 'Hey, boy,' calls him boy like that, y'know, says: 'Hey, boy, where'd you get that co—' and before he even finishes the word Darnell says: 'Yo daddy's asshole. It's a big outlet store. They got all the brands in there.'"

Mousey drummed a short tune on his stomach, tented his hands over his eyes to shade them. "Darnell doesn't even see the sap. Doesn't even have time to stand up all the way straight. Roberts catches him clean. It would have just been a rough concussion, probably. Except Darnell had just started to push himself off the streetlamp, and he fell back into it, which spun his neck the other direction so bad it almost broke. Darnell loses a bunch of mobility in his legs." Mousey made a clicking noise with his mouth.

"Roberts is a cop, and as you know, if you fuck somebody up that bad, they must have done something. So the DA files assault-with-a-deadly charges, says Darnell went at Roberts with the bottle. Bottle broke when Darnell dropped it. Public defender pleads Darnell out, he gets two-to-five, does a month in hospital, twenty-nine months in state prison. Shit. I am talking too much again. When did that start? When did I start being somebody like that? I wonder."

"I'm tired of you. And I want to sleep. Just tell me the rest of it."

"I made a bit of a fuss over it, but I was living pretty hard back then, working red-ball cases, running bag. So I decided it wasn't...it wasn't worth spending all my cards on. So I didn't. A couple years after all that—Darnell is still in pris-on, mind you—I catch a homicide. Home invasion turned rape-murder of a seventy-six-year-old woman. Roberts comes down to my office, no mention of the kid he's fuckin' para-lyzed, and he says he's got a couple of shittums in mind for it, offers to help me. So I say sure, we run down his leads, couple of junkies who've been knocking off stash houses, got bored and started doing normal houses, including our old lady. Don't remember her name. Anyhow, Roberts helps me, we crack it, put these two shittums down for murder one. After we book them, Roberts stops me outside and he apologizes. He doesn't profusely apologize, but he says he's sorry, says that was a fucked-up situation. Situation, he calls it."

Mike's leg had stopped shaking. It would only be a few more hours. A few more hours until he would have beaten Mousey, without having to be anything like him. Without having to turn himself into a thing so hard and so brittle. Without having to turn himself into anything at all. "What did you say?"

"I said what I always say when someone apologizes: 'Don't worry about it.' I say that every fucking time someone apologizes to me. It's like some kind of…I say it every time. 'Don't worry about it.' And then we went to the bar. He bought me a few Jameson and we talked about the 1998 New York Yankees. We were both Chuck Knoblauch fans. Which is a bond, y'know? That's a really weird baseball player to like. I guess what I'm saying, Mike, is it's inhuman. That's what I'm telling you. The world of it. The deals you make, the things you say are fine, what we're doing right now. It's inhuman."

"What ended up happening to Darnell?"

Mousey closed his eyes and then put the thin edge of his hand between them. "I won't tell you that, Mikey. It's too depressing."

The tumbleweed placed the paper gently on the table, leaned forward, and because that tumbleweed had once been a person with a lot of style, blew the note across the table into Mike's open hand.

The boatman had the red, gently lined face of man whose skin has taken a continuous beating from a relatively mild sun for his entire life. He still had most of his hair, all of it white, the front swept to the left in a way that disguised one half of his widow's peak and overexposed the other. He was neither fat nor slender, with a double chin and thin cheeks. He stood in a neutral posture, his hands neither crossed nor directly at his sides. He was not a type of man that looked or smelled or acted a thing like Mousey, but he was a type of man with whom Mousey could deal comfortably and well.

Mousey dispensed with any of his usual flourishes of gait and speech, walked simply up to the boatman with both hands visible. "Are you Mr. Wu's friend?"

Smile lines gouged pleasantly into the tough skin around his eyes. "I'm Mr. Wu's friend with the boat."

The boatman extended his hand, and Mousey allowed his hand to be firmly shaken by it. "Nice to meet you."

"So you've got one man's worth of passenger for me?"

Mousey nodded and counted off items on his fingers. "Yes, one passenger. A nice, able-bodied, calm male. He needs to get to Powell River. Tomorrow a.m. he'll be where we are right now. Tonight at 2100 I need you to go to this address." Mousey gave the boatman a slip of paper, and the boatman took it, stared at it, then crumpled and tossed it behind him without looking. "Pay this two thousand for the shitty blue Toyota Tercel I bought for your passenger." Mousey slipped a slim white envelope with a blue marker stain in the top left corner to the boatman, who moved it casually to his pocket. "And stow it where you plan to dock with the passenger. For this service, you will be paid this three thousand now" — Mousey handed over another slim white envelope, this one marked with yellow, and the boatman moved this one swiftly to his other pocket — "and another three will be with the male passenger, and he will give it to you after you have ferried him over safely and he is sitting in the driver's seat of his shitty blue Toyota Tercel. Are all these details clear?"

The boatman took a thoughtful second and then said yes.

"And are the financial terms acceptable?"

This time he said yes immediately and once more stuck out his hand. Mousey shook it. The boatman said: "It's a pleasure doing business with a professional. And I can promise you Powell River's a lot closer, and a nice, able-bodied, and calm male is a lot better cargo, than I usually have to run."

"Good. I might be here to see him off, I might not. And I hate to break the professional vibe and all, but take care of him. He, uh, he's a nice kid."

The boatman again studied the distance past Mousey's shoulder for a reasonable period before speaking. "I'll see him over. You're talking to a man with six children and seven toes. That doesn't mean anything specific. But it does mean something."

Mousey smiled at the boatman in the same surprised way he smiled at clean babies.

Greta finally realized that she was hungry and returned to the bar to pay her tab and start another one, buying and devouring a huge serving of curry, and then she left to go feel the breath of the wind in the bountiful outdoors again.

Greta decided to lie down on the cool grass by the chess board. Her shoulder holster dug into her ribs in a softly painful way, and she leaned into it, like finding and holding an edge in a Yin Yoga class.

She didn't hear, or see, or instinctively sense Alan Mouse's approach until he sloppily muttered hello. And staring up at the stars with her belly sleepily full, she felt good about that. She missed being spacey. Wandering around distracted, always surprised by other people's bodies coming close to her body, surprised by sounds and bumps and missed bus stops, and never really minding the misses because she was distracted by herself. Her own silent mind. And that, really, was what she missed. Her world as it had been — a world where she gave attention to details she liked, not one where she owed it to every detail, to every bump and creak and footstep. She rolled over and smiled up at him, and he seemed surprised and charmed by it. He slouched to the ground next to her, looking out across the water as he spoke.

"I just wish we didn't have to make a deal. I wish you were a person I could talk to, not deal with, y'know what I'm saying?"

Greta happily did not try to figure out what he was talking about. She would listen to him, and it would feel good to listen.

"I don't really. You kind of just walked out of the night and started talking, bro."

He laughed a bit. "So I figure you know who I am, by now, and I know who you are. And maybe that's better. I've made much sadder trades, if you can believe it, but here's ours. I give you Marlo. Well, I give you his spot, and you go there tomorrow morning to pick him and his precious, precious laptop up. I won't be there myself, but you will take him and leave, and keep my name out of your mouth forever."

The familiar, excited kick Greta felt jangling up her nerves made her feel bad about herself. With men like Alan Mouse it's always a trade. And they'll try as hard as they can to avoid telling you who gives and who gets what. "Why? What do you want back?"

Mouse pulled a bottle of pills out of his pocket and placed it gently on Greta's thigh. As soon as his tiny beautiful fingers released it, the bottle tipped over and fell in the grass. "You want to know, I'll tell you, Manic Pixie Dream Hitman. If you want to know, you deserve to. For a hot second, I thought I'd go to bat for Marlo. Hero it up, get him out of town. And then I remembered: I'm shot. My nerves are shot. By my thinking it would take about six smart, sturdily made moves to get Tommy out of this alive. And I don't have that in me anymore. That's why. What I want is simple: we go back to your room, and you stay with me, and we get lit up like Christmas trees. Like Christmas trees on fire." He reached over and tapped the side of her nose, intrusively. "I'm guessing you have the other half of the speedball with you. But you do have to stay with me tonight, and let me leave alive. That's…" There he was, weirdly looking at his hands again. "That's the whole deal."

Greta flopped to her back and looked at the dark, wide-open sky again. She felt the heft of the baggie of coke in her pocket, and she could sense Mouse beside her, breathing jaggedly in and out. So it came back to this, again. She spoke, mostly, to the openness of the sky. "You were an accomplished, if not respected, police officer and low-level political fixer, right?"

"I'd say that was accurate, yeah."

"Right, so before we go up to my room, I wanted to run something by you. It's a public policy idea."

"Shoot."

Greta raised herself to an upright position. "Elevator pitch: make it 100 per cent legal for women to murder anyone they want."

"That is an idea."

"So let's think about the murder rates. Do you think that'd make the rates of murder equal, as in women commit as many murders as men? Keeping in mind it's totally legal for women to kill whoever they want in this scenario. I'd say it'd get close, maybe fifty-five/forty-five. Those are percents I'm talking about there. The idea is to fully just legalize murder for women." Mousey laughed but nodded evenly as he did so. Greta continued to table her proposal. "If we, as a society, came together and gave women the right to murder other people for whatever reason they wanted, I think they'd kill *almost* as many people as men."

Mousey seemed to be legitimately thinking about it. He tilted his head from side to side and then spoke. "Empirically, I'd say you might be right. About what it'd take to line up the rates."

"But you don't agree, policy-wise."

"Policy-wise, you might need to really put some heads together and think about the logistical side of it before you tried to get it on the books."

"So you don't agree. How? How can't you agree? You've seen, like, a ton of murdered women, right? I'm assuming."

"Yeah, I've spent a fair amount of time with murdered women."

"And you'd agree, based your first-hand experience and all the empirical data that we have and are actually acknowledging today, that we, as a society, have a women-getting-murdered-and-raped-and-generally-accosted-and-abused-by-strangers-and-friends-and-relatives-alike problem, correct?"

"Correct."

"Right, so maybe what it finally takes to curb that species-long and -wide problem would be to just make it so that whenever you interact with a woman, you have to keep in mind that it is 100 per cent legal for her to murder you for whatever reason she wants."

Mousey sucked a smile into the back of his cheeks. "That'd include for money, right?"

"Oooooh, was that supposed to be some kind of half-assed morality jab? Fuck that noise, sir, fuck it. Debate me on the issues."

"I think most, maybe not all, but most of your objections are going to be about logistics and implementation in terms of enforcement."

"At least fight if you don't agree, that's all I'm saying. You might say it's unfair, and I'd say if we don't act, we're okay with the fact that life is unfair, since women kind of have to entertain the idea, not that it'd be technically legal, that a ton of people they meet or talk to or are bothered by could kill them. Life's unfair right now, and you're cool with it. This is just a reformed version of being unfair. I mean, you know this better than anyone, but it's already legal to kill someone under certain circumstances. Those circumstances being a certain level of threat to your life or property, right? So it's not a 'do we ever legalize murder or not' thing; it's an argument, purely, of degrees.

"So a better argument against me might be that I'm, in principle, advocating for a eugenic population-shaping on a global scale on the basis of sex. But that counter-argument is still flawed, son. Because in my scenario the murder is legal for women for whoever, if they're killing a man, woman, baker, candlestick maker, whatever the fuckity-fuck. Take it from someone who knows, you can never be sure who a bitch is going to kill, one moment to the next. You just can't. And whether or not we, as a society, ever succeed in legalizing murder for women in this country, you should know, before we go to my room, that I am both a woman and an entire industrialized nation. And that law is on my books."

"Let's get to the room." He moved to stand and then re-crouched and allowed one of his eyebrows to droop the rest of the way down. "Was that you making a threat just now?"

"Oh, Mousey, Mouse, Mousey. No. That wasn't a threat. It was much, much too classy to be a threat. And what is a classier version of a threat?"

"A promise."

Greta grabbed the drugs and popped to standing using only her core muscles. "Well, look at that. Good for you."

The only measure of how much time had passed was how much of the coke/crushed-up-Percocet mix was left. Mousey stared spacily at the table and realized it had been a while. They were playing a get-to-know-you game.

"Marry, bang, kill: a tree, the word *free*, the number three."

She responded almost before he was finished with the last vowel. "I would fuck the number three, marry a tree, and kill the word *free*. That's, like, so obvious I'm surprised you asked." She dug her chin into the heel of her hand and fixed him with a bloodshot stare. He could tell that he was shaking in her vision. "Do you even respect me a little?"

Mousey's head was swimming, and he was starting to regret the size of the rails he'd done. He leaned forward and brought both hands pleasurably through his hair, then consciously fixed his posture. "Does it count if I'm really, really afraid of you?"

"It does not."

"Oh, then no. You're a real piece of shit."

The hitman laughed so hard she toppled the rickety hotel chair sideways, ejecting and sprawling across the carpet as it hit the ground. Mousey moved to help her, and she pulled her ankle gun, pointed it at him, those eyes still bloodshot like they were an ocean with a leaky oil well at the bottom. "I prefer the term 'sack of shit.' That's what I call myself when I watch *Top Chef* and drink a bottle of wine instead of cleaning my apartment. Sack of shit, please." The gun wobbled a bit, but in a friendly way.

Mousey turned his attention to gathering and gumming some of the scraps left on the table. "I can live with that."

She replaced the gun in her ankle holster, then unstrapped and threw it aside. "I'm going to go to the bed, you're not. You're going to stay there."

"How about you unstrap that other piece there, big boy."

"I'm not big, I'm not a boy, and I'm not doing shit you tell me to do."

"Fair enough."

There was a small part of Mousey that wondered if he had hallucinated Greta doing a straight-up standing backflip onto the bed after she did it. Either way, she ended up in the bed, and he ended up leaning against the wall by the door, not entirely remembering having walked there. To make himself feel a little better, he looked at his hands some more. "So I haven't met a ton of real hitters. A few gangland body droppers, sure, but not many purists, y'know? Assassins like yourself."

She framed her face with two loose-jointed hands. "We are few and far between."

He used one of his beautiful fingers to point at her piece. "Can you draw that thing?"

She rocked her shoulders from side to side, the gun moving in the rig, nudging her left breast now, button undone over the handle. "Like a cowboy? No, that shit's stupid."

"Ah, I get it. You're a button man. Not an assassin."

She rolled over, spoke to the ceiling. "Yeah, chief. Put a small-calibre behind the ear. Two in the chest as he gets out of his car. Sometimes maybe walk up, poke a knife between his ribs. Bread-and-butter stuff. They should change that expression. I don't know a soul who eats bread."

"I remember a time before carbs. I remember a time before a lot of things."

"Motherfucker, I was born in a Costco. Your nostalgia doesn't do shit for me."

Mousey eyed her profile now, saving the smirk for when she was looking. He thought about the janitor at Tommy's building she'd killed, and kept sizing her up. Calm as anything when she was talking to you but quick on the trigger in the moment. Not a talk-your-way-out type, she'd drop the bodies and call the cleanup crew. Must have a serious backer behind her, afford that style.

She nodded towards the bedside table. "Pass the pad. Pen too." Mousey ambled over, knocked the pad and pen over onto the pillow beside her. She snorted and reached over like it was a real effort. "You want to see me draw? I'll draw."

Mousey stayed where he was, trying not to sway too much, and watched as she drew on the pad. When she was done, she flung her arm up, and Mousey plucked the drawing out of her hand. She let the arm drop slowly and limply and in the same kind of way a very heavy bird falls into a swimming pool.

The drawing was one of those sketches that people who are good at art do where the outside lines of everything look frayed. It was a pretty good rendering of her gun, with a long, ornately bordered speech bubble coming out of the muzzle that said: "All birds have to do is move their arms and they fly." The period was as big as the y, the middle of it left white and empty.

"You make me sleepy." Her neck was feeling the Percs now, eyelids starting to hang a little.

Mousey moved over, pushed her softening body backwards and tucked her in. She pulled that rig, sleepy but quick.

"Make your move and I'll make mine, old man."

Barrel pressing into his neck, Mousey slid forward and kissed the top of her forehead.

The hitman laughed. "You just want what everybody wants." Barrel twisting hard into the gaunt skin of his neck, pulling it into folds. "A headless woman with a pretty face who sucks dick." Letting the gun relax its hold on his skin a little, still keeping it pointed at his carotid. Mousey's feet were falling asleep. She continued, a little more softly now. "You ever killed anyone?"

"Depends what you mean by killed anyone."

She shoved him back firmly with her off hand, and Mousey allowed himself to fall, unresisting, into the wall, taking the impact pleasantly against his ribs. "Ugh. What a formless dollop of loose shit you are, dude. Seriously. Say a thing. Not this same tiresome 'depends,' 'does it even matter if,' 'you could look at it that way' nothingness. You open your mouth and fucking soap bubbles fall out. I don't even care what your answer is. Obviously. I asked you so that when it was my turn, I'd say this: the first time I killed someone, I looked down at the body, and my hand was bleeding and I couldn't feel it at all and the blood was dripping down the edge of my pinky nail, in a rich, red, vein-blood line. I took a long look at this kid I'd just deaded, and I had one thought in my mind, and I was calm enough for the thought to be in words: I'll never suck another dick. I will die before I put one more sweaty cock in my mouth."

She shifted her body, bum scooting to the other side of the bed, resting the gun gently on the pillow she'd just had her head on. "That's hope. That's what hope means to me. A long, beautifully appointed hallway of a life, with a gorgeous, useless coat rack, and a huge clock with an unreadable face, and very expensive hardwood floors that I get to walk down alone, forever, with zero smelly dicks in my face."

Mousey gave the speech its deserved moment of quiet, his legs buzzing in a long, rippling sheet. Finally, he stood straight, tipped his imaginary hat on the way out the door, which he almost latched.

The hitman laughed one more time.

Tommy woke up in a sick haze, hanging just on the edge of hallucination. Wrapped firmly in his blankets, he shuffled out of the tent towards the rustling sound that had woken him. The bear who was nosing through the remainder of Tommy's prepackaged sushi bowl was ugly as fuck.

Tommy realized that it was unfair to think of an animal who had never seen a mirror as ugly. But what, finally, did Tommy have but the folds of his brain? All the weird things stuck there that were his, because they were in his folds. If that was how brain folds worked. He was very sick and tired and overwhelmed.

A black bear, the guy was small, but not compact or cutely so, more squat, like an old man who had lifted many heavy things for many heavy years but had also eaten six eggs and three servings of meat a day the whole time. The bear glanced over at Tommy then dug back into the rice and fish.

Tommy didn't know why, but he felt less afraid of this bear than he would a dog off its leash (he'd never been bitten on the ankle by a bear).

"Hi, Bear."

The bear looked up from the meal, sniffed a grain of rice straight up its nose, then settled oddly onto its haunches, nosing slightly forward to Tommy.

"You're, like, moulting. That's the word. Word of the day, man, *moulting*. Maybe that's for birds. Snakes? Like when they shed their whole skin and feel brand new."

Bear swivelled his head in a twisty, sidelong direction that would have put a human neck into spasm.

"Lick me, Bear. Lick me." Tommy extended his hand, and Bear obliged, his tongue seeming to take over the surface it touched, like a very old, very heavy jar of oil spilling across Tommy's hand. "I doubt you can catch a human flu. Well, why? Why do I doubt that? Fuck, I feel bad, Bear. I'm not…"

Bear raised himself, as if in response, and assumed a hovering posture as he began releasing his bowels.

"Timing. Man, you have timing. I know you're just a balding bear shitting in the woods, but…" Bear grunted slightly as he encountered what seemed to Tommy's untrained eye mild constipation. Tommy started shaking his quivering index finger at the bear. "Hey, when you're in a new place, sometimes you have to go the extra mile to make a new friend. Put it out there, right? A real friend."

Tommy rose from his knees, discarded his blanket, waited out the spine-rattling reactive shiver when the wind hit him, and dropped his pants. He stood an extra second, looked at Bear's decreasingly impassive face, and kicked the pants away from his ankles. He moved over, still in his odd, febrile crouch, and squatted next to Bear.

There was almost no chance that whatever caused Bear's locked bowels to release at the precise second Tommy's did actually had anything to do with Tommy. It was almost certainly a pure coincidence. But that didn't mean it wasn't one of Tommy's favourite things that had ever happened to, or near, or because of him.

Now that he thought about it, consciously breathing the fecal air without smelling it through his clogged face, most of the things that had ever happened to, or near, or because of him had been, at least at some point, pure coincidences.

Tommy looked past Bear's partially bald head to the sun cresting over the green, spiking treeline, and he thought that was fine.

At three minutes to nine a.m., Mike stopped in front of the hotel room door, giving himself just another second to breathe, unsure if the way his blood felt thin and fast and empty was excitement or fear, and sure that it didn't matter. The door was a sliver ajar, so Mike walked straight in.

The young cop had obviously been suspicious of Mousey, so he had prepared himself for Mousey and Marlo jumping him, for Mousey to be there shrugging and shuffling and making excuses; he was prepared for Marlo to beg. Mike had run these scenarios in his mind, in the seemingly endless stretch of hours since he'd slept. He'd even imagined an empty room, what he'd do, how he'd search it. He was ready for the details of any of these outcomes; he'd pictured them so minutely that he was prepared for the smallest moments, prepared to act smoothly and bravely and intelligently.

He had not pictured a young woman sleeping with a gun in her hand, and he had not pictured himself making a strange, terrified croak from somewhere deep in his throat. He had not imagined the bullets feeling like two tiny donkey kicks in his chest. And although he had, actually, pictured himself getting shot, he had not pictured his arms reaching aimlessly out, away from his wounds. He had not pictured himself canting over at the waist, his legs bowing in on themselves and somehow holding. He hadn't imagined swaying around suspended like that long enough to see his first aspirated breath splatter the hardwood floor — the boards so old they were fraying around the edges — before slumping rather than falling down.

Tommy had improved a little but was still sick enough to slump forward as he walked or tried to focus on things.

Eventually, he managed to wrestle a granola bar and a decent amount of water down his throat. Then he spent a good while sitting in a nice ray of sun between the trees, warming himself and realizing, abstractly, that being sick was actually kind of helpful. He felt far away from himself but as a result focused on the world a few inches away from his head, and for the first time in what felt like a long time, he wasn't completely terrified. He was just sick.

And it was in this comfortable and oddly emotionless state that Tommy watched Mousey emerge from the bush, weaving erratically towards him before tripping on a root, and in trying to right himself, falling oddly and flatly backwards. Tommy stayed staring at the empty space above where Mousey had fallen for a few seconds before securing his sleeping bag around his shoulders and slouching over to help him up.

By the time he got to sitting up, Mousey was already babbling, reaching a weak, fading hand towards Tommy's shoulder. "Hey, man, it's shit. It's shit, sorry. I forgot your bag. I forgot your bag and your stuff, and the list, the list, the list I made for you, buddy. I just, just forgot it. It's bad. I forgot it. It's bad. It's so bad."

Tommy reached down, held Mousey's face with his left hand and slapped the other side with his right. "How does it feel?"

Mousey was about a day and a half's rest away from remembering the reference; instead he just sat there, swaying softly forwards and back, looking physically numb and emotionally hurt. Tommy reached down and pulled Mousey up as hard as he could, barely getting the guy off the ground before Mousey remembered that he had legs and started to help with the process. They both stood there a second, hunched over and breathing heavily. After he got his breath back, Tommy consciously straightened before he spoke.

"This is my business. This is on me. So I'm telling you we're going to go back to your house, I'm going to put you to bed, pick up the bag. No big deal that you forgot it. And I'll drive myself to the pickup. That's happening."

Mousey shook his head loosely. "It's, it's . . . I gotta take you, I have to make sure."

Tommy took a firmer hold of the detective's shoulder and shook him quiet. "Mousey, man, I appreciate everything you did. You saved my life. I don't know why, but you did and really thanks. Really. But now you need to go to bed, and I need to drive myself to this meeting."

Mousey seemed to totally gather himself for one porcelain-fragile moment. His words came out less mumbled than they did when he was sober, even. He said: "Sometimes I have an intrusive thought where I just remember how powerful milk propaganda was in the nineties…" And then he stopped and just swayed a little more, so Tommy started guiding them, staggering but at a reasonable pace, towards the road to Mousey's car.

At the glass house, he dropped Mousey on the floor by the front door and then went to look for the bag, which was on the kitchen counter. Tommy opened it, took out the day-time cold medication, and grabbed himself some water from the kitchen. It took three pills and about six tries before he could swallow one pill properly. Somehow they kept getting caught up in his throat, like his body's swallowing muscles were on strike. But eventually he choked it down, resettled himself, and looked up the directions to the meeting spot on Mousey's iPad.

Mousey was asleep beside the door when Tommy got back downstairs, so instead of waking him up and having to carry him to bed, which he doubted he'd have the strength to do anyways, Tommy went to the bedroom and grabbed two pillows and a blanket. He rolled Mousey on his side, tucked one pillow under his head and the other behind him to keep him from rolling onto his back, and spread the blanket over him, right there beside the door. Then Tommy took the time to write a short thank-you note before he left.

Driving helped Tommy wake up even more, and he was able to carry himself pretty much upright as he met the boatman, even holding a nice conversation with the guy as he politely deferred shaking hands to avoid spreading the fever around. Tommy only got back to his sick-self after he'd been settled in the boat for a while, tucked low in the back, looking at the island from almost exactly sea level. He knew that he was the one moving, and in spite of the bumps and the feel of speed from under him, Tommy somehow still couldn't help getting the impression that he was still, and it was the island that was moving away from him, so he looked down.

He took to staring at the wake of the boat. The water that kept spreading out in two hard, white peaks, like a mountain getting cut in half, before loosening back into liquid.

Greta waited out the normal period of time for the other people in the hotel to wake up, worry, and then decide that the shots had been a car backfiring and go back to using their phones to geolocate the most wondrous views on the island. She drank a bunch of tap water in an effort to make her head stop spinning. Eventually, she went downstairs and drank coffee until she felt awake and steady enough to eat, then she ate, paid, and went to her car to get the bleach and plastic sheeting.

There was no way she was getting the cop's body out of the hotel. To do that she'd have to piece him up and carry him out over the course of about a week. He was a big boy. So instead she decided to bleach and wrap the body to control the smell and leave it in the tub. This was, actually, the first time Greta had been forced to conceal one of her own dead bodies. Before, it had always been a case of leaving them where they were, or dragging them to an inconspicuous spot and running.

More than anything, manipulating the cop's dead weight as she wrapped it reminded her of the so-called FIIT Farmer's HIIT class she'd attended the previous spring. It had been a workout class held in a back alley, with the basic princi-ple that labour tasks, like carrying a barrel, or pulling a heavy iron hoe with some ropes, were fundamentally more kinesthetically useful than specifically targeted muscle exer-cises. And to be fair, it had been an awesome workout, but somehow introducing the tools of real work and just having them scrape uselessly across concrete, accomplishing noth-ing other than yuppie fitness, really tugged at the already always tenuous edges of Greta's tolerance for such classes. She still went to them, obsessively, as a way to keep herself balanced and not incredibly sad and dire all the time. But still. There are limits.

Eventually, Greta managed to get the body wrapped up, and then she dumped a decent amount of bleach down the open top-end of the rolled-up sheeting, clear but showing its content, like a Vietnamese fresh roll. The bleach stung her eyes, so Greta retreated to the bedroom and carefully lined the base of the door with rolled-up towels. She slumped back onto the carpet and was almost immediately overcome with exhaustion and the nasty after-effects of all of Mousey's sad drugs. She crawled to and up the bed, and fell asleep.

As usually somehow happened when she woke up, Greta managed to forget that she'd killed someone. She got up and immediately took to pacing around the living room before noticing how profusely she was sweating, and she laughed as she re-entered the bathroom and saw that the source of her anxious sweat was also occupying the shower. She stripped and used the towels to dry off before replacing them under the door and finally changing her clothes. She loaded up her weapons, carefully checked that they were concealed, and fixed her hair into an extremely unattractive, ultra-tight topknot that she could feel pulling on her skin all the way down to her eyebrows. She put on some clear, large glasses with very dark and defined frames, then she packed up her things, went downstairs and extended her room rental by a week, and recklessly swerved her way to the ferry terminal.

She would wait until she was at least two hours away before she called Sergei. She imagined Darillo flexing pliers for no reason, alone in an undecorated room.

She was early to the ferry terminal and so was forced to sit, staring at the ocean, fuming. The thing that got to her, specifically, was how wrong Mousey was. He had a way that he thought it had all gone down, and what made Greta angry was not that he'd gotten the best of her, but that he thought he knew why. He thought that snorting highballs and talking and hanging out on that edge that lets everyone feel like they could have gotten laid if one thing had gone differently was what she'd wanted. For herself. He thought the whole night, doing it that way, was anything at all but just easiest. And that was an impression Greta couldn't stomach.

She watched the ferry float into view, slowly drifting at a gentle angle towards the hard line of the dock. The hitman laughed, started her car, and peeled rubber back across the empty pedestrian walkway. She blew past the waving ferry workers in their fluorescent-highlighted vests, and floored it as soon as she hit the open road. Mousey's assumption, his misinterpretation of the situation, was a thing she couldn't, and didn't, have to take. Eventually, she thought, you should stop just taking everything all the time.

At first, Greta made the approach to Mousey's house with extreme caution. Watching her angles, moving in from the treeline, making cautious darts between cover, until she could get a bead on the house. She pulled out her view-finder and cased what was literally the most strategically vulnerable home she'd ever seen. All glass, mirrors behind the glass. She assessed the whole place from ten yards out, through the windows. He wasn't in the house. She moved in closer, staying cautious until she finally saw the thin, meagre pile of him, slumped back against the rock. She couldn't see his face, but she knew. There was no trap here. He'd played all the angles he had it in him to play. He was waiting. Not waiting to, not waiting for. Just sitting still.

Greta relaxed her posture, letting the gun dangle loosely from her side as she walked up on him, even taking a second to crest the slight incline before she got to him so she could see the view he was seeing. He must have lit a cigarette or a joint, because she could see smoke rising and getting blown quickly away. She stayed stopped for a few more seconds, looking at the ocean, thinking about the space where she knew he was, but couldn't see, before finally walking around the side of the rock to join him. No angles, no soft steps, just a nice, normal walk — her head tilted up enough to catch the green of trees in her periphery.

"How are you feeling today, Mousey? All I can see from here is that you look like shit."

Mousey dropped the joint to his feet, and it somehow didn't set the moss on fire. He didn't look away from the view, just let a few words flop out of this mouth. "Well, y'know, I *feel* like shit. But I feel like one of those shits that feels just wonderful, after you drop it in the water." Eyes pinned out, head bobbling loosely on his skinny, sucked-out neck. He looked ready to go, pleased with himself but just as pleased to put his head in an oven. "I thought maybe you'd hustle off the island. Grab the ferry. That was the smart play. Lowest risk, anyway."

"You really bet the farm on that?

Mousey waved loosely at her with both hands, then he spread one arm out and let it drop, weakly gesturing at the trees around him. "What farm?"

"Where's Marlo?"

Greta guessed that maybe a nineteenth-century Russian writer's corpse would call what he did with his face right then a smile.

"I'll only tell you that if you can promise, promise, promise me you care about the answer." For almost a minute, there was just trees and wind and the sound a gun makes when it's not being used for anything in particular. "I didn't think so. You got me, you got me. It's all right, though. The only infinite thing in this world is the threads you can pull out of the bottom of cut-off jean shorts." He awkwardly plucked a thread off the bottom of his shorts with his ring and middle finger, and let it get picked up and moved only slightly by the wind. "What I wanted to tell you about is hair.

Right? You want to hear about hair? My dad was a barber. He was barber and he had this broom... And hair grows back, it always grows back, and all scissors do is rust and rust and rust..." He lost his train of thought, suddenly and totally. Let his voice trail off, and went quiet. In sharper times, Mousey had been quiet a lot, talking when he needed to, and enjoying talking, but listening more than anything.

At that time of the afternoon, with the sun coming through the trees, the occasional pine-tinged wind blowing through the hot day, it was so *nice* on Mousey's property. He took a deep breath and looked like he was about speak, he moved his head like he was speaking, gestured in a small way with his hand, the way people do when they have something to say.

The whole thing, every single thing about the world around him, was so beautiful; it was almost as if Greta didn't take a stride closer, cup his shoulder gently with the emptiness of her palm, put a gun against the back of his head, and fire it, leaving him faceless, down in the dirt.

Acknowledgements

The line "Lick me, Bear. Lick me," is from possibly the greatest Canadian novel of all time: *Bear* by Marian Engel.

Quadra Island is not technically a Gulf Island but rather a part of the Discovery Islands. Over the last couple decades, however, it has become common in British Columbia to include Quadra Island as part of the Northern Gulf Islands, along with Denman, Texada, Lasqueti, and Hornby.

* * *

As always, I'd like to thank everyone even remotely involved in making this book happen. But, to name a few, I'd like to thank my agent Adam Schear for finding this book a home and Bethany, Susanne, Peter, Jill, Martin, and Julie at Goose Lane for being that home.

Many thanks to the Regina Public Library, whose support was essential for the completion of this book

I'd also like to thank my friends, who are all very nice and fun and good people. I'd like to thank my family, who, in addition to being very nice and fun and good people, have been incredibly supportive of my writing, and, well, my whole life.

Finally, I'd like to thank Zani—for the partnership.

790018

Andrew Battershill's first novel, *Pillow*, was long-listed for the 2016 Scotiabank Giller Prize and the 2016 Sunburst Award and shortlisted for the 2016 Kobo Emerging Writer Award. *Pillow* was also selected by the *Walrus* as one of the Best Books of 2016 and by CBC Books as one of the Best Debuts of the year. Battershill is the co-founder and former fiction editor of *Dragnet* magazine. He is now the fiction editor of *This Magazine*. He lives in Vancouver and Quadra Island.